Praise

"Lucy Monroe ~~is one of my favorite~~ indulgences."
NYT #1 Bestselling Author, Christine Feehan

"The [Children of the Moon] world is magical and definitely pulls you in. The characters are engaging and the plot is rich. For me, I have found another author to add to my anxiously awaiting list."
All About Romance

"I have a new favorite historical author and she is Lucy Monroe."
The Best Reviews

"Lucy Monroe captures the very heart of the genre. She pulls the reader into the story from the first to the last page."
NYT Bestseller Debbie Macomber

"Lucy Monroe writes smart, sensual, emotional books
for intelligent women."
NYT Bestseller JoAnn Ross

"Thank you for writing those alpha heroes I love."
NYT Bestseller Lori Foster

"Ms. Monroe never fails to deliver a story that is overflowing with emotion and sizzle."
4 Stars, FAR

Children of the Moon Series

MOON AWAKENING

MOON CRAVING

MOON BURNING

DRAGON'S MOON

WARRIOR'S MOON

VIKING'S MOON

Viking's Moon

Children of the Moon
Book 6

Lucy Monroe

For my daughters, two of the most amazing women I know, personally powerful and strong, and wonderful inspiration for Neilina, champion of her people and protector of the Chrechte.

CHAPTER ONE

Mist swirled around Haakon's lower legs, the pre-dawn light casting the forest of this *other* place in shadow.

The soft moss upon which he walked was hidden from his sight, but he knew from past visits it was a brilliant green, the trees so tall their tops could not be seen even in the full light of day and the flowers so vibrant with color, they had none of their like in Groenland.

Would she come? His sacred mate, the one woman destined to be his above all others, the woman who had spent nearly a decade refusing to give him her name or a clue to where she lived. When they were together, they both spoke the ancient tongue of their people, so he could not tell if she was of the Norse or another land entirely.

He did not even know what animal she shifted into as she had never allowed him the privilege to see.

Her dress was as if she were as ancient as the language, her body covered in leathers and furs, her feet clad in boots that reached her knees, burned with old runes and symbols only their kind would recognize. His mystery woman wore her dark hair long, but with the braids of a warrior, and she carried a walking stick topped with the sharpened antlers of a powerful buck.

His reminisces of her were interrupted as the woman herself, flesh and blood though he did not understand how it was possible in this *other* place, walked out of the mist, her beautiful face set in stern lines.

"You call to me in my dreams when I have other things to concern myself with."

"Are we dreaming then?" he asked, knowing the answer was both yes and no.

They both slept, but this was no dream. This was Chrechte magic, a spirit realm which was as real as his sword, but which he understood less than his ability to shift into a giant cat of prey.

"If you would tell me where you are, I would come to you in person and then we would not have to meet here," he told her, not for the first time.

Fear flashed in her green gaze, gone so fast if he had not been watching her so closely, he would not have seen it. It was always thus when he mentioned anything about them meeting in person.

She frowned, her green eyes now dark with annoyance. "I will never reveal my home to you."

"You are mine." Not that he believed that mattered to her. Haakon did not doubt that his mate spoke the absolute truth when she said she would never tell him how to find her.

Her grip on the staff tightened. "I belong to no man."

"You belong to me, just as I belong to you." It was not about ownership as if either were a slave, but the trust and companionship that only a true mate could bring. "You are my sacred mate."

"I will have no Norseman for a mate." The revulsion twisting her lovely features had long since stopped surprising him, but it still nicked his soul, drawing fresh blood.

"And yet that is exactly what you do have." He was tired of the old refrain, had long since lost hope he would change her mind, but felt compelled to point out what she had to know as surely as he did.

For her, there was no other, just as he could never give in to his uncle's urgings and take a mate from among their people.

"Whatever fate has decreed, I will not be your mate in truth. No matter how many times your soul calls to mine in this place."

"Have you ever considered it is your soul calling to mine?" he provoked her, knowing she would not like that explanation.

"No."

"And yet, as often as I am the first to arrive, I come, drawn by an unseen force. And you are already here. Our souls have been linked these past nine years." Interest in other women as bed partners had disappeared after his first time here, not long after his eighteenth summer and his first shift into the *asmundr*.

Haakon had forced himself to try, he'd been a young man after all, his body rife with unfulfilled sexual desire, and he'd been angry. Angry and hurt, though he would not admit the last aloud to another living being.

After the third time his green eyed warrior-woman had rejected him, Haakon had been seething with rage and the unfamiliar emotional pain, when a lovely young widow had invited him to share her furs. He'd accepted, hoping to erase the craving that tormented his sleep as well as his waking hours for a woman who wanted nothing to do with him.

But he'd been unable to perform sexually with the widow, despite her well-versed efforts and attractiveness.

Just as the Chrechte wisdom claimed would be the case. But it was supposed to happen that way *after* mates had claimed each other for the first time, not when they'd only met in the Chrechte spirit world.

"It is not *I* that draws us both to this place, but you," his mate claimed, her expression saying she believed her own words, regardless of evidence to the contrary. "You, Viking, with your stubborn will and refusal to accept that I will *not* be your mate. You do this."

"What are the other things that worry you so much you find your time here especially onerous?" he asked, rather than engage in an old argument with his mate.

She never gave ground, never admitted her need was as great as his. Never acknowledged his claim on her, or the claim she had made on him simply by existing.

"Other Chrechte are in danger, not that a Viking like you would care about that."

"I am not a Viking." But he'd said as much many time before.

His countrymen had stopped pillaging the lands they visited decades before he'd even been born. Not that she seemed to accept that fact. To her, all Norsemen were Vikings and all Vikings were evil. Though he had no idea why. In nearly a decade, she had not told him the source of her antipathy for his people.

Just as all the times before when he'd reminded her he was not the thing she seemed to loathe most, she ignored him now.

Glaring into the distance, as if she could see what he did not, she shook her head. "They seek to save our race, but if they are not cautious, they will destroy their own packs."

"Packs? So, they are *uffe*?"

Her head snapped back around so her gaze, as brilliant and hard as emeralds fell on him. "I know you would not stir yourself to save a wolf."

"You are wrong. I want no Chrechte to perish."

"You would have me believe you are so different from your brethren?"

If he could trust the evidence of his ears, she *wanted* to believe that, but he was past making up fairytales about them. This woman would never trust him to be the honorable *asmundr* that he was.

Still he told her the truth because not to would be to deny it. "My pride values all life, but the Chrechte most of all." He sighed at the expression of doubt on her beautiful features. "We find it difficult enough to bring children into the world."

Their numbers had been dwindling for generations, or so his father had always claimed. All Haakon knew was that the old stories told of a thriving and well-peopled race, but his pride was small, numbering less than a dozen in Groenland and only about five times that number in all lands where Danes might dwell.

The old legends spoke of *paindeal* who had left for the Land of the Sun, seeking a more hospitable place to dwell, searching for a connection to ancient history even the oldest stories could shed little light on.

His father said the wolves had much higher numbers as had the Éan at one time, but they could not know how the flying shifters fared as he had not come across any in his travels as the Viking warrior she had accused Haakon of being. The wolves Bjorn had seen, many of whom the older *asmundr* had killed before realizing the error of his ways.

Her expression said she did not believe Haakon's claim of valuing all life, but then when had she ever believed a single word he had spoken? Though he was fairly sure they could not lie here in this place of *other*, that their souls spoke to one another as surely as their mouths.

Which was how *he* knew she meant it when she said she would never be his mate.

For nine years, he had tried to change her mind, tried to get her to see him as a man, a warrior who protected all Chrechte, though he'd never told her he was *asmundr*. How could he share his most deeply held secret if she would not even tell him her name? Besides, she had not shifted her view of him. Not even a little.

"Will you help them?" he asked her, having gleaned from their time together over the years that she kept from all society, human and Chrechte alike.

"I have no choice. My dreams tell me I must live up to my nature."

"Your nature as a Chrechte?" he asked, not sure what one woman could do, no matter if she dressed like a man and was trained in combat as this one so clearly had been.

She turned away rather than answer and he knew it was because she could not lie, but there was something she did not want him to know.

"I have been dreaming of other Chrechte as well," he said to hide pain-inspired anger at yet more proof his mate would never trust in, or rely on him.

"You dream of your murdering brethren?"

His people, the Norse, were known for their brutality in battle, for their lack of reverence for those most would never think to attack, even after their leaders had accepted the new religion brought by Rome in the centuries past. But that did not make them murderers.

And he said so. Again.

Eyes the color of emeralds scorched him with heated antipathy. "Tell that to the pack of my birth, destroyed by your *asmundr*."

Her claim did not shock him. He'd long since surmised that his mate had a strong and personal reason for hating Norsemen. But the fact she made it, exposing her own Chrechte nature in the same sentence, left him speechless with disbelief.

Finally, after so many years, she revealed something important about herself. Something he found difficult to believe. Not that she was a wolf shifter, of the *uffe*, but that her pack had been destroyed by the *asmundr*. His father. For he knew she could not be talking about him.

She'd used the word for their protector in his language. And that gave him pause. She knew Norse. *Was* she a Dane then, even if she was a wolf? He had never quite convinced himself of that possibility and thought it more likely she had been exposed to his brethren in an outreach settlement. Groenland was one of many places the Danes had established themselves since the beginning of the Viking's travels nearly three centuries before.

"*I* am *asmundr* to my people and I have destroyed no *uffe*." Haakon had never even met a wolf shifter before her, much less battled with an entire pack.

She blanched, the cold light of pre-dawn making her skin take on a ghostly cast. "You are *asmundr*?" she demanded, the revulsion so strong in her voice, it washed over him like acid, burning his skin with her revilement.

"I am." And despite her reaction to that truth, it was a great honor he would never be ashamed of.

He had been chosen by fate to protect all Chrechte with strength greater than even that of *kotrondmenskr* like his cousin who shifted into the large white tigers known more commonly to the Ruske peoples.

"And the other *asmundr*? The one who *did* murder my family and friends. What became of him?"

"The only other guardian of the Paindeal that I know of was my father." There could be others in the land of the Danes, but his father had claimed those who remained on the continent had no *asmundr*. "He died five years ago, after only a few years training me to be *asmundr* with him."

His uncle had succeeded his father as *jarl* and his cousin would come after. Though Bjorn had been war chief more than a century, Chrechte wisdom dictated that the *asmundr* should not be pride alpha. Pride alpha was always *jarl* of his area. It was the way of things.

His father had broken with Chrechte teachings on that and many other things, but come back to appreciate the ancient ways in the twilight of his many hundred year life.

Finding his sacred mate in his seventh century of life, had humbled him. Or so he had always said. Haakon had never noticed Bjorn, the Firebrand, to be anything near humble. However, there was no denying that he had espoused the ancient ways and denounced his own actions over the centuries that did not abide by them.

"No, it cannot be possible. How could fate be so cruel?" she demanded, sounding more vulnerable than any time in the past nine years, her voice husky with broken pain that was too real for him to mistake it for anything else, her eyes haunted with memories only she could see. "Your *father* murdered my pack? My family and friends and all I held dear?"

"Impossible." Haakon knew Bjorn had done things like that in centuries past, but not since she had been born. Haakon would not believe it. "My father had not gone on a raid since decades before my birth. He stopped when he found my mother."

Haakon's mother had demanded his father stay in Groenland and make a life with her, one not marred by violence and bloodshed. Because she was his true mate, Bjorn listened. And yet, despite being sacred mates, they had not been able to conceive a child until Haakon, who was only twenty-seven.

"You believe I am young, like you?" Haakon's mate demanded with a harsh laugh. "I am older than the settlement in which you live."

She knew he lived in Groenland because he'd told her, when he'd still been free with information about himself, before he realized she was never going to reveal anything about herself. Not even her name.

But she had just told him something even more important. If she had been alive for centuries, she was a guardian as well, capable of shifting in a half-wolf, half-human form. If his father's stories were true, she would also increase in size until she was taller than any Norseman.

"Your father was a betrayer of his own kind," she said with pure loathing. "No doubt you are just like him, willing to murder innocent Chrechte to further your own ambitions. You are *not* my mate."

"You do not mean those words. You know I am not that Chrechte."

Hatred imbued every line of her being. "You are everything I despise."

Pain sliced through him. And that pain sparked a rage unlike anything he'd allowed himself to feel since the hotheaded days of his youth. It welled up in Haakon, nearly choking him.

How dare she make those accusations against *him*? Part of him understood that her hatred for his father was well-deserved. She carried a burden of grief too heavy for most, but Haakon had not placed it there.

The other half of *his* soul believed that soul was black. After nine years meeting, talking, arguing…in this place, she must know by now how important honor was to Haakon. How much he revered their people and the ancient ways, even if he had never before revealed his *asmundr* nature to her.

Haakon drew himself to his full six and a half feet, his big muscles bulging with the effort of holding his anger in check, his jaw so taut it hurt. "I have never murdered. I have killed in battle and to protect my people, but I have never taken the life of an innocent. *I have never taken any life for my own gain,*" he gritted out from between clenched teeth, space between each word.

His words came out tense and strained with his effort to hold back the shout he wanted to give. He wanted to swing his fist at one of the giant trees of this place, but even that outlet, he would not give himself. An *asmundr* had to control his temper at all times. The Berzerkers of legend had not been *asmundr*, but most had been *kotrondmenskr*. Norsemen who shared their nature with the largest cats of prey.

"I don't believe you." She said it so starkly, so certainly.

Suddenly Haakon was tired. Tired of the strife, the hatred, of fighting against an absolute certainty that he was not worthy of her time, not even her name. They had been mates for nine years and for every one of those years, she had refused every claim he had on her.

Now she denigrated the very core of his being. His honesty and integrity as *asmundr*. He did not care if she realized the impact of her words. How they flayed him like a whip tipped in iron. She meant them and that was what mattered.

Fury born of the knowledge he would never know his mate as such, burned through Haakon, leaving nothing but the ashes of cold certainty behind.

This woman would *never* claim him, never allow herself to be claimed by him. She would never give him her name, much less the most important and longed for benefits of finding the other half of a *kotrondmenskr's* soul. He would never know the joy of fatherhood. He would never know the pleasure of sex again, had not known the release of even his own right hand in nine long years.

And she did not care. Nay, she probably reveled in the fact she denied him these things. She refused to believe his words, even in this place where nothing but truth could be spoken between Chrechte, mates even more so.

His soul would always be hungry, but he would be damned to the hell the priests claimed was such an inferno of pain and suffering if it remained that way in the presence of one who he now saw as enemy, as certainly as she had always seen him.

He took the ancient sword he always carried, even to this place of *other* and planted it in the ground between them with one powerful thrust. "So be it. I will not call you to this place again. Can you say the same?"

Then he turned and walked away, leaving his sword an uncrossable barrier between them.

Haakon woke from sleep, his face inexplicably wet, eyes burning in a way they had not since his childhood and his father had trained emotion out of him.

The knowledge he would never have a mate was an icy reality that would chill the edges of his every waking hour. The loneliness he'd learned to live with from the first day after the first dream-walk to the Chrechte place of spirits would always be with him. Children would never be his, no matter how many hundreds of years he lived as *asmundr*.

That could not be changed.

But he would stop pining for that which would never be. Haakon *would* stop craving a woman who could not see beyond her own hatred to the gift that could have been theirs.

He looked to where he stored his sword at night and the dawn light glinted off the well-polished, oiled metal.

So, he had not left it in the *other* place despite walking away from it. Yet, somehow, he sensed that the barrier between him and the intransigent warrior-woman was still there. That she could not go beyond it and he never would.

Never again would he seek her company in his dreams or the *other* place.

He would live without his mate; he would not live without his pride.

CHAPTER TWO

Neilina woke with a start, her body jerking into alertness and away from the Chrechte land of the spirit.

Haakon, her mate and despised *asmundr* of the Norse *kotrondmenskr* had thrown his sword down between them, saying better than the words he spoke that he wanted her no more.

That knowledge should delight her. After nine long years of her denying him, he had finally given up the idea of them being mates. Why did she feel a terrible, hollow regret rather than relief?

It made no sense. No Norsemen could be trusted, particularly the Chrechte among them. They did not value life as he claimed. They were murderers and marauders, destroyers of the innocent.

She had seen firsthand how they treated the people who inhabited the lands they wanted to make new homes in, to plunder for their resources.

She'd spent centuries despising the Norse, particularly *kotrondmenskr*, for what they had done to her pack, to her Pict village. Newly turned *conriocht*, she had tried her best to protect her people and the humans that dwelt with them in the small island settlement.

It had not been enough.

Her skills as a warrior were neophyte and the Norse war chief came with an *asmundr* who had the power of a god and the fighting skills of Thor himself.

Knowing Bjorn was finally dead should give her some peace. How could it though? When she knew his son was her true mate, the one person fate had decreed the other half of Neilina's soul?

What fresh cruelty was this? After all she had lost, to lose any hope of happiness in the future because of who fate had decreed her sacred bonded?

At least they had never claimed one another. She had at least a tiny seed of hope for companionship over the centuries she would live as *conriocht*.

Something in her spirit cried out in pain at even the thought of sharing her body with another, but they had never claimed each other physically. She could overcome her own inclinations and find some sort of contentment with another.

She wanted that to be true, but a feeling deep in her soul said it was not.

"Are you well?" Freya, her adopted daughter, asked from the other pile of furs in their bedchamber, deep in the forest cave. "You whimpered in your sleep and it was a sound so unlike any you would make, it woke me."

"I did not whimper." Offense she made no effort to hide laced Neilina's tone.

She did not make helpless noises, or those of fear, or sadness. Not for centuries. Not since losing all she held dear in one bloody, defeated day.

Freya struck a flint to rock and lit the tallow candle beside her, the soft yellow light illuminating her face, lovely despite its scar, as her expression filled with disbelief. Freya pointed at Neilina. "There are tears on your cheeks."

"Impossible. I do not cry." Not since waking in that boat the *asmundr* had left her in, no doubt expecting her to perish at sea.

Neilina had known in that moment that her honor, her pride, her very place in the world, as well as her people, were lost forever to her.

Only now, hundreds of years later, her dreams demanded she act as *conriocht* again. Who was she to protect the Faol? But the dreams would not leave her alone.

Freya shifted in her furs, sitting up against the wall of the cave. "If you say so."

"I do."

"When do we leave for the island?" Freya asked, rather than pursuing the conversation.

Something Neilina appreciated, if she didn't quite trust it. Freya would revisit Neilina's supposed tears and whimper later, digging for answers. Answers Neilina could not give, not even to the protegee she had taken under her wing the very same year Neilina had begun to meet Haakon in the Chrechte land of spirits.

She had more important things to consider than the man who claimed to be a mate to her.

There were packs of Faol fighting the order of the Fearghall. That terrible secret band of other wolf shifters who believed the purity of the Chrechte must be maintained by destroying all whom they considered weaker. They despised those whose parents might shift but had been born with what they considered a fully human nature. Anyone who they thought would dilute the bloodlines of the Chrechte with some perceived weakness, or another.

The Fearghall considered the bird shifters inferior and were responsible for the decimation of that race.

They murdered without conscience, destroying and practicing the reprehensible act of murdering human true mates. Ostensibly, so the Chrechte could still have children with others of their kind, but just as likely to prevent the birth of children with diluted bloodlines from such a mating.

These evil among the Faol were far more treacherous than the clans set on fighting them realized. The Fearghall were more than willing to kill entire packs to preserve their way of life.

Neilina's dreams told her she must go to these clans to warn them. She must fight beside them as *conriocht*, something Neilina had not done in over two centuries.

A terrifying prospect, far more worthy of her attention and worry than the fact Haakon had thrown his sword down between them. Nelina would not concern herself that her supposed mate had left with every evidence he had no intention of returning.

Haakon's father had murdered her pack and the humans who relied on the Chrechte who lived among them. Just like the Fearghall, Bjorn the *asmundr* had been a shifter without honor, using the strength meant to protect others to destroy them instead.

She wanted no part of the son.

No matter if her heart, that dried and shriveled organ in Neilina's chest, tried to dictate otherwise.

She climbed from her furs and began to dress. "We leave for Balmoral Island tomorrow. It is urgent we reach the pack as soon as possible." She strapped on the weapons she wore under her leather tunic. "The Fearghall have planned something terrible."

"Your dreams will not tell you what?"

"No. I am *conriocht*, not *celi di*."

"They have a *celi di*, don't they?" Freya asked, knowing more about the Chrechte packs than any human not mated to a Chrechte was supposed to.

Considering the twenty-year-old woman who had lived with Neilina for nearly a decade was as close to a daughter as she was ever likely to have, Neilina felt no guilt for breaking Chrechte law in that regard.

"I believe they do, yes."

"So, why hasn't she been warned in her dreams?"

"I believe their *celi di* is a man and I do not know." Neilina put on the leather straps that held her sword in place and slid the weapon given to her by her great grandmother into position.

Why Bjorn had left all her weapons with her, when he sent her adrift, Neilina did not know. But they were all she had left of her heritage.

"Who knows why God sends a message to one and not another? Why fate decrees the things it does?"

Like that Freya herself should have been born to parents who died before her sixth birthday and then taken in by an aunt and uncle who did nothing to protect her from the sexual interest of a married clansman three times her age. Or that Neilina should be mated to a Norseman and an *asumundr* at that!

Fate had much to answer for, in Neilina's opinion.

"Are you nervous about the sailing?" Freya asked, her brows furrowed, bunching the scar over her left eye that she'd carried since the fateful day Neilina had taken her under her wing.

"More to the point, are you?" Neilina asked with what gentleness was left in her warrior's nature.

"*You* don't get scared about stuff like this," Freya observed rather than answer.

"I don't allow anything to frighten me anymore." She had nothing left to lose.

Though looking at Freya, Neilina realized for the first time in centuries, that was not quite true. The young woman before her was too important to be dismissed as *nothing*. Only for the past nine years, Neilina had entertained no doubts that she could protect her charge. Now, with their quest before them, that might not be true.

If she could deny the quest, she would, but Neilina knew that when fate called one of her nature, she had no choice but to follow.

Freya bit her lip. "I've never been on such a long voyage. Are you sure our boat is secure?"

"It is a Viking boat, of course it is seaworthy." Neilina had stolen it decades ago and maintained it as she'd seen the Vikings do on her spying expeditions, taking supplies when necessary from their settlements.

Freya strapped on her own weapons, a woman's sword and knives Neilina had ventured far from the safety of their forest retreat to obtain. "But don't they usually have a bigger crew than two?"

Neilina shrugged. "It's a small boat, meant for a small crew."

"But two?"

"Yes, two will sail her just fine. You must trust me, Freya. I cannot leave you here." Part of Neilina wished she could, but how could she be assured of her adopted daughter's safety if she was not here to protect her?

A human woman, even one trained to battle, was far too easy a target if she was discovered by a hunting party. And the hunters moved deeper into the woods every year. "Besides Dìonach accompanies us."

"Your pet bear is a lot more likely to set the boat tipping than help us." Freya began putting out food with which to break their fast.

Neilina noted to herself that they would need to make bundles of their sleeping furs to take on the journey with them. "Her weight will give us necessary ballast."

Besides, the bear she had raised from a cub was fiercely protective of Neilina, hence her name. She had fought by Neilina's side on more than one occasion and the bear's protective manner had extended towards Freya as soon as Neilina had brought the girl to their cave.

Dìonach would stand with Neilina, between any harm and the girl she loved as daughter.

Freya shook her head. "You should think about leaving her behind."

"I cannot. Our souls are connected as surely as my wolf is within me." She had bonded with Dìonach through the *Faolchú Chridhe*, extending the bear's life to match hers.

It was a mystical ceremony she understood no better than the moment she became *conriocht*, taught to Neilina by the *celi di* who died the same day as the rest of her pack.

The woman had foretold the destruction of their people, if only Neilina had realized it. No one had.

No one could conceive of a guardian using his power to murder and destroy.

Dionach had been with Neilina these past fifty years and had not aged at all.

Freya poured water into cups Neilina had carved years ago. "She's a bear, not your mate."

"I have no mate."

"Are you sure about that?" Freya's expression challenged Neilina to speak the truth. "We share a bed chamber."

"We live in a cave."

"That is not the point. The point is that I am there when you wake from your dreams of this man you claim is not your mate."

"They are not dreams. He drags me to the Chrechte spirit world."

"So, he's some kind of *draoidh*?" Disbelief and a hint of mockery laced Freya's tone.

Despite what she'd been through, the young woman was strong and confident. Neilina was ridiculously proud of Freya's attitude and inner strength. Not that she'd tell the girl and give her a swelled head.

"He is not a wizard. He's Paindeal and that is bad enough."

"Why?"

"You know what his people did to mine."

"I know what human men tried to do to me. I know I'll wear this scar for the rest of my life because of the darkness inside those men." She indicated the thin scar that bisected her eyebrow and marred the top of her left cheek. "But I also know that I do not hold all men responsible. You taught me that."

Neilina had tried, but had never been sure of her success. "Do you not?"

"No."

"Yet you've told me you have no desire to marry, to have children."

"My parents' deaths left me to the not-so-tender mercies of my village. Why would I risk doing the same to my own child?"

But Neilina knew it was more than that. She'd rescued Freya when the girl was maybe eleven summers and they'd been together almost a decade. Freya had long since reached the age at which she could marry, but she'd denied any interest in returning to the human settlements.

She did not have a choice.

Neilina had no idea how long this journey would take, how many days or months she would have to live among the other Chrechte wolves if she hoped to save their clans from annihilation.

The one certainty she did have was that she would not allow to happen to them what had happened to her birth pack.

"Our ancient teachings exhort Chrechte to value all life and to respect the other races. The *kotrondmenskr* do not do that. To set an *asmundr* against other Chrechte for the purpose of overtaking land or possessions is anathema to our kind."

"Surely not all Paindeal are responsible for the actions of one man, no matter how evil he might be," Freya continued. "You have always claimed there are good as well as bad men. That humanity is not reflected in only the evil, but in the good. Do you not believe that any longer?"

"Of course I believe it, but this is different."

"How? One *asmundr* broke his vow to protect the Chrechte and turned his strength toward conquest and power. That does not mean his entire race is corrupt. By that reasoning, all Faol would be as evil as the Fearghall we travel to fight against."

The reminder was not welcome, but Neilina could not dismiss Freya's reasoning. It was sound.

Even if Neilina did not want to admit it, so she said nothing.

Freya nodded, as if Neilina's silence was agreement. "The terrible actions of that *asmundr* were more than two hundred years ago. Even if his...pack?" Freya paused as if unsure of her terminology.

"Pride," Neilina supplied.

"Even if his pride believed that was acceptable then, couldn't they have learned their lesson and changed by now? The rest of the Vikings have. They no longer plunder our coastlines, or even trade in slaves as they once did."

Neilina wanted to say, "No." To deny any hope of goodness among the Paindeal, but if she did, it would perhaps undo all her efforts convincing Freya that not all men were slavering monsters bent on sexual conquest.

"We need to eat and then finish preparing for the journey." Neilina sat down before their repast, taking an oatcake into her hand.

She was no more ready to face the possibility that the murderers of her family might come from a race that was not all evil than she was prepared to verbalize her true cynicism to her adopted daughter.

The pain of their loss had not dulled with time, nor had her guilt for not being the *conriocht* they needed. Neilina had lost her battle with the *asmundr* and the consequences for her people had been devastating.

***

Haakon woke before dawn, reaching for his sword even before he was fully conscious. He had his blade to the throat of the intruder into his family's longhouse a second later. His eyes adjusted to the darkness quickly and he recognized their pride's Seer, the old man's face etched with impatience rather than fear.

"Get that blade away from my throat, boy. I've had a vision and you must act."

Haakon let the sword drop, but he kept his grip firm on the handle, his body still tense and ready for battle. "Can this not wait for morning?"

"No." Osmend made no effort to speak quietly and allow the others in the long house to sleep as Haakon had done. "It is a matter of life and death for a Chrechte."

Haakon understood the Seer's visit, regardless of the hour. They could not afford to lose even a single of their numbers if the loss could be prevented.

"Explain."

"Do not take that tone with me, boy. You may be *asmundr*, but I was *seeing* for this pride before you were a twinkle in your father's eyes, may God rest his soul."

Considering the fact Bjorn, the Firebrand, had never accepted the religion from Rome, Haakon was not sure how much rest their God would give his soul. "Forgive my impatience, but you did say the matter was urgent."

"Did I?"

"Life or death and it could not wait." Didn't the old man even remember his own claims?

"I suppose that could be considered urgent."

What else? Haakon wondered, but did not make the mistake of asking aloud, uninterested in another rebuke from the old man.

Osmend clasped his hands against his belly and took a deep breath, let it out and then breathed again. "There is a boat. It is filled with Chrechte."

"Where?"

"Somewhere on the sea."

"And I'm supposed to do what? Use a divining rod to figure out where?"

"Do not be impertinent. These wolf shifters are on their way to Groenland."

"Wolf shifters?" Like his mate? Could they be from her pack?

No, she said her pack was gone. That his father had killed them all.

As quick tempered as Bjorn could be, Haakon could not imagine his father doing these heinous acts. He knew the man had been a Viking, that he had battled and killed Chrechte, but a murderer of entire packs?

It did not fit with the *kotrondmenskr* he knew, the *asmundr* that had taught him so sternly to live by the ancient ways of their people.

Haakon forced the disturbing thoughts from his mind. His mate was not his mate and had made it clear she never would be. What his father had or had not done to her pack was not what he needed to concern himself with right now.

Haakon had Chrechte to save.

"*Ja,*" the old Seer affirmed. "They are *uffe,* but that makes no difference to your responsibility to them."

"I never said it did." His father had admitted to living by a different code centuries before, but he'd taught Haakon that *his* role was guardian to all Chrechte.

Osmend nodded his grizzled head, his once red beard, now grey touching his chest when he did so. "That is as it should be. You are *asmundr.* Chosen by fate to protect all our people."

"So you said the day you touched my hand to the *Paindeal Neart.*" The day he'd first shifted into the giant cat of prey with fangs longer than his human hand and sharper than any sword he'd ever owned.

"You need to get traveling if you are going to save the *uffe.*"

"Traveling where?" Haakon demanded, doing nothing to stifle his irritation at the Seer's roundabout way of making a point.

"They are headed to the wrong side of our land."

"The township where no Chrechte live?" They were Norseman, just like Haakon's people, but none of the Chrechte had settled on the opposite coastline.

"Yes."

"They won't harm the *uffe* just for coming." The townspeople in both settlements answered to a priest and a bishop now. The way of the Viking was no longer *their* way.

Or so the humans claimed. They lived much as any man or woman on the mainland, or so his father always claimed.

"They are not Norsemen, but Scots, and strangers. I do not know the why of it, but my visions do not lie. You must meet that boat and stop the *uffe* from going to the other township."

"Then that is what I will do." Because unlike what his *kamerat* believed, powerful warrior he might be, Haakon valued all life, Chrechte most of all.

#

Neilina settled Dìonach into the center of the boat, nodding to herself as the animal's weight gave the craft necessary ballast for stability. She and Freya *could* make this journey. They had no choice.

Her dreams said that the safety of the Balmoral clan and its allies depended on her doing so.

Freya stepped gingerly into the boat. "I still think this is mad."

"Your opinion has been noted. Would you have me ignore the plight of the Chrechte who need my protection because reaching them will be dangerous?"

"Nay. You did not ignore my plight despite the numbers being overwhelmingly against you in the fight."

"And still I won."

"Well, you are *conriocht*."

"And they were treacherous human males, blinded by their terrible lusts."

"There is that."

"I fought and won that battle, taking you away from the village which had not taken your protection seriously since your parents' death. I will fight the battle against the sea if need be."

Freya smiled, her face young and carefree for that moment. "If anyone can fight against the sea and win, it is you."

***

Haakon rode his large black stallion, bred for the colder climes of his homeland.

Though he was not sure Groenland could boast the warmer summers it once had. The land of the Danes would have to be cold indeed to be considered more frigid. He would not know, never having been anywhere but the place of his birth.

But he knew the land he and his stallion traversed as well as the four corners of the longhouse in which he lived. He would reach the nearest beach landing spot to the other Norse township tomorrow before the sun was high in the sky. According to the Seer, that would get him there in time to intercept the Scottish *uffe*.

What had brought the other Chrechte to Groenland? Why were they in danger if they made it to the village?

Not for the first time, Haakon contemplated the separation of the Chrechte races and what had caused it to happen so many centuries before. Even his father hadn't been entirely clear on the why, just that there were other Chrechte and ancient wisdom said they should not seek them out. But why?

Fate was sending Haakon to the aid of *uffe* now. Eventually, the wolves would realize they were dealing with another Chrechte. *If* they were any good at putting the pieces together. Haakon could hide his nature, but it was not a skill all the *kotrondmenskr* were taught. Not for centuries, as no Chrechte enemies lived near enough to make the skill desirable for any but the most elite warriors. For them, it was a rite of passage.

Had Haakon not been able to hide his nature, he would not have been given his second chance at the *Paindeal Neart* and become *asmundr*.

Under the strict taskmaster of his father, Haakon had worked hard to master that skill and all that made a warrior strong and capable of protecting his people.

Being *asmundr* had been written by fate into Haakon's destiny since before his birth. His father had said so many times.

Haakon had felt the truth of Bjorn's words from an early age though. So strongly that he never balked at the rigorous training.

He camped that night, rolled in his furs, beside his horse on the ground, the stallion sleeping more peacefully than the beast within Haakon. It was not the cold that kept him restless, though the near freezing summer night temperatures would have kept him awake if he were human.

He was not, and his *sabeltann* nature kept him warm. He had always been less affected by weather than even his brethren. Only his cousin, Einarr, who shared his soul with the giant tigers of the Rus, could withstand the cold as well as Haakon.

No, it was thoughts of who he was going to meet that kept him awake as the moon climbed in the sky.

Uffe. Men who shared their spirits with the wolf. Chrechte that the *asmundr* had never thought he would meet, much less be called on to protect.

Finally, he slept, but his dreams tried to take him to that *other* place. He could sense his mate pulling at him, her soul calling to his, but even in sleep his will was too strong, his denial too great. He'd had almost a decade to hone it. His beast might gnash at the restraint, but Haakon's mind refused that journey. And so then did his body.

And his beast? The *sabeltann* settled into sleep, even his Chrechte nature recognizing the repeated and final rejection he had been dealt by his *kamerat*.

***

Her heart filled with a trepidation she would never allow Freya to see; Neilina looked over the supplies she and her adopted daughter had loaded onto the boat in the hour before dawn.

The tide was right for sailing, but in a couple of hours, the water of her inlet would be too shallow for an easy launch.

They had packed enough food for the journey and a few days beyond. Their sleeping furs were stowed neatly, their weapons, as well, including plenty of arrows for each woman with their unique fletching. Everything they needed to care for the weapons resided in a small cask in the boat near where her bear lay, sleeping.

They had brought their most important possessions because there could be no guarantee they would make it back to their cave home. Though they had not brought everything, just the things both women would grieve if they did not return.

"It feels like we are saying goodbye to our home," Freya said, her voice hushed in the early morning quiet.

"We will be back," Neilina said more in hope than in certainty.

The pile of things in the boat gave lie to her words. She had a terrible feeling they would not be returning to her island, that she would never again know either the peace or the loneliness of her self-imposed exile.

The Faol needed all their *conriocht* to fight the coming battles and not succumb to the will of the Fearghall to destroy them.

Freya gave her a look. "If you believed that, I wouldn't be going with you. You wouldn't risk it."

"It's a bigger risk to leave you here and chance a hunting party coming upon you."

"The hunters don't venture that deep into our forest. Our cave is unknown to them."

"But they come deeper into the woods every year."

"Did your mate bring you into the Chrechte spirit world last night?" Freya asked, clearly uninterested in debating the habits of the village men.

"He did not." Neilina had come to the magical place to have her eyes fall first upon the sword he'd planted in the ground and then onto the mist beyond. Mist so thick she could not see through or beyond it.

Something cold had settled in her chest at that sight, something that had not dissipated with her warm porridge for breakfast. A cold that even now made Neilina draw her cloak more tightly around her.

"So, you are not denying he is your mate?"

Neilina shrugged. "What would be the point? You do not seem willing to believe me."

"You taught me to discern a lie from the truth."

Neilina sighed. "Perhaps I should have taken my own advice."

"What do you mean?"

Neilina just shook her head and indicated that Freya should step into the boat before Neilina used her *conriocht* strength to push it from its mooring.

She wasn't going to tell the girl about the sword, or the now impenetrable mist. Revealing that Haakon had finally given up on their mating would not change anything.

Not that she wanted anything changed. She was content as things were.

If her wolf howled in protest, Neilina pretended not to hear.

CHAPTER THREE

Haakon rose as the sun turned the sky shades of pink, yellow and orange. He'd slept deeply and felt no fatigue, despite the short number of hours spent somnolent.

Breaking his fast with dried elk and the grainy bread his aunt had provide for the journey, Haakon washed it down with water from his holding skin. After, he tended to his horse and then was on his way again. He rode at a steady pace, pushing the battle trained stallion, but not more than the animal could safely withstand. It would do Haakon no good to exhaust his horse.

He arrived at the coastline the Seer had described to him mid-morning, more shocked than he should be by the boat being dragged up onto the rocky beach some distance away. He'd never known Osmend to be wrong in his visions, but in this case, Haakon had doubted.

Men in three different colored plaids, that marked them as Scots, pulled the boat ashore, doing a fair job of making sure it would not float away on the next tide. So, not only Faol, but from the land of the Gael as well.

Riding his horse forward, Haakon was unsurprised when the men all turned to watch him arrive long before he was in normal hearing distance. He concentrated on suppressing the scent of his own Chrechte nature and hailed the men in Gaelic, a language, like English and that of the Franks, his father had taught him, insisting on fluency.

"Well met, travelers. What brings you to Groenland?"

A man came forward, only an inch, or so shorter than Haakon's six and a half feet, the Faol had dark hair, eyes the color of good, aged whiskey, and a sword that would please a Viking. "I am Maon. We are here, looking for our cousins."

Haakon cocked his head to one side, giving the man in the yellow, black and red plaid along with his companions, a steady look. "You do not have the look of any in my township, or the one nearest this landing point."

It was a good story if they were here to find the Paindeal though. There were many settlements in Scotland established by the Norse. The idea these men might have distant family among the Norse of the Groenland was not so hard to accept.

Maon shrugged. "You said there is a township near here? We will start there, looking for our family."

"It is not such a friendly place. You should come first to my township. You will be welcomed, though you are not from the Norse."

"Is that nearby as well?" one of the men wearing a blue, yellow and green plaid asked.

"It is a fair walk. It took me a day and a half of riding." Haakon realized that convincing them not to go to the other township without admitting his nature and that a Seer was directing him might not be possible.

He'd already admitted there were none in his village that had the look of them.

"You must be on your way to this other village then. We'll travel with you, if you don't mind." Maon spoke to Haakon, but directed the Faol who had travelled with him to their tasks with signals from his hands.

The men's discipline impressed Haakon, but he needed to get a better sense of their intentions before he would be ready to reveal his nature to these strangers. Though he'd known what they were, he'd noticed that they kept their nature hidden from him. Was it because they were generally cautious, or for other, more nefarious reasons?

He would no doubt have to reveal his Chrechte nature if he wanted to protect them as was his duty. Once his beast was settled.

Right now, it prowled around inside him, agitated at having a group of powerful Chrechte so close to him.

He watched them unload the boat in silence before admitting, "I am not going to the township."

Maon stopped directing his men and gave Haakon a penetrating look. "You've not given your name, Norseman."

"I am called Haakon." He was also called *asmundr* and the nickname his cousin had saddled him with, Hand of Thor, for his prowess in battle and with the sword. "Nephew to the *jarl* of my area."

"And you are not from *this* town, but you have travelled more than a day to reach this shore. Why?" Maon frowned. "If you don't mind me asking." Though his tone and expression said very clearly he didn't really care if Haakon minded, or not. "And how is it that you speak our tongue so smoothly?"

Haakon had to respect a man who would stand up so easily to him. Even those ignorant of his nature walked a wide path around him because of his size. His speed and strength only enhanced the attitude of caution he was usually met with.

He put his hand out to Maon. One of Haakon's Chrechte gifts was the ability to read the soul of a man when their palms pressed. He could not read minds, or sense emotion any better than the next Chrechte, but he knew if a man, or woman, had a black soul, a pure soul, or something in between, as most did.

"Wait!" the man who had spoken before shouted as Maon went to take Haakon's hand.

Maon looked at the soldier. "Why?"

The man did not answer but walked up to Haakon. "I am Artair, grandson of the Seer of the Balmoral pack." The others gasped, or glared, when the young man used pack instead of clan, but one soldier, who wore the same plaid, sent burning coals toward Haakon with his gaze. The brown-haired man waved the others off and met Haakon's gaze. "I have seen you in my dreams."

"I've been dreamt about by the women of my village, but not the men." Haakon made the joke even as he questioned in his own mind what the young soldier had dreamed.

His skin now awash with color, nevertheless, the younger man took a step forward, so he stood only inches from Haakon. "I am Artair. You are protector of your people. I am not, though I am Chrechte and charged to protect my pack as all members are. Even so, you and I have much in common."

Haakon narrowed his eyes at Artair. "What?"

"Both our sacred mates deny us."

Haakon felt the weight of Thor's hammer slamming into his chest. "You cannot know this."

"I have dreamt and while I am no Seer, my grandda has taught me how to tell when a dream is prophetic and when it is nothing more than mists in the brain burned away with morning's first light."

"Where is your sacred mate?" Haakon asked, more to give himself time to digest the claims of the young Balmoral soldier.

Artair cast his gaze to another man, the one whose glare grew only more furious the longer Haakon and Artair spoke.

"He is here with you."

"He is my best friend."

"But he has denied the pull between mates."

"Aye."

"I am sorry." Haakon knew firsthand the pain of that situation, not that he'd ever admit to such a thing.

Artair shrugged. "We cannot change the heart of another."

"Or their mind when it is set against us," Haakon agreed, thinking of his own Norse-hating mate.

"You've dreamed of this man?" Maon asked, his tone suspicious. "You say he's a protector of his people. What does that mean exactly?"

Haakon allowed his big cat's nature to come to the fore and watched as the wolves reacted with varying degrees of unease. All but Maon. His grin split his face. "You are *Paindeal*. We have found you."

"You have found a *Paindeal*. Artair speaks true when he says I am protector, but not only of my people. I protect any Chrechte as any guardian should."

"You're a Griffin?" one of the soldiers wearing a plaid in blue and green with black stripes asked with undisguised awe.

Did these Chrechte not know anything about their people's protectors? "A Griffin can only come about if the Paindeal and the Éan mate, then both their sacred stones must choose her, or him."

"Females can be guardians?" Maon asked with shock.

"Do you have no female *conriocht* among you?"

Maon blanched. "You know about the *conriocht*?"

Haakon turned and began heading toward a place up the beach they could arrange their packs and eat a meal before they headed toward his uncle's territory. "More than you know about the protectors from our race it would seem."

They followed him as he'd assumed they would.

The young soldier who had seemed to be so awed by Haakon's nature asked, "What are you if not a Griffin?"

Haakon looked back at them over his shoulder. "One day perhaps we will hunt together and you will see for yourself."

Maon nodded when the younger soldier merely looked on in dumbfounded silence. "Fair enough. Did your dreams send you here to us?"

"No. The visions of our Seer." Haakon led his horse to a stream he knew was fresh water, near where the animal could graze, before turning back to the men. "He claims that if you go to the nearby township, some, or all of you will die."

Maon's expression turned harsh. "What? Why?"

"I do not know. If you believe the wily old bastard, he doesn't either." Haakon wasn't entirely sure he did.

"Your Seer sent you to us?" another soldier asked, likely trying to understand this odd meeting on the shore of the dangerous sea that surrounded Groenland.

Sailing these waters was not for the faint of heart, or any who lacked experience and the sturdiest of boats.

"He did."

"To protect us?" Maon confirmed.

"Such is my duty."

"But you are protector to the *paindeal* not the Faol."

"Who taught you that any guardian was protector of only one race? When we are called through our Sacred Stones to the shift others of our race cannot make, we are called to a higher purpose. We become protector of *all* Chrechte." Even complete strangers who did not have any more sense than to cross the waters on a whim, searching for a branch to their family tree that had broken off so long ago, the trunk showed little sign of it ever having been there.

"Why did the Paindeal leave?" Artair asked, as if reading Haakon's mind.

"Even my father, who had lived nearly a Millennium when he died, did not know." Or perhaps, he had not wanted to tell Haakon.

He'd often wondered how his father, who must have been alive when the separation first took place, did not know why it had happened. He'd been adamant nothing good could come of bringing the Paindeal back together with the other Chrechte, but Haakon had to wonder at that too.

Their people were dying out, their numbers so low, men like Artair who had sacred mates of the same sex were required to mate in the fur with a female in the hopes of pregnancy before being allowed to consummate their true mating. And still, every generation, there were fewer of them.

He wondered if the wolves had similar laws.

Maon looked at Haakon intently. "So, the *conriocht* are meant to protect all Chrechte, not just the Faol."

"*Ja.* And were a dragon alive today, he would be not only King of the Éan, but grand protector of all Chrechte living."

"What about the Fearghall? Are we meant to protect them too?" Maon asked with distaste lacing his every word as his soldiers set out the food they had brought with them.

Haakon would not have blamed them if they had needed to hunt, but these Scots showed they were as prepared as any Viking who had travelled the seas.

"This Fearghall, they are the ones that believe only the Faol should live, that human mates should be killed to protect the Chrechte bloodlines? *Ja?*"

Maon looked shocked that Haakon knew of these Chrechte whose beliefs were an abomination.

"My father was *asmundr* before me and lived many centuries. He travelled far and wide before settling here in Groenland."

"You said he is gone?" Artair asked, sympathy in his dark brown gaze.

His mate, who wanted only to be his friend, grunted, gave Artair and Haakon a glare and then stomped off to fill skins with water from the stream where Haakon's horse drank.

Haakon nodded at Artair. "He is."

"And your uncle? Is he as old as your father?" Maon asked.

"*Nei.* He is my mother's brother." Haakon pulled oatcakes and smoked fish from his pack for his own repast. "Bjorn, the Firebrand, did not find his sacred mate until he had lived centuries."

One of the soldiers asked Haakon, "He had a fiery temper?"

"Your mother was Paindeal as well?" Maon asked at the same time.

Recognizing that Maon was the leader of this band of travelers, Haakon answered him first. "She was not a shifting Chrechte, but yes." He flicked a gaze to the other soldier. "My father had a temper as volatile as the sea storms that drowned many a Viking sailor."

The young solider nodded, giving Haakon a look that obviously questioned whether he shared his father's temperament. Haakon thought it did no harm to have the soldiers cautious of him, so he said nothing to allay fear.

Not that their leader showed an inkling of it. "One of her parents was human?"

"*Ja*. The Paindeal do not share the views of the Fearghall."

"Nor do the Faol who follow Chrechte law," Maon assured Haakon.

"That is good to know."

They ate together and Haakon learned that two of the clansmen were Sinclair, two from the Balmoral and Maon and one other of the MacLeod pack. He learned they had been traveling for three years, searching for the Paindeal. Starting in Norvegr, which they called Norway, moving to Islandia or Iceland and finally coming to Groenland, in search of his people.

What he had not yet learned was why Maon and the others sought the Paindeal. Maon had alluded to being on a quest sent by his clan's *celi di* who was also Seer.

Now they discussed their travel to his township, but Haakon still wondered at these Faol's motives for seeking out the Paindeal.

"Wouldn't it be easier to take the boat along the coastline?" Maon asked when Haakon suggested they begin their hike.

"The waters here are treacherous."

"Aye, they're a challenge to be sure, but we've crossed the sea, sailed the coast of Norway and landed on the shores of both Iceland and here." Maon didn't sound like he was boasting, merely stating a fact.

Haakon shrugged his agreement. "Perhaps you are experienced enough sailors to manage it."

Artair's mate, who Haakon had discovered was called Gart, snorted. "Perhaps we are," he said with a bite and no little amount of sarcasm.

Maon frowned at Gart, while Artair scolded him. "That the protector of our people shows concern for our welfare is naught to mock, Gart of the Balmoral."

"We have only his word *he* is *our* protector. For all we know, he intends to lead us into a trap."

"To what purpose?" Haakon asked, more out of curiosity than annoyance.

"Mayhap despite your words to the contrary, the Paindeal share the views of the Fearghall. There's a reason our peoples have been separated these centuries."

Artair gasped with clear affront on Haakon's behalf. The other soldiers looked on with wide-eyed uncertainty, but Maon frowned and opened his mouth to speak.

Haakon waved at him to remain silent. He would answer this foolish soldier's question. "If we did...if I meant you harm, you would all be dead and I would be on my way back to my pride, not sharing a repast with you."

"You couldn't kill us even if you are this *asmundr* you claim to be."

"*Ja*, I am *asmundr*. Have been for nine years and none, no not even a group of *uffe* can defeat me in battle."

"We have our own guardian," Gart sneered, shooting a sidelong glance toward Maon.

Haakon had wondered, but he shrugged, not wishing to denigrate the prowess of the other protector, but knowing the truth. "A *conriocht* is not likely to defeat an *asmundr* in battle."

A giant tiger of the Rus, like his cousin Einarr? Yes. But Haakon's beast was half again bigger and his fangs could rip through the flesh of even a *conriocht*, his strength so great, even two *conriocht* would find it more than difficult to subdue him. They would most likely pay with their lives.

"You said you are not griffin," Maon observed, again showing no signs of concern, and Haakon's respect for the other guardian grew.

"I am not, but it would take a griffin, or the dragon of legends to easily defeat me."

The way all the soldiers went tense at that proclamation made Haakon think they had some experience with one of those two ancient and powerful beings. He could not be sure which one, as their assumption he was griffin could be due to the fact they had met one. But it was equally likely they knew or knew of a dragon guardian.

If they did, this being was someone Haakon would like to meet. As, according to ancient Chrechte law, the dragon stood above all pride, pack or flock alphas. If a dragon walked the earth, Haakon owed him his allegiance and said so.

Either was possible if they were in contact with the Éan.

"You have Éan living among you?"

"We do, though their joining of the clans is recent."

"You mean a dragon is supposed to rule all Chrechte, like a King?" one of the soldiers asked.

"Not *like* a King. He *is* king, but he is also the ultimate protector and all guardians submit to his will, even above their own alphas."

"I don't think the Sinclair is going to like hearing that," one of his soldiers muttered under his breath.

Haakon gave Maon a questioning look, but the other Chrechte merely shook his head. "We will speak more about our reasons for being here and the discoveries we have made since the Éan and Paindeal joined again once we have the ear of your *jarl*."

Haakon nodded, understanding why Maon would wish to tell his tale only once, but felt the need to warn them, "*Ja*. I will wait, but understand this, if your intentions toward my pride is in any way to do them harm, you will all perish for your error in judgement."

Gart sputtered his anger, a couple of soldiers paled, but Maon simply nodded his agreement. "We mean you and your pride no harm."

Haakon acknowledged Maon's words with a noncommittal inclination of his head. "Sailing to our shores will not necessarily take you any less time and there is risk."

"But we will have our boat to hand and everything in it." Unlike Gart, Maon did not boast of their prowess at sea, but showed no sign of concern about taking to the water again either.

And he made a fair point. "*Ja*. Follow the coastline until you see..." Haakon gave them directions on where best to land nearest his uncle's holding. "Wait for me there. If I arrive first, I will wait for you."

The young Artair looked longingly at Haakon's horse before casting a frown at the boat. This Faol was no Viking, excited to take to the water again, but Haakon did not blame him. Not all were meant to spend their life aboard ships, looking for fortune and adventure. The Viking Way had all but died out among the Norse anyway, just as the Paindeal.

"Come with me," Haakon said to Artair. "You can tell me about the Faol and why you have come to Groenland looking for the Paindeal."

"I'll leave that explanation to Maon, but I'm happy to tell you of our people."

Accepting that Maon wanted to be the one to share his *celi di's* visions, Haakon nodded. "Come, we will let the horse rest from riders for a while before we take to his back."

"Wait!" Gart demanded. "Artair, you should stay with us."

Artair adjusted his plaid and the weapons he wore for the hike ahead. "I would be happy if I never had to get on a boat again, but since that isn't possible, I will at least avoid one more trip."

"You don't need to go with *him*."

Haakon's patience with the recalcitrant mate was rapidly disappearing.

But before he could put the Faol in his place, Artair growled at his fellow clansman. "Your words are offensive! He is *asmundr*! Guardian to all our people. I couldn't be safer with another Chrechte."

Gart winced, as if Artair's words hurt him. But having experience with the rejection of a mate, Haakon had no sympathy for the Balmoral.

"Tell him, Maon. Tell him he has to come with us," Gart implored their leader.

But Maon's expression was dark as he turned it on Gart. "Artair is a grown man, a Faol trained in battle. I trust him to make his own decisions, Gart. Just as every Chechte must follow the dictates of his own conscience."

Well, that was pointed and not easily misinterpreted. There could be no doubt that the leader of this group of Chrechte explorers was aware the two Balmorals were mates and that Gart had denied Artair his place in the other Chrechte's life.

Gart scowled at them all before turning and stomping away.

"He acts like a jealous lover," Maon observed to Artair.

"He isn't one." Artair's tone was tinged with bitterness, but his expression had not turned sour.

Like Haakon, the other Chrechte had long since accepted the condition of his mating, or lack thereof.

"He wants children?" Maon asked.

"That is what he says." Artair looked around them with pointed regard. "He's not going to build a family hundreds of miles from the females of our packs."

"Nay. He is not." Maon sighed. "It is not always easy for a wolf to accept the dictates of his Chrechte spirit."

Artair grabbed a pack to carry. "If you say so." He turned to Haakon. "Are you ready to be on our way?"

"*Ja.*"

They left without another word between Artair and the other Faol.

***

Their second day out to sea, neither Neilina, nor Freya was feeling particularly confident as sailors, or the certainty of reaching their destination. A squall had erupted out of nowhere. One moment the sky had been blue and clear to the horizon. Minutes later, ominous grey clouds blocked the light of the sun and powerful winds sent waves crashing over the sides of their boat.

"Quick, bring the sail down," Neilina yelled above the wind, already working on the ropes.

Freya helped her, the sails whipping to and fro as they worked. Had she not had the strength and speed of a Chrechte, they would have lost the sail and perhaps the mast as well. But she and Freya managed to get it tied down.

Even without the sail, and against their best and most stringent efforts, the force of the wind took the boat off course.

As the wind and waves drove them further and further from their original heading, the women fought the storm. All that afternoon and night, they bailed water out of the bottom of the boat so they did not sink and did their best to keep dry what they could so all their supplies were not destroyed by the driving rains.

They worked in silence, neither woman prone to hysterics. After all, for all intents and purposes, Neilina had raised Freya. And she had not raised her daughter to fall into a fit of vapors at the first sign of adversity.

Dìonach made up for their silence, however. The bear growled and sent awful keening sounds into the wind in accompaniment to their efforts, but she did not move from her position in the center of the boat.

And for that, Neilina was unutterably grateful, for surely they would have capsized. When the winds finally died down and the waves no longer sent buckets of water into their gunwale with every gust, the stars had disappeared from the sky and dawn was imminent.

Exhausted, even with her Chrechte strength to buoy her, Neilina took stock of their situation with a considered look at the horizon. They were well off course. Neilina did not show Freya the worry this caused her.

While she could read the signs of the sun and the stars at night to keep them going in the right direction, when it came down to it, she very much feared they would end up sailing right past Scotland. At present, they were on a course toward Iceland, if she was not mistaken. Or maybe Greenland. Certainly, they were not headed south as they should have been to reach the Scottish mainland in what would otherwise have been no more than a day or two of seafaring.

"I think we should drop anchor and sleep. The skies are clear, and I don't have the strength to guide the boat even if you do." Her face cast in grey tones, dark circles under her eyes, Freya looked as exhausted as she claimed.

Neilina nodded. "Later this day will be soon enough to raise anchor and sail to get us back on course for Scotland." She only hoped she was not lying to her charge and had not allowed her dreams to lead them both to a watery death.

***

Artair turned out to be a pleasant traveling companion. Easily keeping up with Haakon's pace, despite being several inches shorter, he did as promised, telling Haakon about the Faol who lived among the clans in Scotland. His love for his island home was apparent, so Haakon asked him why he had been sent on this journey, one from which all who embarked had to know there was no guarantee of surviving.

Of the original 25 ships that had set sail with his forefather, Eirik the Red from Iceland, only 14 had landed on Groenland's shores. The other 11 had perished along with all those onboard.

"I volunteered to accompany Maon on this trip. All of us did."

"Had any of you been on a sea faring journey before?"

"Nay."

"Either you are Chrechte of laudable courage, or fools."

Artair laughed. "A little of both, I think. The journey had to be undertaken. The ultimate survival of our race depended on it."

"This is what you wish me to wait for Maon to explain?"

"I would, yes. He was commissioned by the Sinclair *celi di* to contact the Paindeal and reunite the races."

"This is the *celi di* who is also a Seer?"

"Yes. She belongs to the Sinclair clan, but she was born a Donegal." He opened his mouth and then shut it, like he wanted to say something but thought better of it.

"So, your Chrechte move between the clans?"

"They do now. We didn't before, but the Balmoral took the Sinclair's first intended along with his sister."

"That sounds like an instigation to war, not something that would make your Chrechte begin shifting between packs."

"The Balmoral is a superior alpha."

"For the Sinclair alpha to forgive the insult, he must have more patience than any pride alpha I have known."

"There were misunderstandings, but our alpha ended up married to the taken woman's sister. Our lady has brought nothing but joy and good things to our clan."

"And so these two powerful alphas are now friends?"

"Aye."

"And the Donegal alpha?"

"He trains for his role under the former Sinclair second-in-command."

Haakon shook his head in wonder. He had been raised in a pride that never sought out other Chrechte. None in Haakon's lifetime had left the pride; none had gone wandering since long before his birth. It was hard for him to conceive of this openness between the packs. "And all of your packs have *celi di* that are Seers as well?"

There had to be many more of the Faol than the Paindeal.

"Nay. The Sinclairs have a priest. He is human, and a Seer who used to be human, none that claim the title of both."

"Used to be human? He was of Chrechte heritage and chosen by your Sacred Stone to complete his first shift?"

"*She*, but aye. You knew that was possible? We didn't until the *celi di* had a vision."

"The wolves are plentiful, but you've lost much of your history." Haakon inhaled the scents around them, letting his beast seek out any potential danger.

Though he could detect nothing to cause his beast concern, his gums itched and his joints ached with the need to shift. Something was causing his beast to be agitated, something calling to his beast that he could not smell, see or hear.

"The Balmoral Seer is your grandfather, you said?" he asked, rather than give into the beast.

"Aye. He has trained many Seers. The one who used to be MacLeod but is now Sinclair, and most recently the Seer who serves the MacLeod clan. She's wife to the laird and pack alpha."

"The Sinclairs have *two* Seers?" Haakon's pride's Seer was a very old man, though few knew how old. Certainly, Haakon did not. His father had.

But in all his years, not another Seer had been born to their pride for him to train as replacement. When he died, the *kotrondmenskr* would be without one.

Something else the Faol had said caught at Haakon's attention. "You said laird and alpha, are not pack alphas the lairds of their clan?"

No pride alpha would allow another to be *jarl* of the territory, no matter the rights of a blood descendant.

"Aye, they are. At least in recorded memory."

"There was a time when the Chrechte were not part of the clans." They had lived independently in the forest. Haakon's father had told him of the ancient days when all Chrechte lived closer to their animal counterparts than they did in the modern world.

"We are a fierce and contentious people."

"*Ja.*" The Vikings had gained a large part of their ruthless reputation from the actions of many Paindeal among them. "But our numbers are dwindling."

"Are they?" Artair asked. "Do you still have use of the *Paindeal Neart.*"

"We do." Though the one they used was a small fragment of the larger stone that the Paindeal who had left to journey south to the Land of the Sun had taken with them so many centuries before.

Unsure how much he trusted these Faol, Haakon did not mention that fact.

"It's just that the Éan admitted that if they didn't go through the coming of age ceremony with their stone, they could not father or give birth to children who shared their Chrechte nature."

Haakon considered that in silence as they walked. His father had once said that the coming of age ceremony was naught like it once was. That the light emanating from the stone was a small flicker compared to the glow that had surrounded him when he'd come of age.

Could the size of their stone have something to do with the lack of new Chrechte children born to their people over the past generations?

It was something to consider. What would the Seer say?

Certainly, Haakon had every intention of asking the wily old man.

CHAPTER FOUR

It took Haakon and Artair the rest of that day and the better part of the next to reach the landing spot he'd sent the other Faol to in his uncle's territory. Although they'd run in their shifted forms part of the previous day and all of that one, Haakon had been too eager for information only available when talking in their human form the day before and they'd spent most of it walking. They'd stopped to shift back when they were over a single rise from the landing beach he'd directed the rest of the Faol to.

When they arrived, the ship was there, and the others were waiting. Gart, the mate who wanted a wife and children, rather than to claim the great gift fate had laid before him, paced on the beach. He stopped and tilted his head, spinning to face them as Haakon and Artair came over the rise.

Maon, the other MacLeod soldier and the Sinclairs noticed them after Gart.

Artair had said that none of the Donegals had come on the journey because their laird was just coming into his own at the age of twenty-five and still training under the Sinclair's former second-in-command. Artair had not shared that the man was both Éan shifter and Faol, but Haakon had guessed.

He had not expressed his belief for confirmation but was sure it was true. The description of the Chrechte's prowess in certain areas of battle and battle readiness, the slips about flying, never quite said, but allusions a man of Haakon's knowledge could not ignore.

Gart came striding forward, Maon and the others a few steps behind. "Finally. I thought something had happened to you two."

"What do you think could happen to an *asmundr*?" Haakon asked, humor at the man's foolish belief filling his voice. "Even a griffin would pause before attacking me."

Arrogant? Perhaps, but also true.

Artair nodded his agreement, his expression holding some of his initial shock at seeing Haakon's shifted form for the first time the day before.

Gart sneered. "Whatever you shift into, it can't be that impressive. You're not a dragon."

"No. Only the Éan can bring forth the Dragon guardian, but as I told you yesterday it would take a *conriocht* of uncommon skills and size to defeat me alone." He stepped forward until Gart took a single step back, pacifying the beast roaring inside Haakon. "But you? You are no *conriocht*. My patience with your idiocy will not last much longer."

Gart glared at him, refusing to respond.

"He isn't *conriocht*," Artair confirmed. "Gart is too interested in his own welfare to be called by our sacred stone to protect the Faol, much less all Chrechte."

Once again, Gart looked hurt by his mate's opinion, but he said nothing in his own defense.

"No one knows who the stone will find worthy, even a former soldier of the *Fearghall* who sought to destroy what he did not understand." Maon whiskey amber gaze was haunted.

And Haakon had no trouble working out that it was himself he spoke of.

Haakon turned away from Gart, his action in itself an insult as it reflected how unworried he was to have the Faol at his back, and faced the alpha of this small group. "Even after the call, guardians can make terrible mistakes." His father had fought his own people, had murdered the Faol in the pursuit of land and riches on behalf of his king, if Haakon's mate was to be believed. "You chose to turn from that path and the Spirit that guides us all now leads you on another."

"And that Spirit never makes mistakes?"

"I am sure the Faol my father killed during his years leading soldiers for his Viking king think a gross error happened when Bjorn, the Firebrand, was given the near unbeatable form of *asmundr*."

"Your father killed the Faol?" Maon asked, his expression going wary.

"I told you he could not be trusted!" Gart's strident tones did nothing to appease Haakon's beast.

"He did." He would not share all his mate had told him because he was still hoping she somehow had misinterpreted his father's actions.

"But you said *asmundr* protect all the Chrechte."

"And that is what he taught me. My mother brought him back from the lost place he lived in for so many centuries." That much, Haakon knew to be true.

"*Ja*, your father, he had his reasons for not respecting the other races of our people." The Seer's old, creaking voice came from behind Haakon. "For hating them."

Shocked he had been unaware of the other Chrechte's approach, Haakon turned to face the old man. Stooped before them, under the burden of his age, his grey hair tied into a braid by his great-great-grandaughter as it always was, his long beard a mix of silver and white, his furs enveloped him like a living shroud.

The Seer had suppressed his nature, but more than that, no scent at all came off him and he moved as silently as the specters said to haunt the ancient places.

"He never said anything like that to me."

Osmend nodded, as if he expected nothing else. "Your father had a sacred mate and another son centuries past."

Haakon stepped back, staggered by the blow of the words against his mind. "My father did not find his mate until my mother. He told me so."

"No, he told you he did not find your mother until he was many centuries old."

"He had *two* sacred mates?" Artair asked, his tone breathless, something like hope lighting his eyes.

And Haakon knew why.

Osmend gave Haakon's traveling companion a knowing look before turning his gaze to Gart, which seemed to make the other Balmoral uncomfortable. "*Ja*. Our sacred mate is a gift from fate, but should we not claim that gift, or should it be denied us..." He paused to cast his aged gaze on Haakon. "There is a chance for every Chrechte that another mate lives for him, or her, to claim."

"So, a man might have a female mate if his first mate is male?" Gart asked, his hope bright as a candle in the darkest hour of night.

The Seer gave Gart a sorrowful glare. "You crave children so much you will deny the mate you've been given?"

"What? Who said I have a mate? I was only asking." Gart moved away from them as if putting distance between himself and the supposition he had a mate.

Osmend shook his gray head. "Do you not realize that if children are what you crave, fate will care for that as well? But if you deny your destiny, *nothing* is certain but that you and your life will be less for it."

"You said Chrechte could have more than one mate."

"Did you not also hear me say that Haakon's father did not find his second mate for *centuries* after the first was stolen by a Faol, their baby with her."

Varying sounds of shock sounded around Haakon, but it was as if those sounds came through the distance of a deep cave. His father had truly had another mate? A son, he had lost? But how could he? He was *asmundr*, who could take his child from him and live?

"Surely he tracked them?" Maon asked, his tone and expression saying he'd witnessed atrocities as great.

He no doubt had. By his own admission, he'd once followed the way of the Fearghall.

"The Faol was no fool, he took to the water." Osmend leaned heavily against his walking stick, taking a deep breath of the sea air. "Even an *asmundr* cannot track scent across the sea."

"But how? The Faol of centuries past did not have seafaring vessels." That was one of the other soldiers.

Haakon cared not for such details though. His father had hidden this terrible thing from him. What else had the man hidden from his only…no not only…but *only living* son.

Osmend gave Haakon a long look before answering the soldier. "You forget that in those times, we were one people. The ability to build a ship was something our Chrechte brethren brought with them from the Land of the Sun."

"But that's not what *our* historians tell us." Maon didn't sound like he was arguing, but trying to understand.

"And are your historians old enough to have seen a sunrise a millennium past?" Osmend demanded imperiously, even as his body sagged against his stick.

The walk from his home to the coast had worn the old Chrechte out.

Though Haakon had not realized the Seer was *that* old. His past and life was shrouded in secrecy and mystery. He had family in the village to be sure, but no one spoke of his age, or his past. Too many feared his ability to curse them, despite their beliefs and supposed trust in the priests from Rome.

"But I won't live that long," Gart said with every evidence of disappointment.

"No. You may well live long enough to find a second mate," Osmend said as if admitting it pained him. "Not one as perfectly in tune with your soul as this worthy soldier, but someone with whom you can have those children you are so worried about."

"All Chrechte should be worried about having children. Our race will not survive if we do not." Haakon found himself spouting what he had been taught even as he wondered at its validity.

According to Artair, the wolves had no trouble bringing forth new generations of Faol.

"Seeking truth, living in a way that benefits others, fighting for peace, these goals will make certain our race survives." Osmend's voice rang with certainty and something *other*, something that called to Haakon's beast. "The laws that require procreation as we have in our clan do nothing but engender division and unhappiness."

"You are required by law to procreate?" Artair asked with shock.

"If two men are mated, they must first attempt for at least three moons to impregnate a female in the fur before they can consummate their own mating and be incapable of helping to grow the pride."

"That is barbaric." It was not Artair speaking that time, but Gart. "You would have your pridemates give up their children to be raised by another because they are mated to men."

Haakon had never considered it in that light. They were such a small pride and all lived close to one another. He hadn't thought it was a great sacrifice, but there was no question Gart believed it would be. And if the looks on the faces of his fellow Faol was any indication, they agreed with him.

Nevertheless, Haakon shrugged. "We are of the original Vikings, that is not the first time our pride has been called such."

The Seer snorted. "Do not be arrogant, boy. The foolish Faol has a point. Your father made many mistakes and perpetuated injustices because of his own pain. Some of those injustices continue to this day."

"But he taught me the right way to be Chrechte." Haakon needed to believe that. For the possibility that he was not the honorable Chrechte he believed himself was a live coal in his chest.

Perhaps his mate had been right to reject him as coming from tainted stock.

"He did at that. But that does not mean everything he said was true, right or of honest benefit to our people. He allowed the law of procreation to stand."

"I don't understand."

"He lost his way after he lost his first mate."

That much Haakon had always known, though the why of his father losing his way, he had not. "Did she never return?"

"Oh, aye. She returned. Pregnant with the Faol's child. She was human and she could marry outside her mating, which is what she had done. Your father was a hard man, dedicated to the welfare of the Chrechte. She was young and beautiful, believed she should be the center of your father's life."

"What of my brother?"

"The Faol and your mother petitioned the Chrechte council for the right to raise him. Considering your father's position and what it required from him, their petition was granted. One voice dissented. The Paindeal councilmember. He argued vehemently against allowing the Faol to take the child with them back to his people."

"And my father?"

"He abided by the council's decision, but refused to turn his hand to protecting the Faol after they allowed his mate to be taken from him."

Haakon could not believe what he was hearing. "Is that when the Paindeal left Scotland?"

"That is when the Paindeal drove the Faol out of Norseland."

"What of the Éan?"

"Their councilmember had voted against the *asmundr* as well. She said she understood the woman's needs better than any *asmundr* could."

"So?"

"So, your father told the council that the Faol and Éan had one month."

"One month until what?" Maon asked, his tone saying maybe he knew the answer.

Haakon thought he did as well and really did not want his suspicions confirmed, but knew he must listen to the truth. It was the Viking way and while most Norse now lived by a different code, the Chrechte still followed the old ways.

Osmend sighed, long and hard, his expression reflecting an ancient grief. "Then he would turn the full fury of his *asmundr* beast on any that remained."

"And so they left as well."

"*Ja.* Our people who were mated to them went with them."

"But…"

"No Paindeal exist in Scotland?" Osmend asked with a sardonic look at Maon. "Like no Éan exist among the clans?"

"They didn't. Before."

"Didn't they?"

The Faol were all still with their shock.

"You are saying there are Paindeal among the Faol?"

"There are, but none will ever shift without the coming of age ceremony, which they cannot participate in because they have no *Paindeal Neart*, though at one time they had a fragment as we do."

"What happened to it?" Maon asked.

"That is something you will have to discover, young *conriocht*. After you travel to the Land of the Sun and find our Paindeal brethren, reuniting the races once and for all. That I would live to see that day is all I have hoped for these many centuries past."

"But I thought…"

"That we were the Paindeal?"

That is what Haakon had thought, though he'd been told as a child some Chrechte still lived in Norvegr, but their numbers were small too.

"We are but a fraction of the Paindeal. Those left behind when the others decided Bjorn, the Destoyer, was no true protector of his people and they left to return to the land whispered as the place of our origins."

"Origins?" one of the young soldiers asked faintly. "I thought the land of the Danes was the place of our birth."

"Chrechte come from the Land of the Sun and over the ages have spread far and wide in the world."

"Spread where? England?" Maon asked with distaste.

Osmend lips twisted in an almost smile at the man's disgust for the country to the south of his home. "There are Chrechte in every people, but not all can shift. Some have packs, prides and flocks, others live alone never knowing the ways of our people."

"But we are the Picts, the scourge of Rome." Gart sounded like he could not take in all he was hearing.

For once, Haakon was of one mind with the Balmoral soldier.

"Some of us, *ja*. Some live among the Rus. Some still reside in the Land of the Sun."

"Where is this land?"

"It is far south, across another sea. The ancient and even more ancient stories tell of life beside a river of abundance. A place where all Chrechte lived together as one, revered by the humans around them, but also living among them."

"Surely that is just a fairytale."

The Seer drew himself up and glowered. "I speak history. I speak truth. You doubt me?" His voice reverberated around them as if the very air was alive with it.

Haakon dropped to one knee, his hand over his heart. "No, Seer, we do not doubt your calling or your words."

"Well, I do. This all sounds very farfetched," Gart said with a sneer.

Artair stared at his mate, the Faol he'd told Haakon had been his best friend for most of their lives. "What have you become that you would doubt the one that should be held above others? A Seer more aged than any Chrechte alive in our homeland."

"We have only his word for his age and for that matter, the truth of all these stories he tells."

Artair made a sound of disgust. "And yet one story you want to believe very much, the one where you get to have a different mate than me."

"I never said you were my mate!"

"Nay, and you never will, but still I thought we could stay friends."

"And we will. You are a brother to me."

"I will not call friend a man who disrespects the very core of what it means to be Faol."

"Because I don't believe the old man?"

"Because you would even *think* to doubt him. Because you disparage him like a child who bullies his friends to gain attention. Because we were sent on a quest to find exactly what we *have* found and you doubt even our own Seer by doubting this man so blatantly."

"Your friend is not so bad," Osmend tssked. Though his look toward Gart was not friendly. "It is following without thought behind a leader corrupted by his own grief that caused the split of the Paindeal."

"My father you mean?" Haakon asked, pain searing through him, the memories of his father tarnished by revelations.

"He could not forgive the other Chrechte for the loss of his mate, but even more importantly, for the loss of his son."

"Did he never see them again?"

"His mate was human. She died as human women do."

"But I thought our mates live as long as we do."

"When our souls are joined. Yes. But she never joined her soul with his. If she had, she would not have left the *asmundr* for the Faol."

"And my brother?"

"Your father brought him to the *Paindeal Neart* for his coming of age ceremony. He shifted into a lynx as most of our brethren do. You father always blamed his lack of connection to his son for the stone not choosing him as *asmundr* and he never forgave the Faol for having to suffer not only his mate's death, but that of his son many years later."

"If he shifted into a Lynx, he must have returned to live among our people?" Haakon guessed.

But Osmend shook his head. "The boy lived a long life among the Faol, but refused to stay in Norvegr with his father, the Destroyer."

"He was called the Firebrand." Or was that too a lie Haakon had been fed.

"Even before the Viking raids, your father was known for his ruthless destruction of his enemies," Osmend said by way of explanation. "In those days, indeed until he met your mother, he was called the Destroyer."

"But my brother could have softened him, brought him back to the right path."

"He could have, but he'd been raised to know only what a tyrant Bjorn was, that the *asmundr* was responsible for sending the Chrechte to the land of the clans."

"He never forgave my father?"

"Your father never forgave himself. Your brother? He prospered and had children, sending word of their births to your father even though he had denied him."

"He was his son. He still cared."

"I always believed so."

"And then the raids?"

"Your father felt no compunction about destroying the descendants of the Faol that had betrayed our ways, the sacred bond of a mate."

Haakon felt an urge to empty the contents of his stomach. "He never told me any of this."

"He did not want you touched by the poison of the past, but without knowledge of what came before you cannot help prevent what is to come. Just like if this one does not complete his quest, all Chrechte will perish, Paindeal, Faol and Éan alike." Osmend indicated Maon with his walking stick.

And on that pronouncement, the Seer decided it was time to seek out the *jarl*.

On the way to the longhouse Haakon shared with his uncle's family, he wondered if the *jarl* had known the truth of their past, of his father's deeds. His family had to have been one who chose to stay with the Seer and their *asmundr*. Why had they?

After all the revelations, Haakon only had more questions.

Haakon cast a glance at Osmend riding his horse. He only did so at Haakon's insistence, but the man's age was showing this day and that worried the *asmundr*.

They reached his uncle's lands before the sun had begun to set and Haakon brought the Faol before the *jarl*, Osmend there to explain things in his own irritating way.

Haakon's cousin, Einar, was there, his expression odd when he looked at Artair. Like he was hungry, only it was not so close to the time for their evening meal to cause such a look on Einar's face.

"Why have you come?" Thorsten, *jarl* and pride alpha demanded, his expression not welcoming.

Oh, he knew the history very well and it colored his view of the Faol, even though these were generations and generations beyond the ones who had so grievously betrayed Bjorn, the Firebrand. Thorsten was a loyal Chrechte and his loyalties stretched to old grudges.

Especially on behalf of the man who had mated his sister. Though both were gone now, their memories lived on with Haakon's family. As it should be.

"The *celi di* for the Sinclairs is also a powerful Seer, of the original royal line of our Chrechte forefathers," Maon said. "She has foreseen a terrible illness that will befall all the peoples here, on the continent and in our own beloved Highlands. Only by uniting the Chrechte will any survive when this awful Black Death comes."

"I have seen this also," Osmend said, sadness making his blue eyes even paler than usual. "Many, many will die. There is every chance the Paindeal will not survive."

"What do you mean, unite us?" Einar asked with another piercing glance in Artair's direction.

"Our people will go to Scotland."

Thorsten surged up from his chair. "Leave Groenland?"

Osmend was not impressed with the *kotrondmenskr's* show of temper. "It is the only way, but it does not have to happen in your lifetime, or even that of your son. Teach the children, and the children's children what is to come. Haakon will go now to the Highlands, he will barter peace between our peoples and when the time comes there will be a place among the clans for us."

Haakon spun to face the Seer. "You expect *me* to journey to Scotland? Who will protect the Paindeal when I am gone?"

"You are protector of all Chrechte, not just the Paindeal. We have established this."

"Even so."

"Einar may not be *asmundr* but he is the giant tiger of the Rus. He will protect those who remain behind in his father's territory."

Einar looked pleased by the pronouncement.

But Haakon's uncle less so. "You would take my *asmundr*?"

"You may be *jarl*, but no *asmundr* may belong to you," the Seer scolded. "Or *any* single person, no nor even a pride. He is guardian and he must go to Scotland, if for nothing else than to pledge his loyalty to our king."

"Since when do you call Scotland's king ours?" Haakon found the outrage in his uncle's tone reflected in his own heart.

Like hell he would pledge allegiance to the Scots king.

But Osmend glared right back, his expression and tone righteous. "I do not speak of *political office*." He made the last two sound like foul words in his mouth. "I speak of the dragon."

Everyone in the hall went silent.

Osmend appeared quite pleased with the response, nodding as if such silence was his due. "*Ja*. Fate has seen fit to give us the dragon to lead all Chrechte in the coming times of calamity. Our *asmundr* owes him allegiance and support. More, Haakon will play an important role in saving our people along with his mate."

Now Haakon balked. "I no longer have a mate."

"If that is true, I am sorry." Haakon could find nothing but honest sorrow in his Seer's aged gaze. "But you will *not* make the same errors your father did. You will not allow this lack to embitter you or pull you from your sacred duty to all Chrechte."

Haakon heard the words, but more importantly, he felt them inside and his beast roared in agreement. The Seer spoke Truth, not simply instruction. The *asmundr* was going to Scotland.

His uncle must have seen this resolve on Haakon's features because he said, "It must be an exchange."

The other Chrechte around them looked confused, except Maon, whose expression had turned dark.

"If Haakon has to go to them," Thorsten continued. "One of the Faol will stay here to take his place in our pride, to build a bridge between our people and theirs."

Maon didn't look happy, but he didn't speak up to deny the *jarl*. When they noticed that, the Scottish Chrechte looked at one another, as if determining silently who would stay in Groenland. They would not require their leader to command one of them.

Artair stepped forward, his face set in determined lines. "I will stay."

"No!" Gart's denial was fast and loud.

Artair smiled at him with a surprising acceptance only tinged by sorrow. "I need to do this. For both our sakes. Your path has a wife and children and mine does not."

"No, you'll find someone."

Artair cast a look at Einar. "Perhaps, but it won't be a wife."

Haakon's uncle let his gaze jump from Artair to his son, who still had that hungry look, now colored by a dawning joy in his bright blue eyes. Although the Vikings had considered the idea of being sodomized one of the gravest insults, the Chrechte among them had never had issue with same sex unions. Fate decreed what fate decreed. If that was a true mate of the same sex, then so be it.

Haakon did not know how his uncle would react to this new development, though. It had been a generation, or more since there had been a two-male mating in their pride.

The two were old now, the children they had given to the pride raised by them and the mothers and *their* mates in the same longhouse. Not as barbaric as Maon had been thinking, but not ideal either.

Haakon would destroy anyone who tried to touch his mate in an intimate way, even in the fur. Even if they never claimed each other physically.

It was no doubt better for all concerned he did not know where she lived.

"You are welcome to my land and to our pride," Thorsten said to Artair, proving he had a true Chrechte's view of mating.

Artair dipped his head toward Thorsten, dropping to one knee before the *jarl*. "Thank you. I will do my best to be a benefit to your pride and territory." He pounded his fist against his heart.

Gart made a sound of grief but did not speak another protest.

"Another Faol will stay," Osmend decreed. He gave Gart an almost pitying look. "Of another clan. And two of our pride will accompany the *conriocht* Maon and submit to him as alpha in his search for our brethren in the Land of the Sun."

Murmurs from others in the great hall sounded around the large space, some wondering who would be sent, others questioning the wisdom of such an action when their numbers were so few. But Thorsten remained silent, his expression now stony.

"I will stay." One of the younger Scots soldiers stepped forward. He wore the plaid of the Sinclair. "My beast tells me this is our new home for now."

His fellow Sinclair clapped him on the shoulder. "You will be missed among our people, but you must follow the dictates of your destiny."

"While there is no doubt fate has plans for each Chrechte and human, a man may also influence his destiny." It wasn't the Seer speaking, but Haakon's uncle. "You will be welcome, but stay only if you are certain of your course."

The young man nodded.

Thorsten sighed. "Destiny calls to all of us, but even a mating between those called together by fate in the sacred tradition is a disaster in the making, when one is reluctant."

"You did know about my father's past," Haakon said, unable to keep the accusation from his voice.

His uncle's head jerked then he looked to the Seer and something he saw there made him nod. He directed his words to Haakon, however. "It was his story to tell you, nephew. He loved you and did not want your regard for him influenced by his past mistakes."

"The truth is always better than a lie."

"Is it?"

"*Ja.*" Haakon had no doubts on that. Truth might wound. It might cause division, but deception caused all that and more.

"Nevertheless, it was not my place to tell you secrets your father preferred to keep."

"But now the time has come for the past to be revealed and all Chrechte to once again be united." The Seer looked between Thorsten and Haakon. "Whatever choices our former *asmundr* made, Haakon must choose to live for the good of all his brethren, Faol, Éan and *kotrondmenskr* alike."

Haakon inclined his head in agreement, his own fist going to his heart. "I so vow."

The Seer looked nearly joyous for a brief flash. "You are true guardian, Haakon, of the *kotrondmenskr.*"

"The *Paindeal Neart* called me and I will heed its call, wherever that takes me." Even if it meant giving up his pride and going to live among descendants of the Faol who had treated his father so cruelly.

The Seer laid a hand on Gart, whose face was set in lines of obvious grief, with eyes that reflected haunted uncertainty. "You will find a mate among the Paindeal and bring about the first joining of our two peoples with children to share both natures in many centuries."

Gart stared, like he could not believe the Seer's words. "You... Is that true? A vision?"

"It's true," Artair said as he stood, his own expression a mixture of grief, acceptance and newfound hope. "I dreamt about it last night." Artair gripped Gart's forearm. "So long as you do your best by our brethren, you will always be a friend I hold dear, but our lives are destined to go in different directions."

Gart grimaced at the qualifier on the proffered friendship, returning his packmate's forearm grip. "What of the mate pull?"

It was an unexpected question, considering how determinedly the Faol had denied any such thing. But Artair did not look surprised by it, showing just how well he knew his packmate.

"The Seer said it earlier, at the beach. If a true mating is not accepted by one or both, then fate allows for a measure of happiness regardless."

"Only a measure?" Einar demanded, speaking for the first time, and not sounding happy.

Artair turned to him. "That is up to the Chrechte, I think, how much happiness he allows himself."

"You will allow yourself to be filled with joy at your good fortune." Einar crossed his arms, looking immovable.

Haakon would have laughed at his cousin's arrogance, but he understood Einar was staring his future in the face and he wasn't sharing that future with anyone else, not even a memory.

It was not in his tiger's nature, regardless of how cats of the wild lived. Among the Paindeal, a mate was sacred, regardless of whether or not they shared the true bond. There would be no other for Einar and he would allow no other for Artair, not even an old love held too tightly in his heart.

"You believe our future is set in stone?" Artair asked challengingly.

"My beast knows his mate."

"And I am simply supposed to fall in line?"

CHAPTER FIVE

Einar stared down at the man fate had decreed would be his. Defiance lined the handsome young soldier's face and stance, but Einar *would* have his mate.

For whatever reason, the other soldier they called Gart had not claimed the mate decreed to him and now that mate found the sacred connection with Einar's tiger. Einar was no milktoast. He would claim his mate and destroy any who thought to separate them.

He frowned down at the man that fate had blessed him with. "Do not pretend your wolf is not drawn to me as strongly as my tiger draws me to you."

"I do not follow every dictate of my nature."

Perhaps Einar had been wrong. Perhaps it had been this man who refused to claim Gart.

"You would deny me?"

Artair looked up at him, his dark brown gaze filled with a surprising vulnerability. "I've heard about your law of procreation."

"An abomination the time has come to set aside," the Seer said in tones that left no room for argument.

Not even from Einar's father, the *jarl*.

But argue his father did. "We cannot allow our race to die out."

"It will not. As I have assured you all these many centuries. Bjorn would not listen, his grief coloring his thoughts, but you must, or you will lose far more than you hope to gain."

Einar's tiger gnashed at him to shift at the idea of another touching or being touched by his mate, something his great beast would not tolerate. "I will eviscerate any Chrechte who think to claim what is mine."

His father stared at him, shock rounding his eyes. "But you know the law."

Einar rounded on his father, fury making his voice harsh. "The law will not save the life of *any* who seek to take my mate from me. Even for a single night under the moon."

For the first time, he let his tiger stare his father, his pride alpha, down.

Thorsten fell back on his chair, his face drained of all color. "You would challenge me for my position?"

"If you force my hand, I will. This law will not stand." It was not Einar's desire. He had no pleasure at the thought of being *jarl* before his time.

"Our council—"

"Take their lead from you and our Seer."

"Don't you want children?" His father asked, sounding bewildered.

"Who says we will not have them?"

"But—"

"In the last winter, two children lost both their parents." Their mother had died in childbirth and their father, a human, had fallen, broken his leg so grievously he died from the injuries.

"You are talking about Jorgen and Marie," his father said. "Their Chrechte heritage is many generations past."

"Does it matter?" Einar demanded. "They live now in a longhouse already crowded with children, aunts and uncles more concerned with their own families than giving comfort to grieving children."

"You sound like you really care about these children," Artair said, wonder in his tone.

Einar looked down at the man he planned to make his mate. "I care about all in my father's territory, human and Chrechte alike."

But yes, these two orphans had a special place in his affection. Perhaps because their father had been a good friend before his death. Perhaps simply because they were so much like their parents and yet entirely like themselves.

"The boy, Jorgen, is four and while his parents were not shifters, his spirit is as fierce as any of our greatest hunters. His sister, Marie, is so small, not even quite two summers, but she speaks and shows in so many ways how smart she is."

He'd spent time with the children every day since their parents' deaths, unwilling to let them languish in their overcrowded home surrounded by family who cared out of duty but not enough affection.

"You are enamored," Artair breathed, like stating such a weakness was giving the greatest compliment.

"They are good children."

"I would like to meet them."

"You will." And then they would bring the children back to his father's longhouse to raise as their own.

"He will make an honorable guardian for the pride when the *asmundr* leaves." The Seer also spoke with approval, surprising Einar.

His people were not known for their sentimentality.

His father was looking at Einar with dawning understanding. "You spent so much time at that longhouse, I thought you were courting the youngest daughter."

Einar could not help the look of repudiation he gave. She was barely old enough to be courted and of no interest to him whatsoever. "*Nei.*"

"She was not your mate," Artair said, his expression certain.

"I met my mate today."

Gart made a sound of distress. Or was it simply disagreement? It did not matter.

Artair was no longer *his*. Friend? *Ja*. Einar could tolerate such, barely and because the man would be leaving for the Land of the Sun soon, most likely never to be heard from again.

But any claims other than friend from anyone, on the new member to their pride, Einar's Rus tiger would not tolerate.

"You accept our mating. Just like that?" Artair asked, disbelief running through his words. "Announce it before your father, the alpha?"

"*Ja*. How else?" Even as the question left his mouth, he knew the answer. "How long did you live with the knowledge one who wanted a different life was your mate?"

Artair winced, pain clear in the depths of his dark eyes. "I have known since our first change."

"That is a long time to live with that burden."

"Aye."

"He is no longer your mate." There could be no question about that.

"My dreams told me last night, but..."

"But?"

"I did not expect to meet the mate who *would* be mine today."

"And yet you have." Einar waited to hear Artair agree.

His mate would acknowledge their bond before witnesses.

"Aye. I have."

Unmindful of the others around them, Einar grabbed Artair by the shoulder, pulled him into his side, taking one of Artair's hands in his as they faced their *jarl*. "Father, I present my mate. Artair, once of the Balmoral, now pridemate."

Thorsten inclined his head in acknowledgment, his expression not revealing if the mating pleased him, or not. But he stood and placed his staff against where Einar held Artair's hand. "I acknowledge and accept this mating. The ceremony will be in one week's time."

"A week?" Einar demanded.

His father frowned at Einar. "You will give your mate time to know you and our people before joining your lives forever."

Einar opened his mouth to protest, but Artair squeezed his hand. "I appreciate that. I would also like formal acknowledgement before your pride that the Law of Procreation has been stricken from existence before the formal ceremony takes place."

Oh, his mate was every bit as possessive as Einar, whatever reservations he might have about their mating. Einar's tiger purred at the knowledge.

"It will be done at our council meeting and pride run the day after tomorrow," he promised his mate, daring his father with his eyes to gainsay him.

Thorsten drew himself up and glared at Einar. "You do not speak for me, unless you wish to challenge me for my position as *jarl* as well as pride alpha."

"That is not my desire." But his father knew what would force him to do so.

Thorsten nodded and then turned to face the rest of those assembled. "It will be as my son has stated."

Einar let not a single flicker of satisfaction he felt at his father's words show on his face. It would not be respectful. But he felt Artair's relief in the way he sagged into his side. Did his mate not yet realize Einar would always protect him? From anything that might harm him.

Perhaps this week to get to know each was a good thing.

"Tomorrow, Haakon will set sail with a merchant ship of humans, who plan to trade in England. They will first take Haakon to the island of the Balmoral."

"We aren't going with him?" Maon asked.

"You must begin your journey to the Land of the Sun soon. Time is of the essence."

"Why?" Maon asked, but Einar could have told him the wily old Seer was unlikely to answer.

"You question my visions?" Osmend demanded imperiously.

"Nay, I merely seek to know what they are."

"If they had been meant for you, you would have had them," the Seer informed the alpha testily.

Maon did not back down. "But they concern me and those who travel with me."

"*Ja*." But Osmend did not elaborate as the Scotsman clearly expected him to do.

Perhaps their Seers were more accommodating.

***

Haakon felt the pull to that place of *other* as he slept that night. Burdened with his new knowledge of his father's past, he heeded the call, coming out of the dense fog to find the woman who would have been his mate pacing.

Her head jerked up at his arrival, her green gaze showing relief before she masked the emotion. "What are you doing here?"

"You called me." He would not play games.

"And you are so weak-willed you cannot ignore my *supposed* call?" The words were caustic, but her tone was filled with worry, her gaze haunted.

"I learned the truth of my father's past. I have questions for you and perhaps answers."

She stared at him, but then gave an affirmative jerk of her head. "Speak your answers."

Typical of the arrogant warrior-woman to expect him to speak first.

However, Haakon saw no reason not to do so. He told her all he had learned.

"Because the Faol sided with the human woman to set aside his mating, he murdered all my people?" she asked with clear disgust.

"He saw them as his enemy, not the Chrechte he'd been fated to protect. He was still grieving the loss of his mate and son, and mad with it." So insane, Haakon did not think the haze of madness had cleared from Bjorn's mind until some time after he met Haakon's mother.

"That should excuse him destroying an entire pack of Faol?"

Haakon sighed, knowing it didn't, knowing even this truth probably meant little to his mate. He shook his head decisively. "I am not offering excuses, merely an explanation. My father regretted his action."

"How can *you* know. You're still a boy, wet behind the ears." But the look she gave him said he was anything but.

"Hardly that."

The desire in her eyes was nothing new, but the other emotions...something like regret, longing, even almost approval, was. A frisson of unfamiliar worry traveled down his spine, his instincts telling him something was wrong.

She shrugged, looking away, but not before he saw a stronger desire for *more* between them than he had ever seen reflected in her gem-like green gaze.

"He let you live," Haakon pointed out, his mind only half on this all-important conversation.

The other half worried the problem of her strange behavior, not least of which was simply talking to him and listening to his answers.

His point was a solid one though. There had to have been some kernel of sanity in his father left when he spared her life.

She looked back at him, her eyes flashing derision like lightning in the night sky. "He put me in a boat with my weapons. No doubt the *asmundr* expected me to die at sea from my injuries."

"*Nei.*" She had it all wrong. "That was a sign of respect for your strength. He gave you what amounted to a Viking burial *and* a chance to live at the same time. He was showing he respected your strength and heart as a warrior."

"Nay!" she denied with vehemence. "He wanted me dead."

"If he wanted you dead, he would have killed you and left your body on the field of battle." Brutal his words might be, but there was undeniable truth in them.

"He destroyed my people."

That too was a truth that could not be denied.

"And there is no excuse for that," Haakon assured her, his own honor demanding that acknowledgment. "But neither is there an excuse for that long-ago council to take his mate from him and give her to another, *to steal his child*. He had to live with both their deaths and the unbounding grief that came after."

"As I have lived with the grief of loss of my entire pack for all these centuries."

He stifled another sigh, not wanting her to think he was dismissing her words, but knowing she would never be moved in her attitude toward his father and then toward Haakon by default. "*Ja.*"

"He was terrifying in his fury." Her gaze turned haunted with old memories. "I had never known fear before. I was *conriocht*. Invincible. And then I was not." Emotion laced every word. "I have not experienced anything like the terror and grief of that day since."

Haakon was shocked she shared with him so freely, that she allowed him to see her feelings.

"Not before today," she admitted quietly, though in no way sounding like she was acknowledging weakness, only truth.

The ice of the glaciers infused his soul. "What happened today?"

She stared at him like she wasn't going to answer, but then all pretense of stoicism left, worry and grief washing over her beautiful features. "We lost sight of land."

"You are in a boat?" he demanded, terror unlike anything he'd ever known turning his blood to water.

She gave a barely perceptive nod.

"How many sail with you? Does your captain not have the experience to redirect your ship's course?" Surely even his independent mate would not take to the sea alone.

"It is not a ship. It is a boat. The very Viking boat your father set me to sea in."

"But that was more than two centuries ago."

"I have kept it repaired."

How? That was a question for a different time. And there would be a different time, he vowed to himself. "You are alone?"

"Nay. Two others sail with me." Her demeanor said she held herself accountable for those lives as well.

"Two?" Haakon asked faintly. "In a boat so far out to sea you have lost sight of land?" It was beyond imagining even his stubborn mate had taken on such a foolhardy journey.

"We were heading for Scotland, from my island." She was revealing more than she ever had, but it did not please Haakon.

If something did not change, the woman and her companions would die an unpleasant death out on the open expanse of water.

"What land did you last sight?"

"I think it was Iceland, I used it to correct my course, but…" She let her words trail off.

Haakon didn't need her to say she was lost now to know. The terror she spoke of lurked in the depths of her emerald eyes. And it was not something she was comfortable with.

"Tell me your name."

"I am called Neilina."

Her words sent shards of more fear lancing through him. She had offered that much too easily after nine years of denial. She had not changed her mind about their mating. Her attitude toward his father spoke as much. She would never forgive Haakon for being son of the *asmundr* responsible for the loss of her pack.

But she believed she was going to die, so telling him her name did not matter.

"I will not let you die," he vowed.

"You cannot prevent it, arrogant Paindeal."

But he knew he could. He did not know how. It did not matter. She would *not* die. Perhaps their souls had been called to one another for this very moment in time.

He gave her a level look, letting not one tiny bit of his own fear show in his steady gaze. "Tell me everything."

And she did. She told him of visions in which she was called to protect the packs of Scotland, to leave her cave sanctuary. She spoke of smooth sailing following by a terrible storm that blew them off course, of sighting what she'd thought was Iceland, but unable to make it to shore because of another storm. Of losing sight of land and not being sure of where she was despite her ability to read the sky. She could not read the stars when clouds blocked them.

The sun had never broken through the clouds either and she had only the barest of an idea what direction they sailed because of it.

She spoke of her companions, both of whom she would be devastated if she lost to death. Though she did not name them.

When she was done, she collapsed to the ground, sitting with her arms around her knees, her staff laying beside her. "I never thought I would face a foe again I could not defeat."

"And you have not." Haakon walked forward and took his sword in hand, ripping it from the ground, he wiped it against his thigh before sheathing it once again in his scabbard, then dropped down to sit beside her, surprised again when she gave him no glare for doing so. "Your will brought me here and that action may bring you out of this peril."

She stared up at him, though tall for a woman, still her head only reached the top of his shoulder. "Are you calling me stubborn?"

After nearly a decade of refusing to tell him the simplest things, even her name? "*Ja*. Stubborn. Strong." Beautiful. The one woman he craved, no matter how many others showed him their interest.

But not mate.

As his Seer had said, a forced mating, or even *any* mating between two when one was reluctant would only lead to broken vows and pain.

"Can you allow me to see through your eyes?"

"Of what benefit would that be?" she demanded. "Do you think you would do any better in this situation than me?"

"I can offer you my knowledge and perhaps, added to yours, it will be enough." His Viking forefathers had been unequalled in their ability to read the sea and navigate it.

"You think you have knowledge I do not?" she scoffed.

He knew he did. He only wished he could share more than his knowledge with her, but also the sun stone his father had used for navigation so long ago. "Have you taken to the sea before?"

"Aye." She grimaced. "Off the shore of my island, never beyond the sight of land," she admitted.

"That is natural, but though I have never travelled beyond my home, I have been at sea in a boat many times beyond the sight of land."

"You have?" she asked, disbelieving.

"It is part of the rites of passage for my people to become what I have become." His father had insisted Haakon learn all the skills the centuries old *asmundr* could teach him.

Besides Haakon had been given a Chrechte gift he'd never understood the benefit of before this moment. Now, it may well save the lives of his mate and her companions.

"You would have me allow your spirit to join mine?" Her tone made it obvious how little she wanted to do something so intimate. "Will that not force our mating, even though we have not claimed each other?"

Shaking his head in negation, Haakon ignored the twinge in his chest at this confirmation she wanted nothing of their mating, even now, in the face of death. "We are both guardians. We can share our spirits as *asmundr* and *conriocht*, not as mates."

Though there was no question that sharing their bodies would make it easier, and the mating bite would guarantee it, neither was required. So long as they both opened their minds and access to their beasts to the other. He was surprised she did not know this, but then she'd lost her mentors at a younger age than Haakon had lost his father and he still had the wisdom of the Seer and his uncle to draw upon.

"How?" she asked, her voice tinged with equal parts suspicion and hope.

"Do you have your stone?"

She looked confused.

Haakon drew his sword again. Neilina's eyes widened, but she said nothing. He took the hilt and pointed *it*, not the tip toward her. "Touch your stone to mine."

Understanding came first and then a look of determination. She flipped the great fur cape she wore back over her shoulder and drew her own sword, the hilt carved as for the guardians of the Faol, its size perfect for a warrior-woman. With a cautious look at him, she laid the stone in its hilt against the stone in his.

"Now you must allow your wolf to come out to meet my tiger."

She nodded, closing her eyes and he did the same, releasing the ancient and fierce tiger within him toward the power of his stone. Heat like from a raging bonfire washed over Haakon, and he felt his tiger straining toward a wolf in the distance, but frigid mists swirled between them, acting as effectively as a barrier as if they were an eight-foot-high stone wall.

Knowing they needed a deeper contact and limited in how to provide it, Haakon reached out and laid his hand over hers, seeking the connection their beasts needed. The mist became less thick, but his tiger was still unable to dive into it. Haakon did not understand why. The wolf howled in the distance, looking like she longed to cross the cold white fog as well.

Haakon allowed his eyes to open and he found Neilina staring at him. Green light glowed around her, reaching out to her sword, like the red aura around him.

Sorrow filled her gaze. "I cannot do it. I cannot let down the barrier between us."

"You are certain?"

"I'm trying. The mists only grow colder."

So, she was experiencing the same thing as him. "Is it because I am my father's son? Or merely that I am *asmundr*?"

"I don't know."

"You do not trust me." Of that much he was sure.

"I must trust you, though." She sounded like the thought was a hopeless one. "Or our lives will be lost."

Even now, she did not name her companions. Haakon ignored the frustration that fact caused him and tightened his hand over hers. "You *will* trust me."

"I don't know how." She bit her lip in a gesture of uncertainty he'd never seen her make. "Help me."

Less plea than demand, it was nevertheless impossible for Haakon to ignore his mate's request. Whether she would thank him for his help was as uncertain as her future.

Haakon could only think of one way to draw her soul to his. Laying his sword down, he watched in silence as she did the same. He made sure their sacred stones still touched, the ethereal red and green glow luminous around and between them, but not mixing together.

Instinct told him the colors should be mixing, changing, growing stronger.

But the red around Neilina ebbed and flowed like a fast-moving tide, some spots so light they appeared pink, some gaps in the aura altogether. Her inability to trust, her fear for her future, both were fighting her successful merging with his soul despite what he'd been taught.

Would Neilina allow the joining of their bodies? They had no choice if their souls were going to merge, but she still had a choice. Though her barriers against him were too strong, even against her own desire to save herself and the others on her small craft, even the intimacy of sexual union would not accomplish a way across that cold mist without her truly wanting both his body and the outcome.

"Will you take me into your body?" he asked her bluntly.

"It will help our souls to join?"

"Only if you crave me as I crave you. Only if under all your fear and mistrust, you want our souls to join for this brief period."

Her body went stiff, as if his words hit something raw inside her. In Neilina's company, he understood that reaction only too well.

"I must want you?"

"*Ja.*" There was no way around that. "The trust between guardians is usually enough to accomplish this joining. But you fear me."

"Not you." She looked away. "Your *asmundr* nature."

"We are one in the same and if we are to join, my beast must be welcome by your spirit."

"Sex will make that happen?" she asked with sarcastic disbelief.

"Not if you do not want it."

She stared at him then, unreadable emotion in the depths of her green gaze. "I *do* want you. I crave your touch like I have never craved another."

Haakon found it near impossible to hold back his gasp of surprise at the admission. "You've hid it well, warrior woman."

She shrugged. "My hate was stronger than my desire."

He said nothing about her claim she hated him. He had guessed that long ago and the fact she'd never said the words aloud did not make them less true.

"And now?"

"Now, even if your soul cannot merge with mine, I would not die without knowing your touch."

"You will not die."

"You have given me hope." It was another unlooked for admission.

He nodded. "I am glad."

"What about you?"

"What about me?" His brain wanted to hold no other thoughts than images of their bodies joined now that she'd admitted to craving him too.

"Do *you* want *me*?"

"*Ja.* More than air. More than the empty years of life before me."

She grimaced at the last, but desire flared hot and bright in her emerald gaze as well. That was the final bit of confirmation he needed that she would not be offering him her body only as payment to save her own life. She wanted him, even if it did not work.

Despite the dour situation they faced, something deep inside Haakon rejoiced.

"Well, are you going to do something?" she demanded.

And he almost laughed. She could have kissed him first. His powerful warrior-princess mate, but she wanted the homage paid to her of him making the first move.

And in this? He was only too happy to oblige the mate who denied their mating.

He leaned forward, slowly, in case she refused his kiss at the last second, but she took a deep breath and let it out, almost like she was girding herself for battle. Then she met him halfway, her lips pressing against his with untried desire, and unmistakable enthusiasm.

He could rest certain in the knowledge that no matter what else lay between them, there was also desire. Always had been. Always would be.

Carnal need he'd held in check for nearly a decade exploded and Haakon deepened the kiss, his tongue exploring the seam of her lips with obvious intent. She tasted like a new dawn, the sweetness of honey dripping warm in the sun…like *his*.

Her hands came up to his shoulders, grabbing hard, her fingernails digging into the leather of his tunic vest and she gasped. Her lips open, he now pressed inside, tasting his mate fully for the first time. Spicy and wild, her flavor enslaved him as surely as the magic shackles of folklore and he craved a taste of her most intimate depths, something only he would ever have.

She fisted her hands against his shoulders, and he expected to be shoved away, but she pressed harder into the kiss, like it wasn't enough. Her lips molded more firmly to his mouth, her tongue dueling with is for control of the kiss.

Part of him still disbelieving that Neilina not only allowed his touch, but so clearly craved it, Haakon slid his hand under her cloak. He caressed her side from her waist up to where her breasts swelled against her leather tunic. Insensible to the layers between them, he squeezed the curve, measuring her shape with his hand.

Perfect. For him.

Neilina moaned, pushing him backward until he landed on his back on the soft green grass, the warmth of the sky's light in this place of *other* making him prickle with sweat under his own layers. She landed on top of him, never allowing their kiss to stop.

She tunneled her fingers into in his long hair, holding so tight it would have hurt if he could have felt anything beyond the pleasure she was bringing him with her lips and the feel of her body against his.

He forced himself to remember why he was doing this, encouraging his tiger to go forward into the rapidly dispersing mists.

Her wolf surged forward, running toward the tiger.

He broke the kiss. "It's working."

"Aye." Her eyes met his, the message there not one of rejection, or the desire to stop. "If we stop though, they may well be lost in the mists of my distrust."

The admission must have cost her, but it increased his respect for the warrior woman meant to be his. Even as he knew he had to tell her the truth as he knew it.

Before he could say anything though, Neilina began to give him biting kisses along his jaw, derailing thought all together. "We will share our bodies completely. We will not risk the lives of those I care about because of my pride."

"We can at least try," he said, remembering what he had to tell her. "Our beasts will not be lost; they simply will not merge."

He said nothing about the truth that she would never couple with him if they were not in this place of *other* and she were not in such dire circumstances. Regardless of how much she might want him, or even tell herself she wanted *this*. There was a great chance she would regret sharing her body with him anon.

"You are my mate. I will not die without knowing this one joy. *You will couple with me, Viking*."

He would have laughed at her shouted demand, if his cock wasn't so hard it hurt, if every part of his being wasn't longing to do exactly that.

Before he could say anything else, she sat up and tore off her cloak, then with barely perceptible hesitation, she divested herself of her weapons. She climbed off of him to strip out of the rest of her clothes. Her movements were too efficient to be meant to entice, but each inch of skin exposed increased his craving for their joining.

He needed to feel her hot, swollen depths around his now painfully hard sex. He wanted to touch every bit of the beautiful body being revealed to him. The creamy curves of her breasts that would fill his hands, the beautiful dark curls hiding the mysteries of her sex, enticing nipples hard and berry dark.

There were scars too, from that terrible battle? Or something else?

Right now, he did not care.

Each mark meant only that she had survived, his warrior-princess.

"Do you find me too scarred to be pleasing?" she demanded, standing unashamedly naked before him.

He could not speak, his throat was too dry. So, he shook his head.

"Then take off your clothes, Haakon. This cannot happen if you remain covered."

He choked out a laugh as he did his best to peel his leather breeches down over his swollen member. Her eyes widened as Haakon revealed his sex. He didn't bother with his boots or trying to get his bottoms off all the way, but he yanked his tunic vest up over his head and off along with the woolen undershirt beneath.

She came back over him, her thighs spread so she straddled his body, her honey wet nether lips kissing the head of his cock. The evidence of his need for her jutted up proudly, moisture leaking from his slit in anticipation of coming inside her, as he had dreamt of doing every single night for nearly ten years.

Showing no virginal reticence, she grabbed his cock and held it so she could lower herself, taking him inside her. Wet, hot, silk enveloped the head of his cock and it took all his immense self-control not to surge upwards and seat himself fully in her accommodating body.

Neilina stopped, her body poised to lower further, her face covered in concentration, tension filling her body. "It hurts. Why does it hurt? This isn't real. We're in the spirit realm. It shouldn't hurt."

"Were that true, then we should not feel the pleasure either."

She stared down at him, sweat beading on her forehead, her brow furrowed. "I do not like the pain."

Certainty washed over him. "You have been with no other man." He could no more hide the satisfaction that gave him than the pleasure he experienced at the joining of their bodies.

"Who else would I be with?" she demanded. "I have lived in solitude in the forest these many years." Neilina shook her head. "Arrogant Viking."

"I have never been inside another's body," he offered, feeling magnanimous and perhaps, just a tiny bit arrogant. Deny it all she might, she was *his*.

They might never meet in the world of men, but she always would be his.

This joining was her choice. They might not speak the words of claiming, may never give each other the claiming bite, but they would forevermore belong to one another, as they had done from their first meeting in this place.

Still, the pain creasing her beautiful face, could not be ignored. "We do not have to continue," he offered even as his beast roared disapproval. "Our souls will join now." He was sure of it.

She glared. "Think you I am some weak maiden to balk at a course simply because there is some pain."

"I do not want you to hurt," he told her baldly.

"It is part of it, or so I have heard."

Any advice her mother had given had happened so long ago, he was surprised Neilina remembered it.

Something must have shown on his face because an almost soft look came over her fierceness in that moment. "I spent years memorizing every conversation I ever had with my parents, the people of my tribe. I was utterly alone for nearly a century before I found Dìonach."

"You have not been alone for these past nine years."

He expected instant denial, but she gave a short jerk of her head. "I know."

That, at least, was something. Her first, and most likely only concession to their actually being mates.

His thoughts splintered again as she pressed down with her hips, taking him further inside.

But then she stopped. Her face stiff with pain, she remained immobile above him.

"I would take this pain from you," he told her.

She jerked her head. "No. This is my body, my gift to you, *my* pain."

CHAPTER SIX

Did she have any idea what she was really saying? What she was offering him?

It was because they were in this place of *other*. That was why she offered him herself. And even if it was only for this moment out of time, Haakon would accept the gift that it was.

He reached up to cup her face. "*Kamerat*." His mate. *His*. As she leaned over him, her body embracing his, he could not help but claim her with words. "*Du er min*."

Rather than argue with him, as she usually did, Neilina's entire body shuddered and she pushed down with her hips, only to stop with a gasp. "I can't...I want...It's not working." She frowned, her eyes suspiciously shiny, but he was sure tears would never be allowed to fall. "Help me."

It was not a plea, but a demand.

And one he was only too happy to accede to.

He might have never been inside another woman, but he knew what was required to give one pleasure. His father had spoken to him freely on the topic, after Haakon had become a man according to the Viking Way, when he'd taken on his *asmundr* nature.

Reaching down, he brushed his thumb over the tiny nub at the top of her sex, releasing the scent of her pleasure between them, making his tiger growl for the claiming bite. Haakon ignored the beast, as he'd had to do for so many years when it came to this need and concentrated on building the pleasure between them.

Her body moved a little, her lovely breasts swaying, the nipples calling to his mouth. "You are so beautiful, *kamerat*."

"Don't call me that." She looked away, then sighed. "I am no beauty. I have scars on my body, a scar on my face."

Again, she was not arguing against him calling her mate, only beautiful. His tiger purred with pleasure at this tiny acknowledgement of their soul connection.

He gently pulled her head back around so their gazes met once again, hers filled with defiance, but under that? A vulnerability he would never accuse her of. "Your scars proclaim you to be warrior among our kind, strong enough to survive. That *is* beautiful."

"I needed to be strong enough to *protect*, but I wasn't."

"You are no griffin to defeat an *asmundr*, especially one gone Berserker, on your own." Haakon thought pleasure might give better comfort than his words and he cupped her breast, abrading her nipple with his thumb. "Your curves are perfect. This little nub looks so sweet. Is it, I wonder?"

Before she could answer, he leaned up and bent forward to take the sweet berry into his mouth. She gasped in pleasure and he mouthed the curve of her breast, shifting his lips over her heated flesh to taste the other turgid tip with the same enthusiasm. He continued to rub small circles on her clitoris, his fingers getting wet with her essence.

Neilina's body shifted little by little, taking his hard cock deeper inside her, as pleasure overcame pain.

Haakon laid back, bringing his fingers to his mouth. He flicked his tongue out and tasted her essence for her to see. Neilina's green eyes widened, the pupils expanding with shocked desire, making her gaze darken.

Fragrant with her passion, spicier than her mouth, the silky moisture on his fingers was fully and completely *her*. His *kamerat*. Neilina's flavor burst on his tongue and took over Haakon's senses.

Mine, his tiger roared inside him.

Mine, his soul shouted over the rapidly dispersing mist.

Mine, his Viking spirit claimed loudly, refusing any other circumstance.

He *needed* to give the claiming bite, craved it like nothing he had ever craved in his life. And his soul ached to receive it from her as well, but he had to stifle that need. He could not give into it. She would never forgive him if he did and that was something he *would* not live with. Residual hatred was bad enough, he would not engender any on his own account.

Her eyes heavy-lidded, Neilina's head tipped back as she moaned long and low. "Dinna stop, Viking."

"Not planning to." And if he found his own pleasure in the first time she'd called him Viking without it sounding like a curse word, he wasn't stupid enough to say so.

The tension drained out of Neilina's body as a different sense of urgency built in the air between them. Neilina canted her hips, causing his sex to press up into her body more and more. Suddenly he pressed irrevocably against her maidenhead and they both froze. Pain once again made her grimace.

Haakon could not countenance it, no matter that he knew there had to be a tearing for them to join completely. "We can stop," he offered a second time, this time from between gritted teeth, even as his hips tried of their own volition to surge upward.

Yet he managed to remain still beneath her. He was no untried boy, no matter what she said. He was a man, full grown, with years enough to learn to control his *asmundr* beast, much less the urges of his human body.

Neilina shifted a little, and cried out with pleasure as her clitoris rubbed against the calloused thumb tip he had returned to her sensitive nub. He did his best to increase her pleasure by going back and forth over the swollen nub.

"Aye, Haakon. Dinna stop." She rocked against him, taking more of his engorged sex into her slick depths.

He kept touching her, letting her set the pace of penetration, no matter how hard that was.

She was tossing her head back and forth when she plunged downward, breaking through her virginal barrier and enveloping his sex until he pressed against the entrance to her womb with one thrust. She screamed, whether it was in pleasure, or pain, he could not tell, their souls were still rubbing alongside each other, not fully joined.

He grabbed her hips, stilling her. "Give it a minute."

She stared down at him, sweat now trickling down from her temple. "You think to tell me how to do this thing *we've* never done before?" she challenged.

"I think to save you more pain," he growled. "Deny it all you like. You are my mate and protecting you is at the core of my nature."

She turned her head, breaking their locked gazes.

"No," he insisted. "Look at me. We are doing this so that our souls may join to save you." He did not mention that she'd wanted it for herself, had acknowledged wanting *him*, not sure how true that would be on the morrow. "You cannot build new barriers."

She said nothing for a long moment, but then she nodded and let her turbulent green eyes meet his again, the message there inscrutable to him. "No barriers."

And suddenly it was gone, that wall that had held even to that moment between them. Red and green mixed together, streaks of each invading the other as their bodies rocked together in bliss, the glow around them going a rich brown color before flashing the purest white. Seemingly oblivious to how well their souls had merged, Neilina increased the pace, slapping his shoulder and demanding he move.

Giving himself freedom to do exactly that, Haakon took over their joining, though she rode him. He set a powerful pace, pulling her against him as he thrust upward. The scream she gave when she climaxed was the most beautiful sound he had ever heard. He roared with the power of his beast as he came inside her body, their joining complete in this place of *other*.

It felt so real, the scent of blood from her broken maidenhead impossible proof that they had mated in the flesh, even if they never did so at a soul level.

Though, there could be no denying their souls were fully entwined for this moment in time. He could feel her pleasure, thoughts that were not his skimmed across his own, though he only got glimpses of them.

She had enjoyed the sex. It was better than she thought it could be.

Pride burned through him at that knowledge.

Neilina collapsed on top of him and he felt his tiger leap forward, bounding toward the beautiful she-wolf in the distance.

"Your soul is now with mine," Neilina whispered with awe. "I can feel you inside me."

"Will you let me see what you do?"

Several seconds passed before she said, "Aye." Even now hesitating at that last and final joining.

But she had agreed, so Haakon gave his beast full rein to run free. The tiger and the wolf frolicked together and Haakon opened his eyes.

No longer in the place of *other*, the darkness around him was nearly absolute, not even the moon casting its light over the water that made the boat beneath him rock.

Then the clouds parted. It was only a small gap, but he saw stars he recognized. Haakon looked around, getting a sense of where the moon was and the direction of the horizon.

Hundreds of years of Viking sailing knowledge had been gifted to him by the *Paindeal Neart* and he had never understood why his brain would be cluttered with what he was so unlikely to use, but now he did.

He was able to share that knowledge with Neilina, giving her a sense of not only where she was but the direction she needed to take to reach her destination. He looked around the boat and saw an ancient navigation board, but no sunstone to use with it. Haakon kept the one his father had used on his voyages in his pouch, the same pouch piled on the ground beside his weapons in the place of *other*.

Two dark shadowy lumps in the other end of the boat indicated her two companions, but now was not the moment to take the time to try to see them.

He took careful note of all that was within his sight, memorizing the small patch of sky, the boat itself and what he could see on it. Then Haakon allowed himself a moment to revel in the closeness of their joined spirits before forcing his own to return to the place of *other*. This spiritual connection was as good as the sex, though he would have laughed at himself for saying so. A man did not seek the connection of souls over that of the body.

Taking a deep breath and one last moment to enjoy what would, no doubt, never come again, Haakon closed his eyes and sought the connection to his beast, to his human body. He once again opened his eyes, a sense of isolation worse than anything he'd ever known assailing him, even though their bodies were still joined.

For a moment he begrudged his mate the sharing of their souls, as it had given him a taste of what he could not have. But even though they would never be mates, she was Chrechte and it was his duty to protect her any way he could. Whatever the personal cost to himself.

He saw her intention to move before she lifted herself off of him, her blood and his spend smeared on her thighs. She turned from him, as if now feeling the need to hide her nakedness.

Haakon pulled his own breeches up, ignoring the rest of his clothes and weapons. There would be time enough to finish dressing when he'd said what needed saying. "You have a navigation board on the boat."

"What does that mean?"

He explained about the board that could be dropped into the water, the light of the sun casting a shadow to indicate the direction they were headed.

"And if there is no sun as there has not been the past two days?"

He dug through his things, finding his sunstone and showing her how it worked to draw forth the sun's rays even when the clouds covered the sky.

"But I do not have one of those on my boat."

"Take this one with you."

"It does not work that way."

"You are so sure?" he asked nodding toward her body. "You felt the pain of your torn maidenhead, the blood from that wound scents the very air around us."

"No, it cannot…"

"Take it. If there is a chance. Take it. But even if you wake up without it, the memories I was able to share with you will make it easier for you to determine your course."

She looked ready to argue, but finally nodded, putting her hand out for the clear stone.

He released it to her, not regretting the loss of this connection to his father and the other Vikings that had come so many years before Haakon.

His mate's life meant more than sentiment.

It meant everything, though she might never believe him.

Neilina stood, looking at him, her expression filled with determination rather than terror and something that almost looked like awe. "I can find my way now."

"I am glad."

"Thank you." She swallowed, like words were stuck in her throat. "I believe you have saved my life."

"I have given you the gift given to me, no doubt by fate for this very moment. Thank that which made us and touched me during my coming of age ceremony with such a gift."

She nodded. "I will, make no doubt, but I thank you as well. I have never given you reason to offer something of that like to me and I *am* grateful you did."

He doubted the proud woman would make such an admission if they were in the physical world in which either lived, but here in the Chrechte realm, she offered him sincere gratitude. And he received it, knowing that was the best he would ever get from her.

He was no fool. He did not take the gratitude, or even the physical joining that had come before it, as any sort of concession. He knew better. "I will not plant my sword again. If you have need of me, I will come."

She nodded but said nothing.

He had nothing more *to* say, so remained silent as well.

At first Neilina had an inexplicable air about her, like she expected him to say something more. But when he remained silent, merely waited for her to leave him again, a look that could almost be disappointment darkened her eyes.

Whyfore?

There was nothing left to say between them.

***

Artair ran in his wolf form, taking in the scents of his new home. Smells from the town and its many inhabitants, some Chrechte, some human, reached him. Though the town was several miles from the *jarl's* landholding, his wolf's sense had no trouble distinguishing the unfamiliar scents.

And though Artair had left Einar speaking with his father, the *jarl*, the scent of Artair's newly discovered mate teased at those same senses, urging him to turn around and go back. His wolf whined for their mate, but Artair needed time by himself. Time away from this wholly unexpected turn of events.

He'd never thought to find another mate, had accepted the fact he would live his life alone, with Gart as friend, but no more.

Now he had *another* mate, the son of a *jarl* and alpha to the pride. One day Einar himself would be alpha to the Paindeal. Artair would be mate to the alpha; he would have responsibilities he'd never even considered and wasn't sure how well he would uphold. He was a man who was attracted to other men, aye, but he'd never anticipated being in such a place.

Gart was not a leader, he would never be alpha, or even alpha's second.

Einar was not only born to the role, but Artair could not imagine Einar submitting to another Paindeal as alpha, regardless of birth order.

This powerful cat shifter was Artair's mate. *His* mate. And he wanted to claim Artair.

Shouldn't Artair be rejoicing?

Not running, fear and confusion creating a maelstrom of emotion inside him.

But Artair's mate had already been named protector to the pride. Even though the *conriocht* had only just returned to the Faol, Artair knew how important that role was. And he was meant to stand beside Einar. Him. Artair's wolf had never sought to challenge others for leadership. He was content to serve as a soldier.

As Einar's mate, Artair's life was now forfeit to the protection and safety of the pride as much as Einar's. This, at least, was something he had been raised to accept.

If not on the level of a *conriocht*, he had still always believed the protection of the pack was his responsibility and he would have died to do so.

Did Einar realize that? Did he know how committed his mate must be to the protection and betterment of the pride? The role that being his mate would thrust upon Artair.

And *how* big was Einar's cat that he could replace the *asmundr* as protector of his people?

The questions swirled in even Artair's wolf's brain, the usual peace he found in his animal form eluding him.

Einar's beast would be bigger than Artair's wolf, that was for sure. Though Artair was not Omega, he had never been one of the larger members of their pack. He was a loyal soldier, trained well by his laird and Drustan, as all Balmoral were, but his wolf would not strike fear into the hearts of other Chrechte.

It had never bothered him that Gart's wolf was bigger, but the thought of mating a Paindeal who shifted into a creature anywhere near as fearsome as the *asmundr* was daunting.

Whatever the *asmundr* shifted into, it was no animal Artair had ever seen or heard stories about. The giant cat was bigger than some of the bears from his homeland with fangs as long as a child's arm. Fangs that looked sharper than a well-maintained sword. His powerful haunches would easily launch the biggest bear into the air in a wrestling match.

And Artair's new mate shifted into a creature as fearsome, or close to it?

His wolf whined again for their mate, but Artair refused to turn back. He needed solitude. He had to think. Had to come to terms with having a mate that was a fearsome creature. And was not Gart.

Artair had spent all the years since his first change hoping, sometimes even believing, that one day Gart would accept the mating, that he and Artair would become lovers and spend their lives together. Family and mates.

While Artair had told himself Gart had made his choice, that though he might have a destined mate, he was not destined to know the joy of a mating. His heart had still hoped.

It was only the night before, after waking from the dream that revealed Gart's new mate, that Artair had truly fully accepted Gart would never be his. He'd known that Gart would fall quickly and fully for the beautiful Paindeal woman revealed to Artair in that dream.

She was everything Gart had always said he wanted.

Her features were perfect, her skin an exotic dusky tone, her body exactly what would entice a man who found the female form sexually pleasing. As Gart did, no matter that he'd had a male mate first. Her cat was as lovely as her human form, sleek and black, unlike any animal in Artair's experience.

Most importantly she was a *she* and could give the Faol soldier the children of his own loins he longed for. A family the rest of their clan would accept and admire.

Children.

Artair had never thought to be a father, but Einar said there were two that *he* wanted to raise. Far more difficult than offering his body as protection for the pack, was the idea he would be responsible for the wellbeing of two small children and raising them to be honorable Chrechte.

Fear mixed with excitement inside him at the prospect of something he'd never thought to have. Parenthood.

Artair felt like a boat rushing over choppy water, like the seas they'd sailed to reach Greenland.

He hadn't liked sailing and he didn't like the feeling of his life being tossed about like a toy on the expanse of a great ocean either.

How could he mate another after the many years Gart had owned his heart?

But how could Artair deny his mate?

He knew, better than any other, that pain.

Well, no doubt the *asmundr* understood it, but other than the Viking, Artair had never known another Chrechte besides himself that had a mate who refused them.

It was simply unheard of for true mates not to claim one another. The gift of a soul bond was too rare. Too special.

For everyone but Gart.

His best friend had never even contemplated the idea of building a life with Artair, of looking for children who needed parents to love them in order to build their family, rather than fathering his own. Not like Einar.

The Paindeal had been thinking about taking the orphaned children in before today, or he would not have spent so much time at their longhouse.

He was a rare man.

But that didn't change the fact he was also of the Vikings. Highland warriors had repelled Rome in centuries past, but even Artair's people did not have the reputation for violence and ruthlessness of the Vikings.

Knowing one of their *asmundrs* had been a raider, explained part of that ruthless efficiency. Artair could hardly believe one of their own protectors had turned his strength *against* the Chrechte. Knowing of the *conriocht*, the dragon, and the griffin was new to the Chrechte among the clans, but that one of them could destroy rather than protect was still a concept Artair found near impossible to accept.

Just as he was still struggling with Gart's rejection of their mating. He'd let his friend go for Gart's sake, for the sake of the mate he would one day meet and *want*. But being refused so many years had left a wall around Artair's heart. He didn't *want* to trust Einar.

How could he know this Viking would not one day reject him as well?

Yes, he felt the mating pull, but he couldn't be sure it was another *true* mating, an opportunity for their souls to join.

And if they didn't join souls, Einar could set Artair aside. While there were laws and even church ceremonies governing the joining of two men's lives, they were not the same as a marriage blessed by Rome. They had legal and financial bindings, but did not carry the same lifetime inevitability. Required no Papal dispensation to set aside.

He had no protection against heartache but the honorability of a mate he did not know at all. How could Artair trust that?

Artair's wolf reveled in the sights and sounds of this new place and howled with delight at not having to get back on a ship for crossing the sea, even as his mind grappled with his new reality.

Einar had threatened the *jarl*, his own father, with disposition if the law of Procreation was not struck from the Pride, but had he done that to pave the way for Einar to take over as pride alpha, or for the sake of his and Artair's mating?

How could Artair know? He'd met the Viking only today. A week to get to know each other before they consummated their mating did not seem long enough.

Yet, if he put it off, would he do the damage to Einar's heart and belief in his own value that Gart had unknowingly done to Artair's?

An alluring scent carried on the breeze of this place that was even colder than the Highlands of Scotland, growing stronger and stronger. Spicy and feral, it teased Artair's wolf and his canine body changed course to get closer to the scent without conscious thought.

Then to his left, a shape came into his peripheral sight, just a shadow at first, but soon he made out the form of a giant tiger. Not quite as big as the *asmundr*, it was still larger than any mountain lion, or even wild boar that Artair had ever seen.

Artair's wolf's eyes could not distinguish colors, so the tiger appeared white and black to him, its fur bright against the green covering the land. It did not have the *asmundr's* oversized fangs, but his large jaw was filled with sharp teeth that could rip through a wolf's pelt with ease.

Einar.

It had to be. Not only was Artair's wolf reacting on a visceral level he could not deny, but there could not be another beast so large and fierce.

Atavistic fear washed over him, even as Artair ran toward the giant beast, his wolf's legs covering the ground in powerful leaps. This was their mate, this tiger big enough to be a bear.

Einar had to weigh at least thirty stone, his body nearly twice as long and as tall as Artair's wolf, his muscles so powerful, he covered the distance between them faster than Artair. The tiger ran beside Artair, making a chuffing noise his wolf instinctively knew was happiness, or maybe approval.

Their mate! His wolf wanted to play, though Artair had stopped playing in his canine form when he left his boyhood behind.

But his wolf's instincts held sway right now, not his brain.

He feinted a left, but then dove right, rolling Artair and his mate. Artair jumped up and barked with joy at the tiger, even as his human mind filled with uncertainty bordering on fear that the tiger would not understand the play and take his action as aggression.

But Einar rose to his impressive height, chuffing at Artair before nipping at his tail and then darting back with agility shocking for an animal of his size.

Delight coursed through Artair as he returned the play, which finally ended in a wrestling match he could not hope to win. But Einar never unsheathed his claws and though he could easily throw Artair, he kept the wolf close as they wrestled in play. Artair's wolf reveled in the play and the closeness of his mate even as his human heart opened a tiny crack to this fearsome creature that treated him so carefully.

Finally, they stopped, both collapsing to the ground, their panting breaths mingling in the air around them. The tiger sniffed over Artair's body before curling around the wolf in a protective gesture that made that small crack in the wall around his heart expand alarmingly.

But as much as Artair feared opening his heart to his mate, he and his wolf reveled in the nearness of the tiger and he allowed his body to melt into relaxation.

They napped together, out there in the open space, nothing around for miles.

***

Artair woke with a sense of wellbeing that had been missing since the first time he realized Gart had no interest in claiming him as mate.

He hadn't even realized how deeply he and his wolf had suffered under the sense of not being wanted until he woke with a tiger's heart pounding a steady rhythm that went through his wolf's body, telling him all was well, his fears of the great beast for naught.

He moved slightly, nuzzling into the tigers fur. Helpless against his instincts, Artair began to scent his mate. He rubbed his fur against the tiger, mingling their scents and creating a new fragrance he would spend the rest of his life craving.

The tiger woke, but did not move, allowing Artair's wolf what it needed. When he was finished, the tiger turned and groomed him, its scratchy tongue bathing his wolf's body in a way Artair instinctually knew was part of the claiming ritual of the Paindeal.

Einar finished, biting Artair's snout softly in a sign of approval before standing on all fours and shaking his great body.

Artair stood as well, but allowed the shift to overcome him, needing to touch the tiger in his human form as much as his wolf had done. He wasn't ready for the full claiming, but his wolf insisted they finish scenting their mate.

Einar seemed to understand because he did not shift but stood still as Artair ran his hands over the luxuriant pelt. Touching the great beast from the top of his head to the tip of his tail, all the while Einar's tiger purred his approval.

"You are a beautiful beast, to be sure, but fearsome, even to your mate." White with stripes of black and grey, truly unlike any big cat Artair had ever seen or heard about, even from the well-traveled priest that had opted to see out his old age on Balmoral Island, his mate was impressive and powerful.

Einar made that chuffing sound again, before purring and rubbing against his body as any wolf might to mark his mate, further mixing their scents and touching Artair deep inside where he did not want to acknowledge.

He was not ready to give his heart again. Did not know if he would ever be.

And yet he was not sure he had a choice in the matter. "We are mates."

Einar nodded his great tiger's head, then cocked it to one side as if waiting for Artair to continue. How could he know Artair had more he wanted to say? Was his scent giving away his misgivings?

Perhaps. The idea of masking scent from his mate as much of an anathema to Artair as rejecting him.

"I cannot give my heart away again, so soon after accepting the mate I believed was mine never would be."

Would the tiger understand?

The air shimmered around them and then Einar stood there, his big, naked muscular body sending messages to Artair he had been doing his best to ignore since meeting the man.

He did not look upset by Artair's claim, but indulgent rather. "A Groenlander does not concern himself with matters of the heart."

"Doesn't he?" Artair asked, unaccountably hurt by such a dictate. "You do not plan to love your mate?" To love him?

Einar shrugged, his expression supremely unconcerned. "What is love? Some ephemeral emotion women speak of when men are not around."

"I do not think my clan's women would like being dismissed so easily."

"I do not dismiss women. I say only that they have different issues of importance to them."

"So, men do not care about love?"

"We live to protect our homes, to hunt, to seek out trade to better the lives of those in the *jarl's* territory."

"Your father's territory."

"*Ja.*"

"I loved Gart." Artair grimaced. "I still love him. As my best friend."

"I will be your best friend." There was no doubt in Einar's voice and his countenance was not so serene now. "If love is important to you, you will love me."

Artair ignored the arrogant claim about him loving the Paindeal shifter. "How can you be so sure we'll be friends?" Best friends.

"It is the way of mates."

"To be friends but not lovers?" Artair asked, confused.

"Make no mistake, I will claim your body. You will claim mine. We *will* be lovers."

"Aye." He didn't doubt it. Couldn't, no matter what his misgivings.

Einar gave him a look that probably made others quake. "There will be no room in your heart for old loves."

"So you want me to love you even if you have no plan to love me?" Artair asked, even as he was relieved that he felt no real fear toward his overwhelming mate.

He'd been worried, but in that moment, he knew Einar would protect him, never harm him. He tried to ignore the voice in his head and heart claiming such things. He was not ready to trust, but trust was building between them all the same.

Damn his animal instincts.

Einar grabbed his shoulders and moved so close the heat of their bodies mingled. "You cannot love another. You are *my* mate."

"If I'm going to love you, then you'd damn well better learn to love me," Artair demanded, unwilling to compromise on something this important.

Even if his arrogant mate didn't realize it.

"You want me to love you?" Einar asked, sounding shocked.

Wasn't that what they'd been talking about? "Are you daft?"

Einar's gaze narrowed, the hold on Artair's shoulders tightening. "Does that mean you *don't* want tender emotions from me?"

"Nay. Are you *trying* to make me angry?"

"Angrier, I'm sensing. You are already unhappy with me, though I do not know why. And *nei* that is not my intention."

"Then what?"

"You are my mate. I will give you whatever you need to be happy." Einar nodded his head as if affirming the same to himself.

Artair wasn't convinced. "What if you can't?"

"Fate has drawn us together. I am the only one who can."

"Arrogant."

"Thank you."

"It was not a compliment."

"Was it not?"

Artair made a sound of frustration he had never made before. "Nay."

"You want me to love you," Einar reminded him. "If that is what you need to be happy as my mate, I will love you. If these soft emotions are important to a Highland wolf, then I must change my own thinking as my mate is such."

"You really believe none of your Vikings care about loving their mates?"

"My father has always said that tender emotions are for the more tender sex."

"So, the Valkyrie? They are only myth?" Artair had wondered since coming to this place if the Valkyrie had been Paindeal women.

"*Nei.* The Valkyrie stories were born of the Chrechte women who were trained as fierce warriors and collected the bodies of the *kotrondmenskr* from the field of battle."

"Paindeal women are no longer trained to fight?"

"*Ja*, they are trained. Some fight more fiercely than the men."

"Then how are they more tender?"

Einar shrugged. "I know only that men do not speak of love, but women do."

"Perhaps your men only speak of love with their mates?" Or their wives if they were not Chrechte.

"Mayhap you are right, but my uncle swore a warrior could not concern himself with love and be a protector of his people."

And yet Einar had just said he would learn to love Artair. And he was named protector of the pride. What did that mean?

"The same uncle who killed other Chrechte because he lost his first mate?" Artair asked with some cynicism for the former *asmundr's* wisdom.

"And son."

"Aye, and son. Are you trying to say his murdering other Chrechte was *not* motivated by love betrayed and lost? Whatever words he spoke with his mouth, his actions told a different story. Your former *asmundr* had tender emotions and they got trampled."

Einar stared at Artair as if his words were incomprehensible, though they'd been speaking in the language of the Norse he'd learned since embarking on this journey.

Artair let out a harsh bark of laughter. "What did you think? An *asmundr's* damaged pride would be enough to undermine the very nature of his being to protect all Chrechte?"

Artair and Haakon had spoken more of what it meant to be *asmundr* and *conriocht* on their journey from the eastern beach to the one near the western settlement.

"It is likely my uncle learned from those very actions that giving into this tender emotions was dangerous." Einar's expression said he thought he'd made an unarguable point.

"You are saying he did not love his second mate or his son, Haakon?" Artair asked with no small amount of disbelief.

What Chrechte father did not love their son? 'Twas expected of all Chrechte parents to cherish their children *and* their mates. Even among the Paindeal, he was sure. No matter what claims Einar made that he had no interest in tender feelings.

"If I say *ja*, he loved Haakon deeply and his mate was cherished as any mate should be, you will give me that superior look again. I do not like it, mate."

"I do not believe I am superior to you," Artair said in shock.

"Good. There has been enough separation of our people. To bring the *kotrondmenskr* and *uffe* together, we must respect one another."

"Your own *asmundr* thought we needed to be separated. He never forgave the council for their betrayal."

"That is the way my father made it sound, but my uncle has not been our *asmundr* for many years. My cousin believes the peoples need to be united."

"And you agree?"

"Don't you? You came on a perilous journey for naught if you do not."

"I volunteered for the journey because I believed time and distance might give me the ability to move on from the mate destiny had chosen for me."

"He came with you."

"I did not know he would."

"And yet the trip accomplished what you hoped it would." Einar said the words like a statement, but his expression spoke a question.

"Aye, it did." Even if Artair was still hurting some and confused, *and* overwhelmed, he knew for a certainty his life forward would not be as Gart's mate, but as Einar's. "I have found the mate that accepts me."

It was Artair's turn to speak a question with his eyes, while his words sounded more sure than his heart could support.

"*Ja.*" Einar slid his hands up Artair's shoulders and cupped his neck, brushing over Artair's Adam's apple with his thumbs. "I threatened to challenge my father for you."

"For me?" Artair asked, still not sure he believed that.

"For what else? I have refused to mate in the fur with women of my pride since coming of age because my dreams told me my mate would come to me."

"Did you believe it would be a woman?"

Einar grinned, his expression the devil's own. "*Nei.* Never did I believe fate would treat me so cruelly."

"You do not like women?"

"I like and respect the women of my father's holdings, but they do not heat my blood. My nature is as I was born to be." Einar shrugged, like admitting such did not bother him in the least.

Gart would never admit to the desire Artair had seen in his eyes on many occasions. There was no doubt that he was also attracted to women, but he'd been embarrassed by his attraction to Artair. And denied it.

Artair had never felt like he could be open about the fact that he was like Einar. "You don't care? You never thought to take a wife, to have children?"

"We already have children. You need to meet them. My father needs to decree it. Their relatives agree to them becoming part of our family."

"And will they?" Artair interrupted.

"*Ja.* I already spoke to their grandparents, not long after their father's death. I knew the girl and boy were supposed to be mine."

"How?"

"The Seer helped me interpret my dreams, he'd had visions of his own about Jorgen and Mari."

"That's their names? Jorgen and Mari?"

"*Ja.*"

"Jorgen is the four-year-old? Mari's still a baby."

"She's almost two summers."

Artair had to stop himself from leaning forward, his body craving touch with his mate. He forced himself to stay focused on the discussion at hand. "Osmend is not like any Seer we have back home."

"Is he not?"

"Our Seer's do not withhold information about their visions."

"That you are aware of."

Artair considered that. "Mayhap." He had to keep forcing his gaze away from the tempting body of his mate. "So, your Seer told you to adopt the children as your own?"

"*Ja*. Their father was a friend, but Osmend told me my dreams meant they were to be mine and that we are to bring them before the stone once I had taken a mate."

"Do you think it will draw forth their Chrechte nature?"

"I do not know. Osmend has many reasons for the things he dictates, most of them a mystery to the rest of us."

"And your father puts up with that?" Artair asked, shocked, but his voice coming out husky and filled with the desire, no matter how much he tried to suppress it.

Einar's blue gaze said he knew just how much Artair wanted him, but he replied to Artair's words, not his need. "*Ja*. The Seer is the most powerful among our pride."

"Even more powerful than the *asmundr*?" Artair could not imagine.

Einar leaned down, their foreheads touching. "He can lay hands on a Chrechte and the spirit of the cat will never come forth again."

Artair shivered at the thought of losing his wolf, his body trembling even harder with how much he needed the other man.

"Has he ever done that?" he whispered from between dry lips. How did they know the old Chrechte could do such a terrible thing?

"When he was a child, my father knew of a *kotrondmenskr* who went feral. Osmend laid hands on the lynx. He shifted back to his human and then he never shifted again."

Artair rubbed his cheek against Einar's, inhaling his mate's scent. "Surely that is a fate worse than death."

But truly? The only fate worse than death that he could imagine in that moment was *not* touching his mate. He fisted his hands against Einar's chest, gritting his teeth against the need to skim his fingers over every bulging muscle.

"Mayhap, but the Chrechte had killed in his feral madness and would have killed again. It was lose his cat or his life."

"He chose to lose his cat?" It seemed impossible.

Artair was not sure he could even survive without his wolf.

Einar turned his head so their lips were only a breath apart. "Osmend chose, but the Chrechte lived to an old age. I knew him as a boy; he was quiet, but not miserable."

Artair could not imagine. "I would rather die."

"He could have asked for death after his mind returned to him. He did not."

"So, he *did* choose." Artair wanted to press his lips to Einar's so badly, his muscles locked with the tension of holding back.

"*Ja*, I supposed he did." But Einar did not sound like he was thinking about the long ago Chrechte who had lost his cat.

"Osmend has powers our Seers do not."

"More than your Seers know they have." Einar's lips brushed against the corner of Artair's mouth.

Artair shivered again. "Aye."

A solid, muscular arm came around waist, pressing his body closer to Einar's. "Are you cold, mate?"

"Nay. It was thinking of the power to separate a Chrechte from his animal," he prevaricated. Surely that was enough to make him shiver in dread, but that tremble had not been anything but suppressed desire.

Einar purred, the sound so much like his tiger's that it was hard to believe he made it in his human form. "*Ja*. It is a chilling ability."

"You smell good," Artair blurted, unable to keep up the pretense of thinking about anything other than his mate any longer, then felt heat suffuse his face.

Einar growled, pulling Artair into full body contact, their hard sexes pressing together. "You smell like mine."

"You're very possessive," he whispered, feeling lightheaded from his first sexual contact with another person.

"And you are not?" Einar asked, not sounding happy at the idea, and entirely too in control of his thoughts for Artair's liking.

Wasn't his mate as affected by his nearness as he was by Einar's? He let a little of his wolf's growl into his voice as he declared, "If you touched another as you are now touching me, I would rip out his throat."

"As it should be."

"You're as bloodthirsty as any Viking of old."

"Have you no taste for battle?"

Artair pushed away from his mate. If Einar wanted to continue talking, Artair could not do it with their bodies so aligned.

Einar's eyes narrowed, he opened his mouth to say something, but Artair put his hand up to stop his mate speaking.

Taking a deep breath, which did nothing to help him clear his head as the scent of his mate only inflamed him further, Artair did his best to think about the question. If anyone one else had asked, he would have denied what would have been an accusation of cowardice. But this was his mate and Einar did not sound disgusted or put off by the idea, only curious.

Finally, Artair stated, "I will kill to protect my people."

"*Ja.* I have no doubt. You are a fine wolf."

The praise warmed Artair and he found himself relaxing, even as he ached for the return of closeness of being held by his mate. "I do not crave battle or war as some do."

"I am glad to hear it."

"You are?" Artair could not hide his surprise.

Einar frowned, his expression serious, his blue gaze sober. "Senseless death can never be taken lightly by my people. We are too few to seek out conflict for the sake of the joy we find in battle."

"I find it hard to believe a warrior like you has never been in battle."

"Oh, I have fought to protect my father's territory, I have killed. But only ever out of necessity. My father does not seek to expand his borders, using force only to maintain them."

"There would not be much point of expanding into land that cannot be cultivated, sparse woods that would make poor hunting," Artair said, remembering how the land on the outskirts of the *jarl's* holding had looked when he'd been running as his wolf.

"Aye, Groenland is not the paradise of riches my ancestor claimed."

"Eirik the Red was your ancestor?"

"Aye, a distant one, but related to the royal line of the *kotrondmenskr* all the same. He settled the eastern town, but eventually all Chrechte moved to this settlement under my father's protection."

"Why?"

"Fewer people made for easier hunting in our animal forms, the greater distances between homesteads give us the privacy the *kotrondmenskr* require."

"That makes sense." Artair didn't really know what he was saying. He was too busy trying to control the reaction of his body to his mate's nearness.

It had never been this bad with Gart, he'd never felt a near undeniable urge to touch and be touched. Artair wanted to press his body back against Einar's with a near-feral passion.

Einar let his possessive gaze travel over Artair, stopping at Artair's tumescent member, his eyes heating. "I smell your arousal, *kisa*, but that…" He nodded toward Artair's sex. "That tells me you crave me nearly as much as I crave you. I have done my best not to act on my urge to claim you, but if you want a week before you share your body with mine, you will shift and return to our longhouse. Now."

"What is *kisa*?" Artair asked, fully aware of how serious his mate was, but unable to simply shift and leave. Not sure he was able to leave at all.

"Baby cat."

"You called me kitten?" Artair asked in indignation, using the Gaelic word.

"If that means baby cat, *ja*."

"I am not a baby."

"*Nei*. You are a fully-grown man and my mate." The heat in Einar's blue eyes was enough to burn Artair from the inside out. "It is an endearment among our people."

"So, you would not care if I called you cub?"

Einar stared at him like he'd lost his mind. "Do I look like a child to you?"

"Do I?"

"*Nei*. You look like a man I want, *kisa*. And like a man I will hold more dear than any other."

And that made him a kitten?

It was an endearment. Endearments were part of tender feelings, weren't they? Einar was trying, in his Viking warrior way, to give Artair what he believed his mate needed.

Artair smiled at his big, gorgeous mate. "You may call me kitten."

"I prefer *kisa*. I do not speak Gaelic like my cousin. Perhaps my mate will help me learn."

"But your father spoke Gaelic at the meeting."

"And I understand some. Enough to talk a bit, but I am not fluent as Haakon is, or even as well versed in the tongue as my father."

"It is a good thing I have learned the Norse tongue then."

"*Ja*. Destiny led you to what you needed to be, my mate."

Or they could have communicated in the ancient language of the Chrechte. When he said so, Einar smiled. "That might draw strange glances from the humans among my father's people. If the newest member of our longhouse spoke to me in a strange tongue none but the Chrechte among us recognizes."

Artair shrugged. His mate had a point. "So, did the Seer tell you that I would be able to speak Norse?"

"*Nei*. It is a happy surprise."

Artair nodded, accepting Einar's words.

His grandfather had not had as many visions in his entire life, it felt like, as the Seers and *celi dis* that had been called to serve the Chrechte these recent years. Was there a pattern to these visions? If there was, Artair hadn't seen it yet. Some were little, some were big. Some were for the present, some for the future and some even dealt with the past.

Artair's thoughts were interrupted by the scent of his mate's arousal as it grew stronger. Did simply standing near him increase Einar's desire? The idea heightened Artair's own need tenfold. To be wanted after so many years of being rejected by the man he believed would be his only mate was a spark to the wick of his desire, sending it burning hotly through him.

His gaze flew to Einar's. His mate's blue eyes were filled with intense hunger.

He *should* step away, but he didn't *want* to.

He wanted to feel Einar's lips on his. He wanted to touch his mate's naked body. More than anything, Artair wanted to be wanted.

And Einar's scent, the look in his eyes, the set of his jaw, the way he held his body as if trying with everything in him not to reach for Artair said that Artair was wanted in exactly the way he so vitally needed.

Einar's gaze fixed on Artair's lips, his expression going even more ardent. "If I kiss you, I *will* claim you."

"Not if I tell you to wait." Artair was no Seer, but he *knew* Einar was a good man. A strong warrior, he was capable of controlling himself.

"You trust me." Einar said it almost wonderingly.

"You are going to be my mate. If I don't trust you, that does not happen." As he said the words, he realized how true they were.

Artair could *not* withhold his trust from the man who would be his mate, not and accept that mating.

Einar's jaw went granite hard as he inclined his head. "To bond our souls, we must trust one another."

Artair would have agreed with words, not just his thoughts, but Einar pulled his body close once again and leaned down to press their lips together. Artair's mouth molded to Einar's of its own volition, instincts guiding him where experience was lacking. Artair had never been kissed. He had never kissed another on the lips. Not family, not a lover. He'd never had a lover.

He'd known his mate since before he discovered sexual desire.

Einar pushed those thoughts from Artair's head as he claimed him as surely with a kiss as he would eventually with his body.

Artair's body suffused with heat, pleasure bubbling through his blood like the natural springs near the Balmoral ceremonial caves. Einar's lips were soft and sure at the same time, his mouth drawing forth a reaction in Artair that was overwhelming and more foreign than the language he'd been at pains to learn these past three years.

This was what it was like to kiss?

This was what it was like to be touched by another who desired his body?

He swayed toward Einar, craving more closeness, needing more touch. Einar pulled him in, the proof of their desire rubbing against each other for the second time, sending sparks of unequalled pleasure throughout his body. Artair felt like he could climax right then, his body was so sensitized and every inch of his skin immersed in ecstasy.

Einar's hands roamed down to his flank, leaving sparks of hot pleasure in their wake.

Artair moaned, overcome by delight in this altogether strange embrace. To have his mate so near, naked flesh pressed against naked flesh, their mouths fused, tongues colliding.

The kiss went on until his lungs burnt in his chest, the need to breathe acute, but still Artair did not want to break his lips from those of his mate.

He *would* love this man, with greater depth than he knew himself capable.

Just as terrifying, he would crave him with everything inside himself.

These were truths he could not deny, but neither would he acknowledge them to anyone but himself.

Einar made another one of those purring sounds a man should not be capable of, the low rumble going right through Artair and the urgency in his loins grew, his lower body thrusting against Einar's of its own accord. His balls tightened, the sense of urgency growing with each second the kiss went on and every movement of his hips.

For the first time ever, Artair's body experienced the pinnacle of pleasure in another's company. Delight exploded out of him even as he broke the kiss to shout his joy.

This was what it was to share his sexual ecstasy with another, to share his body.

It was the most amazing, intimate, physically satisfying moment of his life.

He'd known there was supposed to be more pleasure with a partner than by his own hand, but this? This feeling of euphoria, this incredible sense of happiness as his mate roared out his own climax, shouting *Artair's* name at the last, it was unbelievably wonderful. The fragrance of their shared passion tugged at Artair's wolf, the need to shift nearly uncontrollable.

Artair grabbed Einar's face and pulled it down the few inches needed so they could kiss again. The melding of mouths completed Artair's sense of rightness, his absolute ecstasy in that moment.

Einar's chest heaved as they broke their kiss. "My beast wants to claim you."

"We just...I mean, we..."

"Came? *Ja.* And the pleasure has only made my desire to join our souls stronger."

"Your father said a week."

"My father is *jarl*, I am your mate."

"Aye, you are my mate, but I want my week."

"After what just happened? Why?" Einar scowled. "We are well matched."

"As if we were created one for the other, aye. But I want to get to know you, and not just your body." Though he would not deny to himself just how very much better he wanted to get to know his mate's body. "Before we bind the rest of our lives together."

"I'll give you your week, mate, but mark this, our lives are already joined."

CHAPTER SEVEN

Haakon moved restlessly on his bed, the sounds of the longhouse unfamiliar to his beast, though that was not what kept him awake. Tomorrow he sailed with the Norse merchants to Balmoral Island.

From there, he was tasked with traveling to the mainland and finding the Sinclair clan where a dragon was supposed to reside.

A dragon.

Haakon had been born *asmundr*, but his giant cat was no dragon. His father had always told Haakon that the only being who could absolutely defeat an *asmundr* was the dragon. Even the griffin with its ability to fly was better matched.

The dragon could breathe fire from the sky, incinerating any in its path.

Had this dragon ever killed with its fire?

Haakon knew that to protect those under his care, he would do so. He himself had used his fearsome fangs to do as much.

Beyond wondering what the dragon Chrechte would be like, and thoughts of what his new life might bring was his fear for Neilina. Had his mate found her way on the ship she sailed with her companions?

Haakon wished he'd taken a moment when their spirits were united to look at those who she deigned to travel with, the two who were welcome into her life.

Part of him desperately wanted to sleep, to go to the place of *other* and confirm she was well. His need to protect her would not disappear with the knowledge they would never be mates in the flesh.

And as much as Osmend had said that Haakon might one day find another, the *asmundr* doubted that. His bond was already too strong with his *conriocht* mate. Only one of their deaths might sever it.

And he had no desire for his mate to die, no more so himself.

Not quite sleeping, though not fully awake, Haakon felt the call of the Chrechte spirit world. The energy calling him was harder, darker than when he felt called there by his mate.

Did that mean she had died? Or was in such peril it tainted her call to him?

He found himself walking through mist into a forest glen he had never visited before. The sound of a waterfall mixed with chirping birds and the swish of a warrior's blade.

Drawing his sword and spinning to face his foe in one movement, Haakon leapt back holding his weapon in a defensive pose as he recognized the man facing him.

"Father!" Haakon shook his head, trying to clear the image before him, but Bjorn, the Firebrand, once the Destroyer, remained. "How are you here?"

"I am spirit," his father replied as if that should be obvious. "More to the point, how are you here, my son?"

Haakon saw no reason to withhold the truth from his father's spirit. "I have been many times to see the woman destiny chose as my mate."

"You have a mate." A smile unlike any Haakon had seen when his father was living creased the other *asmundr's* face.

Haakon wished he could confirm such and keep his father's clear delight in Haakon's good fortune intact, but he had never lied to the other *asmundr* and was convinced he could not now, in this place even if he tried to. "*Nei.* She will have nothing to do with me."

Bjorn blanched, pain like nothing he'd ever allowed his son to see haunting eyes identical to Haakon's own blue orbs. "She refuses you?"

"*Ja.*"

"Why? Does she love another?" His father's voice cracked with a torment Haakon was shocked now he'd never recognized.

"*Nei.*" At least Haakon was fairly certain there was no other. "But she hates another enough to paint me with the colors of his brush."

"Who?"

Again, only the truth would do. "You."

"Me? Why would your mate hate me?"

"You destroyed her pack."

"She is *Faol*?" Bjorn spit the Gaelic word for the *uffe* out like it was a bad taste in his mouth.

"Why did you never tell me I had a brother?"

"He died centuries before your birth. What good would come of telling you of him?"

"I do not know, but he was my brother."

"He was part of *my* past, son. Not yours."

"Your past shaped my future. It is only right I should have known about it."

"*Nei*."

"*Ja*. Because you used your *asmundr* power and strength to destroy the very people destiny had called you to protect, my mate considers me and those like me abomination."

"The Faol and Éan stole my mate from me." Again, his father did not use the Norse word for *uffe*, saying much about how disconnected he felt from the other Chrechte peoples. "*They stole my child* and because they did, he did not bond with me enough to call forth the *asmundr*. I had to live on after both died, my heart turned colder than the Norvegr winter in my chest."

"But my mother, your *second* mate, she thawed the ice around your heart and spirit. You told me at least that much." Bjorn had cherished the non-shifting Chrechte woman.

"*Ja*. I would not be in this place if she had not, I do not think. I love her still."

Haakon had never heard his father speak of love and found it a little disconcerting now. "You had great affection for her," he agreed, unwilling to say a word he wasn't sure he'd ever spoken.

"I still do. She shares eternity with me." He sighed. "Or rather, I believe I share eternity here with her."

"Yet you still hate the *uffe*?" Haakon demanded, not understanding. If his mother had thawed his father to such an extent, why had this abiding antipathy remained?

Bjorn scowled, looking very much as Haakon remembered him. Hard and unyielding. "What I gained later did not negate what I lost."

"And what you took? Can anything *I* do negate that?" Haakon wondered.

His father's shoulders slumped, his expression filling with regret. "I should not have gone raiding, but my urge to kill, to do battle was strong. I thought better to follow my king's urgings than to turn on the people around me."

"You thought you might turn on the *kotrondmenskr*?" Haakon asked with horror he made no effort to veil.

"In those years after my son and mate finally passed, I was entirely alone."

"You had a pride."

"I was not connected to them as an *asmundr* should be. My soul roamed the earth without peace and connected to no other Chrechte until your mother brought me back into communion with the *kotrondmenskr* and helped me to feel something other than the dark rage that colored my every waking moment."

"But you were guardian. *You* taught me what that meant."

"I was broken, by bitterness, by loss. I did not see clearly until the day your mother came of age and her scent changed, calling to mine."

"She loved you so much."

"*Ja.* She still does."

"And your first mate?"

Bjorn frowned again. "She said she loved me once, but then after our son was born, she claimed to love another. Our souls bonded, but somehow she ignored that bond to allow another into her furs."

"She was human."

"And they might feel the mate pull, but their bodies do not respond the same way."

"Does she live here now?" Haakon wondered how that reunion had gone.

Bjorn shrugged. "I have not seen her in this land where spirits roam. Whether she is here, or not, I do not know. Her soul bond to me should have brought her to the Chrechte spirit world upon death."

"Or she has already passed on, to where spirits no longer commune with the living."

"Perhaps."

"And your son?"

Pain again creased his father's features. "I have not seen him either. Again, I do not know his eternal fate, but he was a strong and honorable *kotrondmenskr*."

"Perhaps you carry too much anger toward his mother, toward the people he was raised to consider family for him to find you."

Understanding lit Bjorn's face. "*Ja*, mayhap you are right."

"You must release your anger."

"You think that is so easy? For you it might be, you have no great atrocity to forgive as I do."

"Do you think not? I could hate you for costing me my own mate."

Bjorn jerked, as if Haakon's words had taken him aback. "I am your father."

"And *you* committed terrible atrocities for our kind before I was born. These actions have severed my chance of bonding with my mate, of having my own children, of living out the life fate ordained for me."

"I never wanted you to know. You must believe I never wanted you to suffer because of my weakness and the acts it drove me to."

Haakon shrugged. He knew that. While the word had never been spoken between them, he'd always known his father loved him, cared about Haakon's happiness and life. Nevertheless, both no longer had a choice but to live (or exist maybe) with the truth that his father's actions centuries before his birth had dictated Haakon's future.

"I am sorry. Even if she is *uffe*, you deserve to have your mate."

"The *uffe* are not all evil, anymore than all *asmundr* are murderous beasts as you became."

Bjorn flinched, but inclined his head. "I recognized the error of my ways. I gave up those murderous ways."

"You do not believe the *uffe* realized their own errors?"

"It was both the Faol and the Éan."

"Even now, you do not use our words for them. Do you still hate them so much, even after mating another and having a son who *did* become *asmundr*?"

"I am proud you are protector of our people, but it was knowing I would not have to watch you die that gave me my greatest joy when the stone called for the *asmundr*."

"Our stone...it is only a chip off the true *Paindeal Neart*." Haakon knew that now.

"*Ja*. That too was my fault. My actions caused a great schism in our people."

"How could they not?"

Bjorn nodded. "At first, all our people stood behind me, but when I allowed my anger to turn me against other Chrechte, killing them, many said they would not live under the protection of a murderer."

"Osmend did not leave."

"He'd foretold your birth."

"Didn't knowing another mate lay in your future give you some measure of comfort?" Haakon could only wonder.

"I never allowed it to. I didn't believe him. I'd lost my faith in Providence. I no longer believed I had a higher purpose."

"And so you killed without discrimination."

"I let some live."

"Like my mate."

"How is that possible?" Bjorn wondered, his brows drawn together in question.

"She is *conriocht*."

"I battled only one female *conriocht*." Which implied his father had battled male protectors, and defeated them, leaving the *uffe* without their guardians.

No wonder their own people had left their *asmundr*.

"I did not think your mate would survive her sea burial."

"You put her adrift in a boat with her weapons."

"As was only right for a guardian of my people, even if the Picts forgot the ancient ways. Ships were our symbols of travel into the afterlife as well as seeking a better life in the present."

"You talk like a Viking."

"I was Viking before those we plundered named us."

Haakon sighed, the love a son for his father too strong to deny what needed to be said. "You must release your old resentments. Your time here in the Spirit world is hindered by walls your anger has built between you and others. Forgive your first mate. She loved another. Forgive your first son. He did not know you to call you *pa*."

Not that Haakon had ever called Bjorn *pa*. It has always been *faðir*. Father.

"If he had known me as I was after he died, he would have hated me." Bjorn sighed. "And he would have been right to do so. Even before his death, I had turned hard and unyielding. When he came to touch the stone, I could not open my soul to his. It was my fault the stone did not call him to *asmundr*."

Haakon did not believe that. "The stone calls who the stone calls and bestows gifts as the Creator wills. You never had the power to call forth the next *asmundr*."

"It called you."

"Because *my* spirit connected to the stone as it was meant to. My brother's was not. That did not make him less of Chrechte."

"*Nei.* Of course not."

"Did he have a mate? Children?"

"He did. An Éan. I had hoped their child at least would be griffin."

"But it was not?"

"*Nei.*"

"Do his descendants still live among the *uffe*?"

"I do not know. The Éan and the Faol separated...they may live among the Éan."

"You would have done better to watch over your own descendants than kill those of the *uffe* who misused you."

"*Ja.*"

" It was my brother's destiny to live his days out as *kotrondmenskr* not *asmundr*. He would not have hated you. I do not believe he ever hated you. He was *your* son, no matter that he was stolen for another to raise. "

"You cannot know that."

"I can. I am your son too. Even knowing all your faults now, I do not hate you. "

"How is that possible? Now that you know what I did. How I betrayed the very essence of what we are?"

"You are my father and you taught me truth. You taught me how to be a true *asmundr* guardian to all, even when your heart still harbored lies born of rage banked, but not forgotten."

Bjorn nodded. "I did my best. Your mother would not have forgiven me otherwise."

"Is she here?" Haakon had a terrible desire to see the one person in his life who had shown any softness toward him.

Though he would never admit such a need. He'd missed her terribly after her death.

While he'd been certain of his father's love and regard, Bjorn had trained Haakon ruthlessly from the time he could walk (perhaps before, for all he knew), right up to his own death.

His uncle treated him like *asmundr*, not nephew. His aunt had always kept her distance. He'd never known his grandparents, on either side of his family.

"I was not sure why I had been called here, did not know it would be you," Bjorn said, breaking into Haakon's thoughts. "Perhaps next time she will be here as well. The ways of the spirit world are a mystery."

"And yet you believe there will be a next time?" Surely Haakon's visits here were irregular for a Chrechte who was neither *celi di* nor Seer.

"Osmend always said you had some of the Seer in you. You'll return to this place and we will be here to greet you." Bjorn spoke like his words were prophecy, not a guess or a hope.

Haakon chose to believe, but he could only imagine how Neilina would react to seeing his parents if she was the one who called him the next time. He said nothing, however. His father had his own demons to battle.

Haakon would deal with the ones plaguing his mating on his own.

Bjorn could no more change the past than Haakon could. And he was sorry for it, now. Perhaps that was not enough, would never be enough for Neilina, but Haakon could forgive his father.

If Bjorn's past deeds made Haakon even more determined to do all he could to protect all Chrechte, so much the better. He would pledge his loyalty to the dragon king that apparently did not know he was king and Haakon would do whatever needed doing to make sure their race survived.

"I am going to Scotland to live among the *uffe*."

"To be with your mate?" Bjorn asked, making no disparaging comment about the other Chrechte race.

"*Nei*. I do not know where she hails from, her clothes are of the forest, her manner that of a warrior, our words always exchanged in the ancient tongue."

"I only battled one female *conriocht*."

"So you said."

"She was of the island a day's journey north of the uppermost highlands."

"So, she *is* Scottish." Haakon had not been absolutely sure considering his father had gone a Viking to England as well as other countries of Europe.

"*Ja.*"

"But you set her to sea," Haakon pointed out. "There is no telling where she ended up more than two centuries past."

Bjorn nodded, looking thoughtful. "That is true. So, you travel to the land of the Scots for something else?"

"I go at the Seer's behest, because it is my duty."

Again, his father nodded. "When will you make the journey?"

"I leave tomorrow." Haakon couldn't help pointing out, "I'm surprised you aren't upset."

"You are doing as I taught you, even if it is not the way I lived my life as *asmundr*. And you can come to this realm from anywhere."

Perhaps his father was closer to releasing old resentments and pain than he thought.

Haakon vowed, "I will do my best to serve the dragon king."

"You plan to stay in the land of the clans?"

"If that is the will of the dragon and Seers."

"You would leave the *kotrondmenskr* without *asmundr*." But Bjorn didn't sound angry about that fact.

"Einar is strong and powerful."

"He is that. My nephew will make a good *jarl* when his father is ready to step down."

Haakon agreed. He'd never been jealous of his uncle or cousin's place in the pride, understanding to his very marrow that his duty was greater than that of *jarl*, or pride alpha. "He found his mate," Haakon informed his father.

"She will give him many fine children."

"He is *uffe* as well."

Bjorn sighed. "It seems fate has decided the races will be reconciled."

"It is hard to believe my own father is the reason they separated to begin with," Haakon mused without rancor.

"Was it *my* fault? To be sure, I reacted in fury at their betrayal, but it was the Faol and Éan council who ignored Chrechte law to follow the dictates of a human woman's heart and a Faol's lust."

"You do not think he loved her?"

"Even if he did, she was not *his* mate."

Haakon could not imagine how he would respond to his mate giving herself to another. Even the thought made him rigid with rage. But murderous? He hoped never to have to find out.

"Whoever was at fault, it is time for the separation to end."

"Past time, though I never admitted that to myself before."

"Past time."

Bjorn reached out and clapped Haakon on the shoulder. "I am proud of you, son. You are a good *asmundr*."

"I am as you taught me to be."

"You are your own man."

"As you encouraged me to be." His father had been a tough taskmaster, but he had taught Haakon well.

"Your time here is closing."

"You can feel it?"

"*Ja*." His father then did something that shocked Haakon into immobility.

The *asmundr* had never held Haakon as a child. A rare pat to his shoulder, the only physical sign of affection he'd ever received from Bjorn.

But his father hugged Haakon, his embrace strong and not at all hesitant. He held him tight and for several counts before stepping back. "Be happy, my son."

"I will be a good *asmundr*. Happiness is not something I aspire to."

His father sighed but nodded. "I will aspire on your behalf."

Haakon felt a half-smile form on his face. "You do that."

Perhaps wishes such as that were the prerogative of those who lived in the spirit realm.

Certainly, he could never remember Bjorn being concerned about that kind of thing when he'd walked the earth with Haakon.

Haakon expected to return to his rest and waken as usually happened after a trip to this place of *other*, but he found himself in a familiar glen, Neilina standing on the other side of the expanse of grass as she had done many times before.

She wasn't frowning when she saw him. Which, in itself, was unusual enough, but beside her was a large bear, perhaps even bigger than Haakon's beast. Dark brown, it lumbered beside her as she walked toward Haakon, its back even with her shoulder.

She'd never approached him upon his arrival before either.

Haakon felt fear seize his chest, making it hard to breathe. "You were unable to get your craft back on course to reach land?"

Her brows drew together in confusion. "We are on course as well you should know, having given me the knowledge to find our way."

"But you are here." Again. Having drawn him to herself. There could be no denial.

Not even from this stubborn warrior woman.

"I am."

"Your soul called to mine," he pointed out, his fear still a living thing inside him.

Would she call on him if she were not still in grave danger?

"I suppose it must have. Your willingness to share your spirit with mine allowed me to save my own life, but more importantly that of my companions."

Haakon nodded toward the bear, who now sat on her haunches staring at Haakon. "Is he one of them?"

"She, and I bound her to me through my stone many years ago. For too long she was the only company I had."

Haakon had never heard of such, but something else Neilina said was far more important. "Now there is another?" he asked, forcing himself to a semblance of calm.

Glad once again that he did not know where his mate was so he could not seek out her *companion* and kill him.

"I adopted a daughter the same year we began to visit this place."

"Oh." He now wanted to meet the woman she spoke of. Badly.

After all, they were family and the girl's protection was not only the responsibility of his *conriocht* mate now. It was his as well. "By Chrechte law she is also my daughter."

Neilina shook her head, a sound coming from her he had never heard before.

It was a laugh. "Of course you claim her, though we've never met and are unlikely to. Your arrogance knows no bounds."

"It is arrogant to obey the ancient laws of our people?" he asked, genuinely confused.

Her beautiful mouth twisted in a grimace. "I suppose not." She sighed. "She'd probably like you."

"She has no reason to hate those of my people." He assumed she didn't. If Neilina had adopted her only a few years past, the girl was not old enough to have suffered at Bjorn's hands.

"She has reason enough to despise men in general."

"But she does not." If she did, Neilina would not have suggested the girl would like Haakon.

"Nay."

"You could not have taught her to cling to bitterness as you do, for her to be this way."

Neilina shrugged, as if conceding the point. "I did not want her to be as I am, unable to trust anyone."

"Unwilling mayhap. Not unable."

She frowned at him. "Must you always argue with me?"

"Was I doing that?" He'd thought he was only stating an opinion.

She sighed. "Mayhap not. Anyway, I wanted to thank you."

"No thanks are needed between mates. Even if you were not my mate, I would have done my best to help you. You are Chrechte."

"You really are different from your father."

"He regrets his actions deeply."

"How can you know that? You said he was dead." Her face twisted with angry distrust. "Did you lie to me?"

"*Nei.* He walks here, in the Chrechte spirit world."

She looked around like Bjorn might jump out of the trees and attack them, her hand going to the hilt of her knife, the other grasping her walking stick like a spear.

"He wishes you no harm." But Haakon would not claim his father had given up all animosity toward the *uffe* as he was not sure that was the case.

He thought the other *asmundr* might actually be working on it though.

"I will not stay if he is here."

"I do not believe he can come where you are. There is a barrier between you." Whether it was of his father's making, or Neilina's, Haakon did not know.

"How can you know that, have you suddenly become *celi di*, now, *asmundr*?"

He shrugged. There was a reason he was able to walk the spirit realm when other *asmundr* before him had not been able to until death. "You are *kelle*, is that so hard to believe?"

"What do you mean I am *kelle*? I am no priestess."

Haakon could not believe the warrior woman was unaware of her own nature. "You said yourself you are centuries older than me. How can you deny a truth such as this? You are a warrior priestess as in the days of old, your days, I suppose."

"You don't know of what you speak."

"You had visions that led you to sail away from your home, didn't you?"

Her eyes widened as if she was seeing something she had not before. "I did."

"You could not ignore these visions?"

"Nay."

"That sounds like a Seer to me. A normal Chrechte may have dreams and visions, but they are not driven by them."

"How do you know this?"

"Our Seer, an ancient much older than you, has said so to me many times."

"No, I cannot be *kelle*. I know nothing of being *celi di* or..." Her voice trailed off. "The *celi di* said he wanted to train me and I did not understand how. I was a warrior. He was a priest."

"And then he died, along with the rest of your people."

Her face changed again, the memory of something unpleasant unmistakable in her countenance. "Yes, then he died by your father's hand."

***

Neilina and Freya pulled the boat ashore. Dìonach had lumbered over the side and swam to shore already, clearly impatient to feel land under her paws. Neilina was only glad that the bear had not capsized them in her haste to reach land. Not having the added weight certainly made it easier for the women to pull the boat up onto the beach.

Neilina surveyed the rocky expanse of land before the water, her keen ears picking up the sound of approaching feet.

"Men are coming," she told Freya. Two of them, rushing on foot, no horses' hooves clacking against stone, shod or unshod, to be heard. "Go into the woods with Dìonach."

"What if they mean you harm?" Freya asked, worry making her hazel eyes darken.

"Then they will pay with wounds, if not their very lives," Neilina replied without compunction or the least amount of doubt.

She was *conriocht*. Warrior to her people. In the more than two centuries of her life, she had been forced to kill. To protect others. To protect herself.

Even a hermit in the woods might be found with an eye toward taking what would not be given. Whether her possessions or her person, Neilina had never suffered the fool who thought to harm her to live.

Since that long-ago battle, she hadn't killed another Chrechte. No Paindeal lived among the people of her island and few Faol remained. So few, she had only caught their scent on the wind. And avoided them.

But fate had decreed she could not avoid her people any longer.

"They cannot harm me," she assured her adopted daughter.

Freya remained unconvinced. "What if there are too many of them?"

"There are *two*. Do you doubt my ability to handle two men, even if they are Faol?"

Freya shook her head vehemently. "Nay, mother of my heart."

"Don't get sentimental on me."

"I can if I want."

"Get in the forest," Neilina demanded with exasperation even as her heart warmed at Freya's words.

The young woman finally listened, sprinting into the wooded area surrounding the beach on silent feet. Quieter than the men who were approaching Neilina and her boat.

The two men were young, so she might give them the benefit of youth making them less cautious, but she scented their Chrechte nature and suspected they thought, as she did, that they had nothing to fear.

She had been right.

But if Neilina *had* meant them harm, both soldiers would have died today.

She sighed, wondering if she was obliged to tell them so.

She stood still even when they got close enough she could hear the muttered conversation between them.

They wondered at her garments, where she'd come from, if she'd been sent as a *Fearghal* spy.

"If I were a spy, you've done little to protect your secrets from me," she informed them in a tone she knew they could hear, though a human soldier wouldn't have.

Both men stopped with amusing speed and stared at her in shock.

"You know what we are?" one asked.

The other backhanded him in the stomach. "Don't say anything."

"You are Chrechte." She inhaled and smiled, delighted to be meeting one of the Éan for the first time in her life. No Éan had stayed among the Picts who settled her island.

"You are Éan." She pointed toward the sandy haired man on her left with the sharpened antlers on her walking stick. "You are Faol." Neilina tossed one side of her cape over her shoulder, making it easier to access her sword and knives. "Neither of you has shown proper caution."

"We knew it was only you."

She was not impressed. "Was it? *Only* me?"

The Éan glared at his companion. "You're sense of smell is better than mine. What do you scent?"

The Faol took a second to inhale and consider. For that, at least, she could give him a glimmer of approval.

His eyes widened. "There's another woman with you. Where is she?"

"You tell me," Neilina challenged, intolerant of demands from one so young and incautious.

"Her scent goes toward the forest."

"And that is all you smell?" Perhaps bears were plentiful on this island, so her companion would not cause comment.

"There are no men. How did you get here?"

Neilina gave them a wry look. "The boat not three feet behind me did not give you a clue?"

"You did not navigate that craft alone."

"I didn't?" Neilina asked, her annoyance growing.

Did her own Faol brother not even recognize her scent? Yes, she'd masked it, but she'd allowed a little through when they arrived and she had determined fully they would be no danger to Frey or Dìonach. Their scents gave them away as not only Chrechte, but men of decent character.

The Faol's light brows drew together. "You are a woman."

"And a woman cannot take up oars in a boat? She cannot direct the sail?" Were the Chrechte women among his pack really that dependent?

Neilina refused to believe it.

"Of course a woman can do those things," the Éan said with assurance and another frown for his friend. "Women can be strong warriors."

"Ah, so you have been taught the true way of the Chrechte, not followed the way of humans who train their women to helplessness." Neilina was glad. It would make her job easier.

"Our lady is a human woman and don't ever let her hear you say she is helpless," the Faol said with pride.

"And who is your lady?" Neilina asked, wanting very much to know if at least the first leg of her journey was over.

"She is Abigail of the Sinclair."

"And your laird, is he your alpha?"

"How do you know what we are?" the Éan demanded with suspicion.

Neilina allowed her scent to waft in the air around them, her Chrechte power to surround the two men as she'd been taught to do so long ago. "I am protector of our people, here to seek out the Sinclair, the alpha who wears the green and blue colors, and the alpha who wears the red and black."

"The alphas?" the Éan asked.

"Protector?" the Faol asked at the same time.

"Aye," she said to both.

"But you are a woman."

"We have covered this."

"The one who would have been our queen, chose to be warrior instead," the Éan said with some acerbity to his friend. "I have told you this. Your own Lady Abigail is formidable of will if not stature."

"Neilina is both," Freya warned the men as she and Dìonach approached.

Neilina noted the appreciation in the gazes of both men as they looked upon her adopted daughter even as Neilina scolded the young woman. "I told you to stay in the woods."

"You told me to go to the woods. Not to stay. I would have remembered." Freya pushed her blonde hair behind her shoulder, shifting her cloak so her weapons were easier to reach in one movement.

Though she approved the subtly defensive action she'd taught the girl, Neilina glared at her daughter. "You knew what I meant."

"I suppose next time you will spell it out." Freya did not sound too worried about the prospect.

Neilina could not take time to reply.

The two soldiers had suddenly decided to show some caution and had drawn their swords. Had they pointed them at her, she would not have cared, she could disarm them easily enough. But they were advancing on Dìonach, worry strong in the air around them.

Neilina didn't bother to tell them to put their swords down, she wasn't going to risk her companion of so many years getting an accidental injury from overzealous boys.

She used her the antlers at the top of her staff to catch the sword from the Éan's hand and wrenched it, tossing the weapon a fair distance away. Before it landed, she'd kicked the wrist of the young Faol soldier hard enough his hand released the sword as he cursed.

They both rounded on her. "Why did you do that?" the young Eagle shifter demanded.

Neilina drew herself to her full height. Tall for a woman, she was still an inch or two shorter than these young soldiers. From the looks on their faces, that did not in any way make her less intimidating. Good.

Her hand out to Dìonach in silent command to come to her, she instructed the men, "Do not ever draw your weapon on me unless you plan to use it."

"Same goes for me," Freya said, her own sword out now, her body angled so that she could not be as easily disarmed as they had been.

"We were intent on protecting you from the bear."

"Dìonach is my friend." Neilina put her hand in the thick brown fur of the bear's ruff. "Any who would harm her will feel the kiss of my blade."

"Your staff more like." The wolf shifter cradled his wrist against his chest. "That thing is wicked sharp."

"And not my primary weapon. Do not test me," she did the service of warning them.

The Éan lowered his head toward her in respect. "That was not our intention, lady."

"I am not called lady."

"By me you are," the Éan insisted. "You're as fearsome as our own princess. You're probably of the royal line, as well."

Neilina shrugged. Aye, she'd been born to a family directly descendant from their royal lines, but it mattered little now.

Of her family, all but she, were dead and gone.

"You're a princess?" Freya asked. "No wonder."

"No wonder what?" the Faol prompted her.

"My mother is very bossy."

Neilina frowned at Freya. "I am *conriocht*." She took a deep breath and corrected herself and all because her mate had claimed something she could no longer deny. "*Kelle*, and it is my right and responsibility to care for my people."

"Oh, no, not another one," the wolf shifter said with a groan.

Freya looked amused. "Another one, what?"

"She sounds just like our prince," the eagle shifter said.

"Prince of the Éan?" Neilina clarified. Could that be the dragon she'd seen in her dreams?

Both soldiers nodded. "We never thought our laird would suffer another to be leader among his people, but the Sinclair has accepted Eirik Taran Gra as an equal."

"As he should." If Eirik was dragon, all *conriocht* and pack alphas owed him allegiance. It was the way of their people.

***

Neilina learned much about the Sinclair clan and the Chrechte among them on the long walk to the keep. It took two days because of how late they'd started their journey.

The young soldiers that had found her upon arrival were called Everett and Beathan. Everett was the wolf and older than his companion, though he still behaved much as an untried, if not untrained, soldier would.

It confused Neilina until she discovered the soldiers tasked with patrolling that beach acted more as messengers between the Balmoral pack and the Chrechte among the Sinclair, than guardians. Still, the packs would have to take the security of their borders more seriously if their current peril was to be overcome without a great loss of life.

Neilina's arrival with her companions had caused a stir among Chrechte and human alike. Many looked askance at her bear as Dìonach walked beside her, the scent of fear growing with the size of the crowd as they approached the gate to the inner bailey.

It made Neilina's spine tingle with the need to shift to protect. Even knowing they feared, not an enemy, but her bear. And perhaps even her.

Men and women, Chrechte and human alike, watched her and Freya in goggle-eyed wonder. Had they never seen female warriors before?

Not one woman wore any clothing but the plaids that were so long most had pleats that brushed the tops of the women's feet. Not a practical garment for fighting in. Not all of the clan wore the Sinclair colors though. Some wore plaids made up of the colors of the forest.

Neilina wondered if these were the Éan. Even though Beathan wore the traditional plaid of the Sinclair clan, that did not mean all his people had taken on the colors of their adopted clan.

Laird Sinclair, an imposing presence, stood beside his lady wife just this side of the drawbridge that led to the inner bailey. He looked just as he had in her visions, his dark hair long with warrior braids at his temples, blue eyes assessing her, he stood a good six inches taller than her own five-feet-ten. Power radiated off him like the heat from a rumbling mountain. There could be no doubt this man was *conriocht*.

Another woman, young enough to be daughter, whose spirit was a near physical presence around her, stood on his other side. The *celi di*. She stood between the laird and a Chechte that could be no other than the *dràgon* Neilina's visions had sent her in search of.

He might mask his scent, but the blood red sheen to his black hair and glow in his amber eyes revealed his nature for what it was.

This was *dràgonrì*, king of their people, no matter what the humans claimed in their petty wars for territory.

Neilina dropped to one knee, putting her fist over her heart. "I pledge my allegiance and my strength to the protection of our people. I give you my loyalty and very being."

"You're pledging to the wrong man," someone said. "That is not our laird."

"Women do not pledge such an oath of fealty," a masculine voice, craggy with age, opined.

Neilina ignored their mutterings. The humans, and maybe even the Chrechte, would not know that this was the dragon. He could be the one and only king over all the Chrechte races and he would reign until he died. That would not be for many centuries to come because it was near impossible to kill one of his kind. The aura of power around him was too great to be anything other than that which provided the ultimate guardian to their people.

After a long moment of silence, even the children among them did not break, the dragon reached out his hand and touched her forehead. "I am Eirik Taran Gra and I accept your pledge."

The magic of their stones shadowed his voice, going through Neilina's body and leaving her near breathless.

"Maybe she's Éan," she heard someone whisper, too low to be picked up by any but the most sensitive ears. "Some have not yet realized they owe their allegiance to our laird, though they've been among our clan for more than three years."

The wolf shifter did not sound happy, a feminine grumble of assent sounding no more pleased.

Neilina surged to her feet so fast she knew to the humans among them it would seem a blur. She spun to face the offender and her gaze settled on a Chrechte dressed in the garments of blacksmith, his leather apron still covering his plaid.

She stalked over to him, speaking with vehemence but low enough only he or another Chrechte very close by would hear. "Do you think only the Éan pledge their loyalty to the king?" she demanded, her hand on the hilt of her short sword.

That aged voice sounded again. "He's no king." No effort was made to speak low or hide the discussion from the humans among them.

Neilina's gaze went quickly to the laird, who did not look happy at the turn of conversation. But she could not tell if that was because they spoke of matters they should not before the whole clan, or her pledge of loyalty to the dragon had angered him.

"He's a prince, I heard Niall say so." A young voice continued the conversation and the laird winced.

Neilina stared at the mix of Chrechte and humans around her, then back at the dragon and the man who claimed to be his laird. Laird over a king? How could that be possible?

Had the Chrechte lost their way so badly, they did not even know that a dragon was only ever called forth by the stone when all needed to be unified under one leader?

She walked back to the laird. Though her instincts had told her he was also *conriocht,* Neilina did not fear him. She'd pledged her loyalty to the dragon. He had accepted that pledge with more than words, but with the power of his own Chrechte magic. He was now bound by Chrechte law to protect her.

Did he know that?

Not that it mattered. She did not *need* protection. Not even from another of her kind.

She stopped before the laird and bowed her head infinitesimally. "I have much to say, but I believe a private audience would be better."

The Sinclair nodded, sending a glare to some in the crowd. The ones who had spoken out of turn in front of their human clanspeople?

They began walking toward the large building, grander than any the marauders had built on her home island.

"Your pet is not going into my keep," the Lady Abigail informed Neilina, no give in her tone.

Nevertheless, Neilina turned to the woman and gave her a *very* rare smile. "I would consider it a personal boon, if you would allow Dìonach to accompany us. She is part of my family and these people are restless and nervous of her."

Bethean said, "A bear cannot be part of the family."

"Your horse is part of yours," someone else claimed. Laughter sounded around them.

The Lady Abigail did not look convinced, however. "My children are in the keep. Until I am convinced of the bear's tame nature, she stays outside."

"She is by no means tame, but will never hurt your children. Dìonach has only ever harmed those that would do me, or Freya, harm."

"She protects you?" Laird Sinclair asked.

Freya answered before Neilina could. "Aye. My mother raised Dìonach from a cub. She recognizes us as her family. If you give her the chance, Dìonach will protect your children as well."

"I protect my children," the Sinclair said with typical male arrogance.

Neilina approved. She, too, was confident in her ability to protect those she cared for. As she now was determined to do for Dìonach. "Aye, as is your right, but surely your soldiers share the responsibility. Because they are part of the clan, your family."

Rumbles of assent sounded around them.

"That is different, your bear is not one of my soldiers."

"No, and Dìonach will take no orders but mine," Neilina acknowledged.

"Not even his?" Freya asked pointing at Eirik Taran Gra, curiosity burning in her brown eyes.

"Nay," Neilina assured her daughter. "Dìonach is bound to me, no other."

"The bear is bound to you?" the woman Neilina believed to be a powerful *celi di* asked.

"Aye, since I saved her life as a cub. I raised Dìonach in my home." Neilina had also bound her with the stone, but was not going to say so until she knew such revelations were being made in safe company.

"What kind of home was sufficient for a bear? Did you live in a cave?"

"Aye." Freya answered that question, her expression daring the crowd that followed them to keep asking more, or denigrate the nature of their former home. Neilina's daughter had clearly hit her limit of tolerance for idle curiosity.

Nevertheless, she reacted with gentle patience when a small girl came up and asked with wide eyes, "Did you really live in a cave? My lady will gives you a good bed. She takes care of all of us."

The lady in question looked quite taken by the child's statement.

Freya smiled down at the little one, her scar puckering her otherwise flawless features, the expression as rare on her face as it was Neilina's. "Our home was cozy and warm, but Dìonach had her own cavern where she could rest not bothered by the heat of our fire."

The girl looked up at her mother. "I wants to live in a cave. I wants a bear to be *my* friend."

The woman, an Éan by scent, shook her head. "We left our forest home behind when you were but a babe. We've settled in here." Though something in the Éan woman's eyes said maybe they weren't as settled in as she claimed. "Your baby brother has known no home but this one. Now you would have us return to the forest?"

"I don't want to live in the trees," her daughter denied. "I wants to live in a cave."

Why had the Éan lived in trees in the forest to begin with, why were they only recently joined to the clans? And was it safe to discuss such matters in front of the humans of the clan?

"If you will not allow my bear into your keep, we can finish our talk outside," Neilina offered. "But I believe the laird should choose carefully who I tell my story to."

Even the Chrechte could not all be trusted. According to her dreams, the Fearghall had access to the clans and that access was unlikely to come through humans.

Not with the Fearghall believing any but the Faol were inferior to them.

***

Haakon climbed out of the small boat that had brought him and his weapons to the shore of Balmoral Island. The merchant ship, large enough to transport cattle and goods could not land on the beach with no dock. His horse had made the journey with him and swam to shore beside the small rowboat carrying him.

The Norse sailors left Haakon on the beach, his bundles of belongings at his feet. Haakon sniffed out water and led his horse to a natural stream where he washed off all residue of saltwater from the animal's coat before drying the black warhorse with a cloth Haakon had brought with him.

Afterward, he led the animal back to the beach, where they settled in to wait, as Artair had suggest he do, for the guards that patrol the beach to find them.

According to Artair and his clansman Gart, no longer mate, only one clan lived on the island. The Balmoral, led by the alpha of the pack who live among them, Lachlan. Artair had suggested, and the Seer had demanded, that Haakon speak to Lachlan, to warn him of the coming peril before traveling to the Sinclair clan to make his promise of fealty to the Chrechte king.

The dragon shifter who was the Éan prince and mated to the daughter of the pack alpha.

Artair had said the dragon did not consider himself a king and Haakon wondered at this. Even he, who had been raised to only know his own people, knew that a dragon among their kind was meant to be king.

Outside of politics or country boundary lines.

No Chrechte in the world should go against the dragon, especially not the guardians of their people.

Only the dragon could send Haakon back to his own people, but first he would accept Haakon's oath.

Osmend didn't believe the *asmundr* would return to Groenland.

Haakon did not know what outcome he hoped for. He was staring down centuries of life without his mate. He was not sure it mattered where he lived and served his people. His homeland gave him no comfort. His people did not need him. Not like in the days of old and not with Einar there to see to their safety.

But these Faol? They faced a terrible threat. First and most imminent, from those they called Fearghall. Later a devastating plague was coming and only if the Chrechte races were once again united would any survive. Osmend had said that the plague would not come until generations after all those Haakon now knew as family had passed over to the Spirit realm.

The Seer had revealed that he had known of the plague to come for more than a century, but only now was the time right to reunite the peoples of the *uffe*, the *kotrondmenskr* and the Éan.

They must all learn to live together again, share their knowledge of the powers of their Chrechte nature and the ceremonial stones if they hoped to survive the coming devastation. The thought was a chilling one. What disease could be so virulent that even their Chrechte nature could not protect them from it?

"*Tha thu ann.*" A Chrechte soldier wearing the colors of the Balmoral and well past his first blush of youth hailed Haakon as he approached. "Who are you and where have you come from?"

Haakon's senses told him there were three more soldiers, not far off, but out of sight. All Chrechte, but not all Faol.

Smart.

Haakon inclined his head to the soldier, giving him a measure of respect. "I am Haakon of the *kotrondmenskr*. You call my people Paindeal. I have come to broker peace between our peoples and to pledge my vow of allegiance to Eirik of the Éan."

"Peace? Our peoples are not at war. Why does a Paindeal want to pledge allegiance to the Éan?"

Haakon ignored the question about his pledge, guessing it would not be the last time it was asked. "We have been at war for the past six centuries, but your packs have forgotten our past."

"Do the Paindeal mean us harm then?" the soldier asked, his body tense with preparation to fight.

He could not stand against *asmundr*, but Haakon respected his wiliness to try. The wolf did not know *what* kind of shifter Haakon was and yet, he was prepared to defend his clan and his pack.

"We mean you no harm. I have come to reunite the clans."

"If that is true, where is Maon?" the man asked suspiciously. "And the others that were with him?"

"Osmend, our Seer sent Maon to continue on his quest, searching for the rest of my people in the Land of the Sun."

"And the others?"

"Maon took all but two with him, those two replaced by *kotrondmenskr*."

"And the other two? Where are they?" the soldier demanded.

Haakon did his best to remain patient, reminding himself that this Chrechte knew nothing of him. "Artair and Fionnlaigh agreed to join my pride. They begin the process of the unification of our peoples."

"What about Gart? He didn't stay with Artair?" Did the older soldier know the two had been mates? His expression said maybe he did.

"Gart follows a different path, one with a wife and children in his future."

The soldier shook his head. "That can't be right."

"Artair found his true mate in my cousin, Einar, who will one day be *jarl* of our people and pride alpha."

The Chrechte looked unimpressed by Einar's position. As it should be. "But, he already had a mate."

"When the mating is not accepted, a Chrechte *may* find another true mate." Then again, he might not. Haakon knew deep in his gut that *he* would have no other mate but Neilina.

No matter if they *never* saw each other in this life.

"You need to talk to our laird. He'll be able to tell if you lie."

"You cannot?" Haakon asked in surprise. He'd done nothing to disguise his scent.

The other Chrechte should have been able to smell any intent to deceive on him.

"I don't know what the Paindeal can hide, now do I?"

"You are wary," Haakon said with approval. "That is smart."

The older soldier gave a jerk of his head in acknowledgment. "Come, we will go to the keep."

"And the others, will they join us, or follow behind?"

"They'll follow behind, prepared to end your life should you threaten mine."

Haakon was not offended by the threat, more impressed by it. He was going to like this soldier. "What are you called?"

"I am Lyall, and I may as well tell you, I'm not believing this nonsense about a Chrechte having more than one mate. It has never been such."

Haakon did not blame the man for his skepticism. "I had never heard of such a thing either." He'd recently realized there was *much* his father and Osmend had not seen fit to reveal to Haakon. How was he supposed to stand guardian to his people when he'd been left in the dark about so much?

Some of his rancor at that thought bled into voice when he added, "Until our Seer met your Artair and the man who had refused their claiming these many years past, I had never been told that a Chrechte might have another mate should the mating not take for some reason."

Like an *asmundr's* intended hating his father so much she would never trust him enough to bind their souls.

"But they have been the closest of friends. Gart always had Artair's back."

"*Ja*. That may be, but he refused to bind their souls."

Lyall sighed. "The boy wanted children."

Haakon was not sympathetic. "My cousin and Artair have adopted two children left parentless this last winter."

"Your pride did not see to their welfare?" Lyall asked, sounding shocked at the idea.

As well he should be. If it were true.

"Naturally, but Einar said the children would be known as *his*, a gift from Providence he would cherish for their lifetime. They will be raised as grandchildren of the *jarl*."

"He sounds sentimental, does your cousin."

Haakon had to laugh at that description of his usually stoic, very much a warrior cousin. Einar had expressed the same belief Haakon had been raised with many a time. Tender emotions were for women and old men. Not warriors.

"Smart enough to insure he has heirs when his mate was destined to be a man. Besides, to acknowledge a gift from above is not sentimental, it prevents later reprisal for dismissing those gifts as nothing." Vikings understood this and even the Roman church taught such.

"You believe if he did not show his thanks, they would be taken from him?" Lyall asked musingly.

"Don't you?" Did these Scotsman believe they did not have to give thanks for their blessings?

Did their priests speak a different message than the ones sent to Groenland? Regardless, the *kotrondmenskr* might have accepted the Church and its teachings, but they hadn't forgotten everything of the old ways. To give thanks was ingrained in the Chrechte from the time of birth.

Though they no longer offered the animal sacrifices of old, at anything other than their most sacred of ceremonies and in absolute secrecy.

"I dinna ken. Our priest teaches we should give thanks for all good things, I suppose."

"And the bad?"

"England's Church teaches bad happens when we disobey."

"And *your* priest?"

"He says bad comes to every man's life. 'Tis no the result of sin, but can be because of it."

Haakon nodded his agreement with the idea. "He's a wise one, this priest."

"He has many years and chose to live his remaining ones among our clan. He is wise indeed."

Haakon nearly smiled at the arrogance of the soldier's claim. Perhaps living amongst these people would not be so different than among his own pride.

He had leave to doubt that assumption later, after explaining his arrival and where the other Balmorals were to their laird.

Lachlan looked at Haakon with distrust and no small amount of anger. "We have only your word for any of this," he growled. "I dinna believe Artair would stay in that place without Gart."

"He went on that quest with Ciara and Eirik without him," the laird's second, a man called Drustan, pointed out.

"But he came back." Lachlan scowled at Haakon as if it was the *asmundr's* fault that this time Artair had not returned to his clan.

"He volunteered to go with Maon before he knew Gart would as well," a woman, he thought it was the second's mate pointed out.

Drustan nodded at her and touched her shoulder, confirming their bond. No other but mate or family would touch her in front of others. And while she shared the man's scent, she did not have the scent that spoke of a familial connection.

The woman sighed, looking unhappy. "I think he realized that no matter how strong the mate pull is, Gart's desire for children was stronger."

"I think Gart is attracted to both men and women," the laird's mate, a woman Lachlan had introduced as Emily, pointed out. "He didn't want to love Artair *that way* if it meant giving up the possibility of being a father."

So, Haakon explained again about Artair being one already.

The two women got misty-eyed. "That's so wonderful," Lady Balmoral said. "Artair deserves to be happy."

"He deserves to be with his mate, not kept as a sacrifice for our two races to find common ground." The Balmoral looked ready to do battle.

"He is no sacrifice. He and Einar *are* mates and my cousin will kill any who try to take his mate from him," Haakon warned.

"He's not keeping my pack member without my say so," the Balmoral declared. "I dinna accept such an insult without reprisal." Lachlan gave a significant look to both his mate and that of his second that Haakon did not understand.

"You're going to travel to Groenland?" Haakon asked with only a tinge of mockery.

The look he got back was anything but amused. "I'll take an invading force, if necessary. Artair is under my protection."

"He is under Einar's protection now," Haakon reminded the angry pack alpha. "Ask your Seer. Perhaps he has had a vision." Haakon could only hope. He was supposed to be brokering peace between their peoples, not restarting the war the *uffe* had forgotten. "You have a very real enemy among your own people, you would do better to spend your time preparing to battle."

"What do you mean?" the Balmoral asked with even deeper suspicion.

"You call them the Fearghall."

"What do you call them?" Lyall asked.

Haakon did not hesitate. "Anathema."

Thawing just barely in his demeanor, the Balmoral nodded. "That is a better name for them, though they follow the ways of the first among them."

"They kill true mates to prevent a human-Chrechte mating." Lyall shuddered, his warrior's countenance showing just how abhorrent he found such an action.

Haakon agreed. "They would destroy your entire clan rather than allow you to give sanctuary to the Éan." Osmend had impressed that truth upon Haakon, though he'd seen as much in his own visions.

Visions it had taken him many weeks to understand and realize he must act on.

"They can try." Lachlan did not sound worried in the least.

While Haakon admired the alpha's confidence, it was misplaced. "They will not fight you face to face, a battle you would most certainly win. Their ways are sneaky and underhanded and they do not care how many die to achieve their goals."

"What does that mean?" the Lady Emily asked, fear scenting the air around her, worry strong in her violet gaze.

"I have my suspicions, but I do not know. With certainty, I know only our Seer said you faced a more terrible threat than the plague to come. That you and any you call ally are at risk of being destroyed completely if the Fearghall are not routed out and destroyed."

"We do not kill other Chrechte for no reason," Lachlan said, his voice firm. "We have turned the minds of more than one Fearghall."

"*Ja*, Maon said he used to be one of them, but more will have to die than can be allowed to live." That much Haakon knew.

"Says you."

"*Ja*. And our Seer confirmed my own visions."

"And I am to take the word of a stranger, or this Seer I have never met?" Lachlan demanded.

Haakon liked the man's abrupt nature and protective attitude toward those under him, but he was rapidly losing patience. He'd spent his entire adult life as *asmundr*, trusted implicitly by all the Chrechte and humans for that matter who knew him. "I have already said, speak to *your* Seer."

"Don't you think if he'd seen something like that he would have already told me?"

"Not if he's anything like Osmend."

"This Osmend sounds like he holds information to his chest."

"*Ja*. He does that." Too much. There was still so much Haakon did not know.

"Our Seer would not do that," Lachlan said with just the type of arrogance that was bound to get pricked like a puffed-up pig's bladder.

Haakon had his own arrogance so he could find it within himself to feel a measure of sympathy for the shock the man had in store, for he was sure he did have a surprise coming. No Seer told all they saw. Osmend had said so too often for that to be anything but ancient Chrechte wisdom.

A commotion sounded near the door, the sound of shuffling steps came into the hall soon followed by the visage of an old man. While it was unlikely, he looked a great deal older than even Osmend.

He had the look of Artair around his eyes and walked in on weak legs, leaning heavily on his walking stick. "You have come."

Haakon bowed toward him. "Seer."

"My dreams said you would come and you did. But that means the other dreams...they are true." Terror shown in the old man's eyes. "I believed they were the rumblings of an old mind before death."

"Death is sure to come if we do not take action."

"Are you saying you saw the demise of our clan and you said nothing?" Lachlan asked, his voice more growl than human.

"It was too terrible." The Seer did look like he'd seen the horrors of the damned. "I couldna believe it was true. How could we all die like that, in terrible agony, everyone affected, so many dead, the corpses left to rot in the great hall?"

The Balmoral blanched. "This cannot be true."

"Oh, aye, it's true enough. If the guardian is here and he is what my dreams say he is, then the rest must be true too."

CHAPTER EIGHT

"What do you mean?" Drustan asked, eyeing Haakon askance. "What *is* he?"

No patience for being talked around, Haakon answered. "I am *asmundr*."

"What is that then? A new kind of Chrechte?" another of the few soldiers allowed into the hall asked.

"Guardian. First to the *kotrondmenskr*, but last to all Chrechte."

"You are a griffin?" Lady Emily asked, her violet eyes round.

Haakon did not roll his eyes, but it was close. Did none among them know the ancient ways? "Griffins cannot be called forth by the stones unless they have the mixed heritage of the Éan and the *kotrondmenskr*."

"That's what they call the Paindeal," Haakon heard someone whisper to the man next to him.

"Then what is *asmundr*?" the Balmoral demanded.

"He'll have to show you, or you willna believe," the Seer said, then sighed. "I willna believe either, until I see for myself. 'Tis the truth, I hope you shift into a mountain lion, or some such. I dinna want these dreams to be visions."

Haakon frowned and reminded the old man, "A Seer has no choice about what he sees, though according to Osmend he gets to choose what he shares."

The Balmoral did not look happy to hear that, turning a sulfuric glare on the old Seer before him. "Tell me, Ranulf, is that what you believe? What else have you held back from me, your alpha *and* your laird?"

"No alpha, no not even a laird, may dictate to a Seer," Haakon reminded them of this sacred truth.

"That may be the way it is done among the Paindeal, but—"

"No Chrechte will put themselves above the Seer, not even the king." Haakon was done trying to be tactful.

"We have no king."

"*Ja*, you have one, but you've ignored his place in favor of modern human rules and norms. You have forgotten the ways of our people." Haakon let what he thought of that show in his voice and the glare he gave the offending speaker.

The *asmundr* thought the Balmoral might lose his temper at the accusation, but he calmed down instead.

Sighing, Lachlan looked around, letting his gaze fall on a Chrechte Haakon could scent was not Faol. Not *kotrondmenskr* either. Éan then.

"Aye, we have forgotten much over the centuries and welcome the wisdom of others who have kept better record of our people's ways."

"Our guardians live centuries. Their memories serve as our history. Our Seer has lived longer than even a guardian."

"But I've lived no more than ninety years," the Balmoral Seer said. "My life draws to a close."

"Perhaps Osmend would know why this is." And if there was a way to change it. "Until he revealed his true age, I did not know that the Seer and the guardian had the same long life span."

"You are a guardian. An *asmundr* you said?" the Balmoral asked.

"*Ja.*"

"You will shift for us? That we may know this part of history we have forgotten?"

"*Ja.*" Haakon looked for Lyall. "You will guard my weapons."

The soldier's eyes widened and then he puffed up with pride. "Aye. With me life."

That would not be necessary, as none would be foolish enough to challenge his beast, but it did not sit well to strip his weapons and not charge someone with their care.

Haakon began to strip, smiling slightly when he saw the laird and his second covering their wives' eyes rather than send them from the room.

Perhaps the Chrechte here understood the power of women as his own pride, if not the humans of the *jarl's* landholdings.

Haakon removed his vest of furs, the cloak he usually wore over them already with his bundle of belongings. He had to untie the laces that went up his calves around his leather boots. His shirt, smalls and leather breaches were quicker to remove and then he stood proud and naked for only a second before allowing the shift to come over him.

The gasps that filled the hall did not surprise him. These *uffe* would never have seen one of his kind.

"Aye, it is all true," the Seer lamented, collapsing onto a stool.

"He's amazing," Lady Emily said, awe filling her tone.

"He's almost as tall as me and he's standing on all fours," the second's mate said.

The sound of a *conriocht* growling *did* surprise him. So, the laird was guardian, but unfamiliar with their ancient laws and ways? Interesting. Had he not been trained by the *conriocht* that came before him? Or had Haakon's own father killed all the *conriocht* as the Seer had claimed? It was a terribly sobering thought.

I am no threat to you, Haakon sent to the *conriocht* with his mind, practicing a gift he'd only ever experienced with his father before. Bjorn being the only other guardian he'd known.

"You can speak into my mind?" the *conriocht* asked, his words slurred by the changes in his facial structure.

You can as well. All guardians can with each other.

Shift back, the man demanded in Haakon's mind.

Haakon let out a mighty roar, telling the laird he was no lacky to be ordered. Only after those around had taken a step back, showing their respect for his beast did he allow the shift to overcome him.

He gave a real smile when he noted that one of the soldiers had fainted and they all eyed him with wariness.

He was *asmundr*. They would do best not to forget that.

Nevertheless, they needed *another* reminder about his nature. "I am guardian to *all* Chrechte. So long as none of you are offenders of our ancient law, or intent on harming others without just cause, you will never know my beast's wrath."

"What kind of beast are you?"

"It is the ancient tiger from before the time we left the caves."

"Your pride knows such history?"

"Some." Haakon had come to realize how many holes there were in their understanding of what had come before.

"You say you are called to protect *all* Chrechte?"

"Every guardian is. *Conriocht, asmundr,* griffin, and the dragon."

The laird tensed upon the mention of the dragon. So, he was aware of their king, but not that he was king.

"When a dragon is called forth by the stone, it means our people all need to be united under one leader."

"We have lived separated for centuries."

"And if we wish to continue to live, we must unite."

"This peril we face, it is that serious?"

"Has not your Seer said so?"

"He spoke of our entire clan dying in agony."

Haakon nodded, thinking what could cause such a thing. "Poison."

Lachlan nodded grimly. "We need to call a council of the Chrechte."

"You cannot have a true council without a member of the Paindeal there."

"You?" the Balmoral asked.

"I am guardian, not pride alpha. As *jarl* and pride alpha, my uncle would be the natural council member. Though we have our own *kotrondmenskr* council. Our Seer is the council elder."

"Neither could get here in time to deal with the present threat," the Seer opined, his face still white with shock, sweat beaded on his forehead attesting to his worry. "You were sent here for a reason."

"As *asmundr* I have never sat on the council."

"Were you welcome at their meetings?"

"My father was, but he was also *jarl*."

"He passed the position to someone else?" Lachlan asked.

"It is not good for guardian to be alpha as well. A guardian can be called on to protect away from the pack or pride and who leads then?"

Lachlan frowned. "That has not come up for the Faol."

"In your memory."

"We just discovered that *conriocht* are not myth in the past few years."

"None of the guardians are myths, though we are fantastical creatures that stories have been told about since the beginning of our people."

"You will have to represent the Paindeal," the Seer said.

His laird glared at the man. "That is a decision for the council to make."

"Nay. You cannot deny the will of providence."

"My destiny is to protect, not to play politics."

"According to you, if we had a dragon shifter, your allegiance would be to him?"

"*Ja.* This is true." Haakon wasn't entirely comfortable with that thought.

He'd submitted to his own father as a son should, but no one since. Even his uncle understood that it was not his place to order Haakon to a task, but to make the need for his power known.

"He is on the council."

"As he should be."

"Things are not as they once were with the Chrechte."

Haakon shrugged. Peoples were bound to change over time, but the laird in front of him would have to learn to live with the way of things just as Haakon would.

Neither of them had a choice. The good of the Chrecht depended on it.

***

Haakon spent the next days waiting for the other members of the Chrechte council to arrive and getting to know the *uffe* and Ean of the Balmoral as well as the human clan.

Every evening he spent the hours after dinner with the laird and other members of his inner circle answering questions about the *kotrondmenskr*, their history as his people understood it, and explaining about his father's role in their shared history.

"So, a guardian *can* turn on the people the stone called his beast forth to guard?" Drustan, the Balmoral's second, asked.

"Just as a council might contravene the very tenets of our mating bond to allow one Chrechte to steal another's mate," his wife said with some acerbity before Haakon could reply himself. "His father's actions were unconscionable, but so were those of the council that caused his terrible grief. How would *you* respond if the council gave me to another?"

"But if she did not want to be his mate," Lady Emily said.

"She'd lain with him, she'd married him in the ways of her people or she would not have had a child with him."

Haakon nodded. "It was before the ways of the Roman Church set laws down that required a lifetime commitment for marriage, but she had made vows to my father. And it was not just his mate he lost, it was his son."

The Balmoral looked sick at the thought. "I would never allow anyone to take my child."

"My father submitted to the will of the council, but his grief and anger were terrible."

"He could have annihilated them all right then," Drustan mused.

Haakon nodded. "Their *conriocht* would have had to be powerful and many to defeat my father."

"There was no dragon for the Éan?" Lady Emily asked with curiosity. "No griffin?"

Haakon shrugged. In truth, he did not know. "If there were, they did not accompany your people to Scotland."

"A dragon might have prevented what came later," the Balmoral mused.

Drustan's gaze said he agreed with his laird. "So, if no dragon lived, how did your father know they were real?" he asked Haakon.

"I do not know." Haakon had no trouble admitting the truth, no matter how much it irritated him personally. "There is much my father and the Seer have not told me."

The Balmoral frowned. "You speak like you still have communion with your father."

"I have spoken with him in the Chrechte spirit world." And what a shock that had been.

"You can travel there?" the Balmoral asked, his brown gaze narrowed in thought.

"*Ja.*"

"Are all *asmundr* Seers, then?"

"*Nei*. Until recently, it never occurred to me why I traveled to that place of *other* so often." He'd thought his mating bond pulled him to it, and indeed it did.

But it couldn't have, if neither he, nor Neilina were *more* than guardians. The fact they could both go, and call the other to them, was how he knew she was *kelle*, not merely *conriocht*.

"You have no scent of deceit about you, but we cannot know what the Paindeal might mask."

The Balmoral's caution was understandable, but they were past the time when Haakon could indulge it.

"Lyall said as much to me the first day. I can only speak truth and you must decide whether or not to believe."

"Ranulf had visions of him. Surely, we can trust our own Seer," Caitriona pointed out to her husband, Drustan, and to the laird.

Emily nodded decisively. "I agree. This wariness is not going to help you save our people."

Haakon frowned, unable to agree completely, despite how time was against them. "I have to disagree. If there had been more wariness between Chrechte, the Fearghall would not have infiltrated your pack as they have done."

"We have only your word for that."

"And I only have a supposition, but I know the dreams I have had. I know that the threat comes from within, not without."

"We have routed out the Fearghall among us." But the Balmoral did not sound as certain as he had in other matters. How could he? He knew now of his Seer's visions, of the terrible calamity to come if it was not stopped.

"We thought none lived here at all," Emily said impatiently, "and that is clearly not the case."

"You would then have me trust this man if I cannot scent out deception among our own people?"

His lady winced, as did Druston, but Caitriona simply looked thoughtful. "There must be a reason you haven't scented deception among our people. Perhaps this insider is not one of us but connected to the clan in some way. They will gain access to us through that connection, but it's not someone you would normally test for affiliation with the Fearghall."

Haakon had to admire the woman's theory. It made sense and he said so.

The laird sighed. "As much as I would like to believe that, we cannot rely on that being the case."

"*Nei.* You cannot." The man's entire clan's lives depended on him and those he most relied on being cautious.

"You will find the betrayer," the Seer said. The old man had not left the keep since his arrival, but he spent most evenings silent, staring into the fire as the others talked.

"Is that what your visions tell you?" Lachlan asked, sounding disbelieving. "You're the one that told me Haakon's ability to shift into that beast that no longer walks the earth meant we were all going to die a terrible death."

"Our visions can be given to us to help prevent a terrible tragedy to come," Ranulf reproved his laird.

"And this one?" Emily asked with a glare for her husband.

"I have had a waking vision."

Haakon jolted in shock. Waking visions were so uncommon as to be nonexistent. Osmend had told Haakon of them but had never had one in Haakon's lifetime. To his knowledge anyway.

Seers did not tell all, no matter what this laird expected.

"What did you see?" the laird demanded.

"I canna tell you yet."

That did not go over well with any of the Balmorals. Shouting, threats and anger ensued, but the old man stood his ground.

When one of the soldiers got up to stand threateningly over Ranulf, Haakon moved with the speed of his beast.

He threw the offending Chrechte across the room to land with a loud thump against the far wall of the great hall. "You will respect the Seer and his decrees," Haakon roared, his words heavily tinged with his tiger's growls.

Lachlan, who had been on his way to them nodded firmly, scowling at everyone present. "We, none of us, get to choose our nature, only how we make our journey. Ranulf is our Seer. I do not like his refusal to say more either, but we are Chrechte. We respect the elders, we respect the visions."

"And if he lies?" another soldier demanded.

"Are you accusing our Seer of deceit?" Lyall asked, his wolf flashing in his eyes.

"He himself said the betrayal will come from within," the soldier who doubted said truculently.

Lyall's glare was sulfuric. "So, he warns us only to betray us? Use your head, ye daft boy!"

"Enough!" Lachlan thundered before the other man could reply. "We will not fight amongst ourselves."

"Are you going to let the Paindeal get away with attacking one of our own," the same soldier who had accused the Seer of lying asked with a sneer.

Lachlan stalked forward, more beast than man, though he had not shifted. "You question my leadership? You wish to challenge me for my position?"

Paling, the younger soldier swallowed. "Nay, laird."

Laird, not alpha?

Haakon shifted subtly, moving toward the mouthy soldier without appearing to be doing so.

"I am your alpha!" the Balmoral barked. "Kneel before me and give me your pledge."

"Sir, you doubt my loyalty?" the man did a credible job of acting offended and shocked, looking toward Drustan as if expecting him to say something.

The second-in-command merely stared back, his expression stony. He did not repeat the alpha's order, but there could be no question he expected the other man to follow it.

The soldier looked around him as if expecting someone else to defend him, but all the other Chrechte were now staring at him with suspicion.

Haakon had it in himself to pity the young *uffe*, to be doubted by one's own people would be demoralizing. If he was innocent. Very dangerous if he was not.

Lachlan did not move, his expectation in no doubt. The boy would pledge his loyalty or pay the price. It was the Chrechte way.

Glaring around like he felt betrayed, the *uffe* dropped to one knee and pounded his chest with his fist. "I pledge my life and my strength to protecting my clan."

The look that came over Lachlan's face was more than rage, it was hurt. He moved forward, his expression going stoic. "You did not pledge with your hand over your heart and you were too damn careful not to make your vow to *me* or *this* clan.

Rage washed over the younger *uffe's* features. He surged up, metal glinting in the candlelight as he threw himself toward the alpha.

Haakon was in a position to interfere, but he didn't. Lachlan Balmoral moved with the speed of the *conriocht*, fur sprouting on his hands as they shifted into claws. He easily disarmed the disloyal soldier, shaking him with one giant clawed hand around his neck. "You dare to pull a knife on me? You cur!"

"You're just the half-breed son of a misguided Chrechte and his human mate." Had he not already done so, those words would have revealed this soldier's sympathies lay with the Fearghall.

"I am alpha," Lachlan growled. "I am *conriocht* and well you know it."

Hatred and disgust mixed with fear in the boy's eyes. "The stone didn't call you into such a beast form. That is from the lower regions of hell, that is. You are demon not protector."

"Chrechte came before the teachings of Rome, or don't you remember that." Lachlan asked with his own disgust.

"That doesn't change what you are."

"Who taught you such filth?" Emily demanded, unquestionably furious at the man who had dared to threaten her mate. "You are Drustan's cousin, you were raised here in the clan."

"Not always, he wasn't." Drustan sounded as heartbroken as any warrior could. "They got to him when he was but a boy, living with his father's people. When his mother brought him back to live on the island after his death, it was already too late."

"Aren't you going to try to change my loyalties?" the youth demanded. "Like you think you did with the others."

The expression on the laird's face said the boy's sally had not reached its intended target. The Balmoral had no doubts. "I can speak only for Maon, but there is no question he follows the path of the true Chrechte now."

"As he should. He made his vow." Drustan gave his cousin a sulfuric glare. "As did you."

"I never spoke words of loyalty to the pretender half-breed alpha."

A look of near demonic glee came over the Balmoral's features. "And that is how these disloyal curs infiltrated our clans. We will demand new tribute and any that do not vow specific loyalty to the alphas, not just *their* clans will be tested."

Haakon respected that despite the severity of the situation, Lachlan was not proposing they label anyone disloyal without first testing.

"If they make their promise before the *dreki kongr* in his shifted form, they cannot lie. It is the way of our natures. Even if they do not acknowledge loyalty to him, no Chrechte can speak deception directly to our king."

"Are you sure of this?" Drustan demanded, relief and hope clear in his countenance.

"You and your laird can test with your senses and the way every Chrechte conducts himself. By no means, should we leave it all on the dragon leader to know the honesty of his people. We have all been called to our guardianship for a purpose."

"Demons more like," the Fearghall infiltrator spat.

Haakon shook his head. "I have it in me to pity you, boy. You were deceived young and you have clung to those deceptions despite the evidence of your eyes now."

"You think they've proven themselves worthy leaders? They not only allow, but participate in half-breed matings. Soon, no Chrechte will survive but the Fearghall."

"If that is true, then there is no need to destroy those who live now, is there?" Drustan asked with undisguised repugnance.

"We shall not survive the abomination to live."

"Then I guess you need to die," Lachlan said with a shake of his head. Grief aging his countenance for a moment.

"Of course you will kill me," the young soldier spat. "It's what your kind do."

"Nay, boy, that is not what I meant. But by the rules of those you follow, you should die.

you carry the blood of humans in your veins. Your great grandfather on your mother's side was a nonshifting Chrechte born of a human and a Faol."

Drustan's cousin jerked back in revilement. "Nay, that is not true," he denied with all the vehemence of youth and obsession.

"It's true enough," Drustan said, his tone weary and sad, but not disbelief.

These Chrechte had already had too much experience with the subterfuges and hatred of the Fearghall to be surprised by them.

The dragon arrived the next day, along with all the members of the council. They weren't all alphas, though the alphas of four clans were present. An elder, *celi di*, or Seer was also present from each pack.

But it wasn't any of those *uffe* or Éan that caught Haakon's attention as he stood on the beach watching the latest boat of people step onto the rocky shore. It was the bear that came lumbering onto the pebbles beforehand, now shaking its fur clear of water, and turning to watch as the boat approached the beach.

Haakon thought the heart in his chest would seize as he spied the dark hair with warrior's braids on the woman standing with her eye on the horizon. He could not see her face, but he knew every inch of her.

Neilina wore her usual leather clothing more suited to a man, though it was as appealing as anything he'd ever seen on another woman. Her large fur cloak was missing, but perhaps that was because she did not need it in the near mild temperatures he'd encountered since reaching Scotland. She held her ever present staff with the antlers sharpened to points at the top, her stance as though she was the only one on the boat.

Then she moved and turned to face the others, his keen vision picking up the beautiful features he'd been so sure he'd never see in this life. She spoke to someone else in the boat and he realized it was another woman dressed much as she was, but her hair was blonde, her lovely features marred by a scar on one side of her face. They spoke some more, their words carrying on the wind, though it did not look like even the sharp hearing of the wolves were picking them up.

"Do you think this council can prevent what you came here to stop?" her companion asked, for Haakon was sure this woman had traveled with Neilina to the island.

Her adopted daughter. His daughter, though she did not know it yet.

Woe betide anyone who might do the girl harm with two Chrechte guardians as her parents.

"We will see. They have been open to our warnings, though you can tell the alpha and the *dreki kongr* are finding it difficult to believe my visions are true and the terrible calamity that will befall the Chrechte if we cannot avert it."

Their daughter frowned, her consternation clear, even at the distance. "Their *celi di* is very powerful and she has not had the visions,"

"She may be too close to the death." The boat docked on the beach as Neilina shrugged. "It works that way sometimes with the Sight."

"She is more than Seer."

"That too may hinder her. She is charged with the spiritual wellbeing of her people. Foretelling the type of death I have seen might be beyond her ken."

"She saw the coming plague."

The shrug was in Neilina's voice now as she stepped out of the boat. "And I did not. Does that mean the plague is *not* coming?"

One of the men grunted. As big as Haakon, his hair was near black, a color not common among the *kotrondmenskr*. Tinted with a red so deep it too almost looked black, the man's hair alone might have indicated he was dragon, but the power emanating from him left no doubt.

And his eyes glowed amber unlike any other Chrechte's.

Surprisingly Neilina did not glare at the dragon. She must be aware of his nature as well, because though she gave him a look of challenge, that defiance did not make it into a verbal foray.

She respected their dragon king as all Chrechte should.

Their daughter tapped Neilina on the shoulder and whispered near her ear. "Who is that man looking at you?"

Neilina's head snapped up and she looked around, her gaze at first skimming right over Haakon and he felt something inside him freeze.

She did not recognize him? The other half of his soul.

Her head jerked back toward him, her green eyes going wide in shock as her gaze focused on him. She shook her head, her dark hair and braids swinging back and forth as she gave silent denial to his presence.

Haakon found himself smiling.

So, it was destined that he and his mate meet in this world after all. Though it felt as if iron itself welded their gazes together, he looked away from his mate and toward their daughter, his smile growing at the curiosity in her expression. *She* didn't look like she hated him.

Perhaps, after all, he would have a family, if not a mate.

***

He waited for them, like a king awaits his subjects. Standing tall, his boulder like shoulders thrown back with confidence, a Viking's grin on his face, his blue gaze twinkling with inner mirth.

Did her mate find it amusing that she was here?

That *he* was? What was the *asmundr* doing here? In Scotland? He was Norse, from Greenland. He did not belong on Balmoral Island, looking so pleased with himself.

"Do you know that man?" Freya asked. "Is it *him*?"

The satisfaction that flashed in the Paindeal's eyes said his hearing was as good, or better, than hers.

She ignored her daughter and stopped in front of Haakon. "What are you doing here?"

"Is this *your* home then?"

"Nay."

"These are the people you had the visions about?" he asked as if something was making sense to him finally.

"They are."

"Our Seer had visions as well. We must all come together if our people are to survive."

"You are telling me that you were called here as I was?" Neilina asked doubtfully, her body tense.

Haakon's lips twisted wryly, like he thought the question a silly one. "*Ja.*"

"You found out I was Scots from your father in the Spirit land." He had to have, and this man had followed her, intent on their mating.

Haakon shrugged, like that was of no consequence. "I did, *ja.*"

"And yet you claim you came because you were sent by your Seer," she said derisively.

He rolled his eyes. At her. "*Ja.* I was sent." He turned to Freya. "Though your mother denies our mating, you are my daughter. If ever you have a need, it is my duty and honor to stand for you."

The shock in Freya's scent had to be as obvious to Haakon as it was to Neilina.

"You dare claim my daughter as your own?" she asked, not nearly as angry as she should have been.

In fact, not angry at all. Something she had not felt for so long it was nearly unrecognizable unfurled inside Neilina.

Comfort.

For all that Freya was hers. Neilina had cared for the girl these past nine years. She could not deny that having someone else share the burden of the girl's safety in these calamitous times, was a relief.

Not that Neilina would ever admit to it to the arrogant Viking.

"Whatever you wish were true, you *are* my mate. We never have to acknowledge that for it to be true, our souls have already joined."

"Nay. You promised that would not happen when I allowed you into my mind." And she had believed him.

"It happened long before. I've not been able to touch another woman since the first time you pulled me into the place of *other*."

She could sense no deceit in him, but still Neilina had to deny it.

Because if that were true, then they were both doomed.

"Nay, that is not possible," she whispered, even as the thought of him *trying* to touch another filled her with cold white rage. "Faithless Viking."

"Faithless when you have never allowed me to give you my pledge, never allowed words of mating between us?" He shook his head, turning from her. "I will speak to the *dreki kongr* now."

She looked around to see if any had heard his words, worried that the secret their leader had been at so much pains to keep would be out to all the Chrechte on the beach. She could not know whether or not these were people that were aware of Eirik's true nature.

But then she realized that whenever Haakon referred to the dragon shifter, he did so in the words of the Norse, not a language her people were likely to understand. Not the ones here, at any rate.

Those who lived on her island were no doubt as familiar with Norse as they were with Gaelic.

"You're so sure you know who our *dreki kongr* is?" she asked, using the Norse word as well.

"Didn't you? The first moment you saw him?"

She couldn't deny it.

He turned his head to look again at Freya. "Remember, young one, you are *my* family as well as hers. I will protect and care for you in every way within my power and being *asmundr,* that power is great."

Without another word for Neilina, Haakon walked away. He stopped in front of Eirik.

Neilina felt the air still in her chest as the man who claimed to be her mate, the man she now knew to be *asmundr*, dropped to one knee and put a big fist over his heart.

He then spoke his vow of allegiance in the ancient Chrechte tongue, repeating the words in Norse, before bowing his head in a show of true *dìlseacht*, unquestionable fealty.

As Eirik reached out and laid one hand on her mate's head, Neilina felt the connection between all three of them as real as if they were bound with a stout, *living* rope.

Her own heart changed its rhythm to match the dragon's as she knew Haakon's had done as well.

She did not know how she knew, but she could feel the absolute *dìlseacht* suffuse every bit of Haakon's being as he made his promises.

She had vowed her help, but she'd held back, certain that once this crisis was over, she would return to her island, to her life of solitude.

There was none of that holding back in Haakon, he was promising a lifetime of loyalty and service to their *dràgon rì*. And for an *asmundr,* that lifetime would be very long.

It shocked her, the depth of the Viking's commitment to the protection of all Chrechte. His father, the *asmundr* before him, had not been so committed.

Had he been, even the loss of his mate and child would not have caused him to do what he did. To murder all the other living *conriocht* of her time.

She'd learned since coming among the Sinclair clan that until recently, no other *conriocht* had been called forth by the stone in so many years, they had lost their memory of the stone itself in some cases, and *conriocht* in others.

She was not surprised later to hear, as the alphas discussed recent events, that a Fearghall who had infiltrated the Balmoral clan had called the *conriocht* form demon.

How else could they explain the fact there were no guardians among them other than to call the ones that did exist demon, or unclean?

The Sinclair laird voiced that very opinion.

"Aye. How long have the Fearghall known of the *conriocht* and taught their own that to have the third form was to be touched by evil?" Eirik wondered aloud.

"The first Fearghall was *conriocht*," Ciara reminded them all. "Perhaps when he lost access to the stone and knew he could make no more like himself, he began the story."

"How did he explain his own nature then?" the Balmoral wondered.

Haakon asked for the full story as they knew it, listening intently as Ciara repeated all she'd learned from the ancient *kelle* in her spirit communications with the other woman.

Neilina was shocked to learn that one of their own had turned
against the people of the Chrechte as well. A *conriocht* as rogue as
Haakon's father, but with less cause, if Ciara's account was to be
believed.

And Neilina could see no reason to doubt the *celi di* and her
visions, despite the fact that her clan still questioned the validity of
Neilina's claims.

"A guardian can turn against those he is called to protect,"
Haakon said, his voice heavy. "But to destroy his own mother?"

He didn't sound like he could imagine such perfidy. Because of
how her own relatives had treated Freya, Neilina found it easier to
believe. She found it much harder to accept that one like herself had
not used his strength to protect, but to destroy.

The very reason she had hated that *asmundr* and all Norse for
more than two centuries.

Now, she was faced with undeniable truth that *any* might go
rogue. 'Twas not a result of being Paindeal rather than Faol. Or Éan
either.

Her entire thinking was turning on its head and she had no time
for it. Neilina's focus right now must be the salvation of the clans
around her.

"So, the Fearghall teach the *conriocht* are demon," she said, to
bring her own thoughts back where they needed to be. "They have
always believed any but their own select group are abomination. It
is this belief we must prepare for."

"Neilina claims all clans who fight the Fearghall's ways are at
risk." Eirik made no effort to hide his doubt.

Annoyed, Neilina gave her *dreki kongr* a good glare. "My visions
drove me from the solitude I prefer to join your clans, to help you
protect your people. I would appreciate if you would not show such
disdain for my sacrifice."

Suddenly Haakon stood beside her, his big body rigid, his
expression grim. "It is not only Neilina who has had these visions.
I have had them as well, and the ancient Seer who lives among my
pride sent me here for this very purpose."

"Our own Seer has had the visions," the Balmoral laird said, some
anger in his voice as he added. "He told me nothing about them until
the *asmundr* came and proved such a being existed, so the rest of his
visions were real, as well."

The dragon king still didn't look fully convinced. "Ciara has not had the visions."

"Not all Seers are given the same visions," Haakon said, like he knew what he was talking about.

Having been raised around a Seer who knew more of their people's history than these clans, perhaps he did.

"But if it is something so terrible for all our clans?" Ciara asked, her tone wounded.

"You have been called by the stone to protect our peoples into the centuries that many here will not see. Be glad there are other Seers who share your burden, if there were not, the weight would be too heavy to carry, even for a *celi di* such as yourself," Haakon said to the beautiful woman, with more compassionate warmth than necessary, Neilina thought. "The ancient *kelle* made a terrible mistake giving her son the gift of the *conriocht* when she knew his heart to be bent on power and domination, not the good of his people. Any might make such a mistake."

"Which is why we have more than one Seer, more than one *celi di* among our clans. Why there is not just one guardian, but many called from each of the packs and prides." The Balmormal's words were heavy with meaning. "Each are called to their own message and outreach to our peoples, but each one helps to check the others, as well."

"Some cannot be checked so easily." Neilina gave Haakon a hard look. "Your father decimated the *conriocht* of my time."

"How were you called forth by the stone if it had been hidden away?" Haakon asked Neilina.

"Each pack was led by a member of the Chrechte royal lineage. And in each family, small stones were passed down from father to son, mother to daughter, as the case may be. I inherited the weapons with the stones from my grandmother."

"You mean the stones in my sword and knife can be used in the coming of age ceremonies?" Ciara asked in wonder.

Neilina nodded. "They can be used in all ceremonies, but the smaller stones rely much on the magic of the Chrechte in the ceremony as well as those around him or her. 'Tis nearly impossible to call forth a guardian without the original *Faolchu Chridhe*."

"You were called forth."

Neilina shrugged.

"The power of our ancestors lives within her, the same as in me. I did not know our stone was only a chip off the *kontrondmenskr hjarta* until our Seer told me that our pride split more than a century ago."

Ciara, mate to the dragon and undoubted chief *celi di*, looked very thoughtful at Haakon's words. "I had no idea. I knew the emeralds in my weapon's hilts helped me to connect to the ancient *kelle*, but not that they could be used for the important ceremonies. All this time, we've been doing without among our packs and it was not necessary."

The dragon looked grim. "We thought if we lost our stone there would be no more Éan."

"If you did not know to use the smaller stones, there would not have been," Ciara said. "It may have taken the *Clach Gealach Gra* to call forth your beast."

Neilina did not know how much of the dragon being called forth had been need, how much had been Eirik's personal connection to the magic that ran through their people, and how much could be attributed to those who had participated in his coming of age ceremony.

She glanced sideways at Haakon. He had been called forth with a gem, not the larger *Paindeal Neart*. What had made that possible?

His father had been given the *asmundr* gift from the larger stone, as he'd been called forth before the pride split and took the original with them.

There could be no doubt his family was of the royal line, though. Not if they had the smaller stones that had been passed down.

Neilina wished, not for the first time, that she'd had a chance to learn more from the elders of her pack before they were taken from her.

Her sigh was little more than a puff of air, but it brought Haakon's gaze to her. "You are well, *kelle*?"

"Don't call me that." She had no right to the name. She'd spent two centuries hiding from her own people. She was no *kelle*.

"Refusing to speak the word does not change what and who you are. I am *asmundr*. I am Norse. No amount of speaking or refusing to speak will change these facts." His tone was almost like he was giving her a warning.

Mayhap he was.

Never in nine years had Haakon hidden from the truth of what he believed them to be, or who he was. Truly, she had not known he was *asmundr*, but that was because she'd refused to ask about him.

It had taken him very little time to realize his confidences fell on deaf ears. Or so he had believed.

For the first time in centuries, Neilina felt tears pricking at her eyes over the past. Over events that could not be changed.

"I hid from my people. They were without *conriocht* because I wanted only to bury myself in the forest and lick my wounds."

Now the warmth of Haakon's compassion was turned on Neilina. "You have rejoined the packs when you are most needed, there is nothing of shame in that."

"You don't believe that." He couldn't. "You do not even have thirty years yet and you have heeded the call to protect with everything in you."

"I do not have your past." He said it so matter of factly.

Like he did not question that his own life had made his actions possible while she had been hampered doing the same.

She gave him a wry look and sighed. "Wisdom is not supposed to be in the young but come with age."

"There are different kinds of wisdom, *kelle*." The dragon spoke, but the other alphas around them nodded.

Ciara spoke then. "You have knowledge of things we know nothing about. We thank you for sharing that knowledge."

"I am not *kelle*," but the words did not sound true, even to Neilina's own ears.

The dragon frowned, like his head hurt. "You are. Ciara is *celi di*. You are *kelle*, Neilina. And as Haakon has already acknowledged, he is *asmunder*, guardian to all Chrechte. We will serve our packs, prides and flocks for centuries to come. Together."

The words washed over them like a resounding gong and chills rushed over Neilina's body, sending goose bumps up and down her arms.

"We're never going back to our island, are we?" Freya asked of no one in particular.

But the dragon shook his head. "Your mother and father are destined to a life beyond the cave you have been living in this past decade."

Neilina couldn't help the sound of protest that came out of her mouth at the dragon referring to Haakon as Freya's father. The Viking, though, looked well pleased with the legitimizing of his claim.

"You cannot simply say you are her father," Neilina muttered in an aside to Haakon.

"I will gift our daughter with Chrechte nature."

"You cannot."

"With you, with our stones, I *can*."

"Don't you think I already tried to pull forth any Chrechte nature she might have?" She'd done it with a coming of age ceremony, but while the light had sparked, Freya had remained wholly human. "She has no Chrechte in her ancestors."

Haakon cocked his head to one side, his blue gaze going unfocused as if in thought, or that he was listening to some inner voice and then he said, "You were not enough."

Neilina felt the words like a blow and drew herself up, anger making her voice sharp. "I have protected her these past nine years, taught her the ways of a warrior, how to live as a Chrechte even without our nature to sustain her. I am her mother. I am enough."

"Would you allow her to remain unchanged because your pride will not accept my help with our daughter?" For once that infernal control of his slipped and Haakon sounded angry. Truly angry. With *her*.

Neilina's throat tightened and no words of denial would pass her lips. Was it possible that their daughter did have Chrechte blood in her and that she might gain strength and a longer life if she was presented to the stone by Haakon as well as Neilina?

If there was even a tiny chance, Neilina knew she had no choice but to take it.

"It is not only Haakon who will touch the stone with you. Each of your fellow *conriocht* will as well," the Sinclair vowed.

"And I," the *dràgon rì* promised.

Ciara smiled at both Neilina and Freya. "And I. Freya is your daughter for a reason. Let us call her nature forth from the stone."

"But we must have our council, time is not in our favor," the Balmoral said.

As much as Neilina wanted Freya protected in every way possible before the coming peril, she agreed with the alpha. "The laird is right, we must figure out how to stop the Fearghall from perpetrating the atrocities I have seen in my visions."

"As to that, I have some ideas," the Balmoral said.

With that, they all moved to the table and began the Chrechte council meeting with a ceremony of the stones glowing on the table. Haakon was recognized as the representative for the Paindeal and Neilina found herself surprisingly accepting of that.

Perhaps her unreasoning prejudice toward his kind was finally lessening.

The fact she considered it unreasoning was something new and she thought good for her as well as her daughter. It was Neilina's job to set a good example for Freya and she'd long known that she did not want to imbue Freya's nature with Neilina's own bitterness toward the Viking people.

Haakon said they were no longer Viking...but she did not believe it. The Chrechte had longer memories than humans. They would still live by the Viking way, but that did not mean he was a threat to her, or any of the other Chrechte she'd come to help.

Haakon shared what his Seer had foretold. It was so close to what Neilina had been trying to convince the Sinclairs of that she could not doubt he'd been sent to the Faol just as she had been. Then the Balmoral Seer spoke of his own visions, again testimony to her claims.

The dragon's visage grew more and more grim as the discussion progressed, his mate's countenance being taken over with grief.

She was true *celi di*, the spiritual and emotional welfare of her people weighing heavily on her, as well as their overall safety.

When the Balmoral told the other alphas the claim Haakon had made about a Chrechte not being able to lie in front of the dragon, she saw the same disbelief she'd been faced with since her arrival on the mainland.

Frustrated, Neilina pounded the table with her fist. "Because you have lost knowledge of the old Chrechte ways, does not mean they are wrong. We do not have time for these foolish arguments against the truth. The dragon is your *dràgon rì*. He is the ultimate guardian and as such, every Chrechte must speak honesty before him, even those who refuse to follow him."

"We dinna even submit to the whims of Scotland's king. You think we are going to follow the will of any other man without question?" the Balmoral asked her wryly.

"I do not believe our *dreki kongr* would ask you to follow blindly. 'Tis not the Chrechte way." She sighed but couldn't help glaring at the alphas who had discounted Haakon's words. "But you must stop arguing truths you dinna understand."

"Try to lie," the Sinclair said to Circin, the laird of the MacLeod. A young shifter with dual natures that gave him powers she suspected he knew nothing about.

"I am not..." Circin's jaw strained with the effort to get words out. "I canna do it. I was going to claim I was not the alpha of my pack, but even though I am still training with Barr, the words wouldna leave my mouth."

The Sinclair nodded. The Balmoral had not argued with the powers of the dragon, so the lack of surprise on his features was expected.

It was Ciara, *celi di* who turned white. "It cannot be on Eirik's shoulders entirely. One man, no matter how powerful, cannot route out the betrayers among the packs." She scowled around the table. "He will not be responsible for passing judgment on them."

"*Nei*, all guardians stand together." Haakon shook his head. "Our peoples have been separated so long, we have all forgotten different things, but this I know...we are all responsible for finding the Fearghall among the clans and giving them the chance to learn a new way or perish."

The Balmoral nodded. "We can test our packs again, but this time, the vow of fidelity must specifically be to each alpha, not the pack, or the clan. The Fearghall see themselves as the saviors of the pack, so vowing loyalty to those they plan to save from pretender alphas, as they call us, does not give off the scent of deception."

"But if we tell them to pledge themselves to serve us specifically?"

"They canna do it without lying."

"So, it's possible all the packs have Fearghall among them still."

"'Tis a certainty more like," Neilina muttered under her breath.

But those around the long table heard her as they too shared her keen sense of hearing.

Haakon's almost-there smile sent an odd warmth through her, like his approval meant something good to her. And maybe it did.

"*Ja.* Each pack must swear anew and there must be a guardian present for every swearing ceremony."

"And me?" Eirik asked. "We cannot ignore this gift I've been given." He gave a soft look to his wife. "No matter how much we may wish to."

"We begin here. In this room. Every member of the council must pledge their loyalty to you as *dreki kongr*, or *dràgon rì* as you say, our one, true king, and utterly denounce the Fearghall."

An acrid scent of fear wafted over the table and Neilina knew that Haakon's words were true. They could not afford to ignore the very group that had been tasked with protecting their people.

There was a betrayer among them.

Out of the corner of her eye, she saw someone trying to leave the hall by sneaking behind the oddly placed English buttery. Lady Emily's doing, no doubt.

Neilina leapt from the bench on which she sat and ran to intercept the Chrechte thinking he would avoid giving his vow and no doubt planning to warn others of the tests to come.

She caught the older man before he made it to the door leading to the tunnel that, by the smells emanating, led to the kitchens. He twisted in her grasp calling her all sorts of foul names.

She held tight and dragged him back to the table. "I suggest you start with this one."

"Donnan?" Circin asked, sadness and resignation in his tone. "You swore you did not follow Rowland's beliefs and I was sure there was no deceit on you."

The elder tried to get away again, but Neilina had no trouble holding him. She was *conriocht,* after all.

Finally, the old man stopped struggling, glaring at everyone present. "I'm not traitor. Ye canna think this woman who pretends to be a man has the right of it. I was going for a breath of fresh air."

He was a wily one. Neilina allowed that. The alpha Circin looked relieved, but Haakon frowned and stepped forward. "You will not address my mate as you have done again. Or I will end your life."

"She's no mate to you. We all heard her deny your claim."

Haakon didn't flinch. "I know what our souls say. Apologize to Neilina, *conriocht* to your people, *kelle* to all."

The man stood there stubbornly mute.

Neilina didn't care if he said he was sorry. "His opinion does not matter to me."

"You are *kelle*, both warrior and *celi di*. You deserve respect. For him to call you such names shows his deep lack of reverence for our ways. I will not tolerate it."

"Apologize," Circin said, using his alpha voice.

The elder glared at the young alpha, but he muttered, "I'm sorry I called you names."

Haakon's glower did not diminish. "You Fearghall have a way with deceit, I'll give you that."

"You've no right to call me anything but Chrechte."

"Vow your allegiance to this council, to Eirik as your *dràgon rì* and denounce the Fearghall."

"I've spoken my vow of allegiance." Donnan looked around at those assembled, his expression filled with ire. "Asking me to do it again to make this upstart happy is an offence and an abomination."

Circin looked unhappy again. "Speak the words, Donnan of the Donegal. Now." There was no question the alpha expected his elder to do as he had been told.

Donnan glared at Circin and then around at everyone else before opening his mouth. He seemed like he was having difficulty getting the words out.

Neilina shook him a little. "Say it, elder. Either you are loyal to all Chrechte, or you are true to none."

His scowl focused on her, the look promising her death and retribution.

Neilina held back a dark laugh with effort. No matter how powerful this man thought himself, he would not harm her. She would not give him the chance.

"I am loyal to all true Chrechte."

There was no sting to her nostrils from deceit, but then there wouldn't be.

"Denounce the Fearghall and pledge loyalty to the Chrechte on *this* council!" Circin barked.

The elder opened his mouth, but no words came out. He looked toward Eirik and spat, "Demon!"

Circin turned away, dismissing the elder. "He is no clan of mine. Do with him as you see fit."

Barr, the man who had been training Circin came forward. "You are his alpha. You pass judgment on him." His tone was hard, but there was understanding in his eyes. Compassion, if a warrior could have such a thing.

Circin stopped, took a deep breath, his chin in his chest, then nodded as he turned back around. He faced the elder, a man that he had trusted and probably called friend. "Donnan, you have deceived us all, pretending to support your alpha and the Chrechte of our clan, all the while you had a terrible agenda, one which would see us all destroyed."

The man did not deny the accusations, but stood, defiantly mute, only the acrid scent of fear giving away how he felt about what he faced.

"There is no bringing one such as yourself around to caring for all Chrechte," Circin said with grieving finality.

"How dare you pass judgment on me? You are nothing but a carrion bird, your wolf subject to all its weaknesses."

"If the Éan are so weak, how have we lasted despite the best attempts of the Fearghall to kill us all these many centuries?" Eirik demanded.

"You are such a fool," Neilina said to the old man and shook her head. "Those who have three forms, whether they are guardians or dual natured shifters have gifts our brethren wish they all had."

Haakon nodded, the look of disgust in his eyes clear for all to see. "Circin will live centuries, not decades. His strength is near twice that of a normal shifter when he calls upon both natures at once, he can both fly and run as a wolf, making him near impossible to track and kill. You denigrate that which you do not understand."

"Or that which he fears," the Balmoral said in hard tones.

"I fear no Éan," Donnan spat, but his scent gave lie to his words.

The rest of the council gave his comment the attention it deserved, which was none.

Circin stepped toward Eirik, and then dropped to one knee. "I will be first to offer my pledge."

Which is what he did, the other alphas following suit, powerful men promising loyalty to a cause, a people and the Supreme Protector of all Crechte.

The rest of the council also gave their pledges before plans were made to go from pack to pack, clan to clan, requiring new pledges of allegiance to be made.

"We must begin here, on Balmoral island. Every wolf and human alike will pledge their loyalty anew to me as laird and pack alpha as the case may be," Lachlan said.

No one argued, for the visions foretold terrible calamity for his pack soonest.

"We will search the entire island for any who might hide, who may already be hidden, but are not Balmoral," the *dràgon rì* added.

CHAPTER NINE

Artair trained with the jarl's soldiers, glad Einar was not in his line of sight. His mate was far too much a distraction for Artair to fight with any effectiveness.

After he had put his third *kotrondmenskr* on his ass, Artair stepped back to take a breath.

These big Norsemen assumed that because he was smaller, he would be easy prey.

Artair was a wolf shifter, as most of them had to be aware. He'd made no effort to hide his scent from his new Pride. That, in itself, would make Artair a formidable foe, but he'd been trained by the Balmoral himself and Drustan, warriors that would have been shamed had Artair allowed himself to be bested by brawn alone.

The *kotrondmenskr* he'd been fighting stood and came toward Artair. "Will you teach me that move with your feet?" he asked.

Young, and clearly inexperienced, Olaf showed *he* at least had the wisdom to recognize skill when he saw it.

Artair suspected he'd been given the greenest of the lot to train with, because his Einar's second did not have the same wisdom.

Gart would have been furious to be relegated to their ranks, but Artair knew he would prove his own worth in time, and perhaps teach these *kotrondmenskr* something in the process.

He nodded. "Aye, I'll teach you."

He proceeded to do just that, pushing the young Olaf to rely on his cat's instincts as much as his brawn.

The rest of the small group Artair had been training with, a mixture of *kotromnendskr* and human, had stopped to watch Artair and his sparring partner, Nei, by the time he'd got the Norseman squatting low enough and able to swing his foot out the same time in the arc so dangerous to an opponent.

"You're agile, man, I'll give you that," Artair said.

He'd expected no less. The *kotrondmenskr* shared their spirits with large cats of prey. Though Einar had told Artair most of his pride shifted into the Mountain Lynx, nothing nearly so impressive as Einar's Siberian Tiger.

And for as big as these Norsemen were, the Lynxes they shifted into were smaller than even Artair's wolf. But they were still men who shared an animal's nature and had the agility and strength to prove it.

"I see you've decided to help train my soldiers." Einar's deep voice came from behind Artair.

He nodded, without facing his mate, who had spent *his* morning training with the elite warriors of their clan and Pride. "Olaf learns quickly," Artair praised the young *kotrondmenskr*.

Olaf threw his shoulders back with pride. "Your mate fights dirty," he said with relish.

Artair took the compliment for what it was and inclined his head in thanks.

The others crowded around asking him to teach them the ways of the fighting Scots.

"I see I may have made a mistake placing you with this group to train," Einar said, sounding chagrined as men pressed in around Artair.

"Oh? I thought it was your second who made the decision." That put a different light on things, saying something Artair wasn't sure he liked about how his mate saw him.

Nevertheless, he said, "It was no mistake, if you don't mind me saying so. I'd moved into the training ranks before I left my clan and am happy to continue teaching soldiers now."

"It is not for you to decide you are trainer," Einar's second-in-command said gruffly.

Artair spun to face the other man. "Isn't it?" he demanded, determined that all would respect his place as Einar's mate.

"*Nei.* You are new to our holding. It is *my* job to assess your strengths."

"You are second, but *I* am *mate*."

"A female mate would never—"

"I am not female, but if I were, and trained to war, I would still expect deference to my place."

The soldiers around looked on with keen interest to see how their former leader took his demotion.

"Just because Lord Einar wants to bed you, does not give you a place above me with his soldiers," Dag spat.

Einar growled, clearly growing agitated, but Artair put his hand up toward his mate.

"We want to bed each other, if you really want to know, but mating is much more than who shares a man's furs. Nevertheless, I'm happy to fight you for position."

Artair had never wanted to fight for position before, but this *cat* dared to place himself in a position of more importance to Artair's *mate* than he himself held. Neither he, nor his wolf would stand for such.

"*Nei*," Einar roared.

"*Ja*, I accept your challenge," the other *kotrondmenskr* said quickly, giving the man that one day would be his *jarl* a look of pitying defiance.

Artair smiled. He'd never sought leadership in his former pack. Had never craved recognition for being a top warrior, but he would not have been promoted to the training elite if he was not one of the best.

And while his size might be against him, the current second's assumptions and hotheaded demeanor would be a much bigger burden to Dag.

Einar stepped between them, fairly vibrating with anger. "I forbid it."

"We will fight then," Artair said at the same time and then gave his mate a look.

The man had better step back, or they wouldn't be consummating anything after their mating ceremony tomorrow.

Einar must have read Artair's expression correctly because he frowned in confusion. "You can't think to best him? Dag is my best warrior."

"And *you* thought I was better placed with your unseasoned soldiers to train."

Einar grimaced. "Clearly that was in error—"

"Nay, poorly conceived, but not in error." Artair wanted to train these young soldiers. In a few years, he was confident he would have them besting even Dag.

"I will not allow you to fight him," Einar said stubbornly.

"On what grounds?" Artair asked curiously, but with no doubt to the outcome and let his tone say as much.

"You are new to the holding, to the Pride."

"But I am a member of the pride, your father, the *jarl* himself, has said so."

"I am second only to the *jarl* and I forbid it."

Artair smiled, but he knew it wasn't a very nice smile because his intended winced and even Dag looked a little worried. "Olaf, please go tell your *jarl* there is a matter of law only he can settle."

"My father does not need to be bothered with this matter," Einar growled.

"I disagree. If we do not settle it now, we will settle it before any mating ceremony takes place."

"You would delay our mating?" Einar asked furiously.

"To be sure that I go into it with the full protection of the laws of the pride, yes."

"I *am* trying to protect you."

"I concede you believe as much. I do not agree."

"And if I do not allow you to be beaten into the ground by my second, you do not think I am allowing you to be *protected* by our laws?" Einar demanded with disbelief.

"I am a soldier, not a craftsman, untrained in the art of war. I have killed." He gave Dag a look. "And I have faced adversaries a hell of a lot more intimidating than your second-in-command."

"I will not stand the insult, Lord Einar. Your *mate*," the man spit out the word, "is right. Our laws dictate that as a full member of our holding and pride, he has the right to make a challenge and I have the right to accept that challenge."

Einar puffed up his chest and opened his mouth to speak, but Artair forestalled him. "If you threaten him in any way or try to protect me by ordering him not to fight with all he has, I will not soon forgive you and I will *never* forget the insult."

Einar stared at Artair, his mouth snapping shut. Hurt warred with worry in his gorgeous blue gaze, but he nodded. Just once. "So be it."

He turned to walk away.

"You will watch, mate. Despite all your prejudices and preconceived beliefs, you *will* believe in *me*. I will settle for no less."

Einar spun to face him, his glare sulfuric. "You would ask me watch you get hurt when honor will not allow me to step in to save you?"

"Nay. I *demand* you watch me wipe that superior smile right off your second's face."

Artair's wolf was close to the surface and he wanted blood. He had been insulted not only by the Lynx they would fight, but by their mate.

Artair would stop short of killing the other Chrechte in the challenge, but how short he was not sure. His wolf demanded retribution.

"You said you never participated in position challenges back in your clan." Einar's confusion and worry was there for all to see.

It was equal parts annoying and endearing. There could be no doubt in anyone's mind that Einar *cared* for his mate, but neither could they doubt that the tiger doubted his wolf's strength.

And that Artair would not abide.

"And I did not." He'd never had to fight for respect and he had not *wanted* position.

He could sense the satisfaction his response had given to Dag. Which would make the man's defeat all the sweeter for Artair and his wolf.

"You *will* trust me," Artair informed his mate, unwilling to accept any less.

Theirs would be a mating of equals, or there would be no mating.

"I do not want you hurt."

"And I will not accept the place your second would relegate me to."

"I should have challenged him on your behalf, at the first insult," Einar said as if he just now realized that showing solidarity with his mate might have been a better course of action than the one he took.

But even so, Artair did not agree. "He would have learned nothing."

"And you are so sure he will learn something from this challenge you are so intent on fighting in?"

"There will be a lesson." For both his mate and Dag. "Whether he learns from it, only time will tell."

Olaf laughed, along with some of the other soldiers, which gained them a glare from their current second-in-command. Other soldiers fidgeted with a nervousness he wasn't sure even they understood.

But Artair's wolf would make them uneasy, even if they did not understand why.

The beast was out for blood, more than Artair ever would be without the wolf's fury.

The humans especially wouldn't understand the danger charging the air around them like lightening during a storm.

"You realize that once you win this challenge, you will be my second, with all the responsibilities that entails."

"What did you think taking *me* to be your mate would mean?" As he'd already reminded Einar, Artair was a soldier, not a craftsman.

As Einar's mate, he could be nothing less than the man's second and one day, he would rule right beside Einar when Artair's mate became *jarl*.

Understanding flashed in Einar's gaze, his blue eyes widening. He had not considered Artair's role beyond them becoming mates and making a family with Jorgen and Marie, but Einar was no ordinary pride member. He was in line to be alpha, and that truth defined Artair's future role as well.

Artair would have been happy to wait to take his place as Einar's second, but Dag had challenged him and his place by Einar's side in all things. There would be no waiting now.

Artair held back his annoyance at his mate's shortsightedness. It was on Artair not to shirk his own destiny, but it was entirely Einar's responsibility to support Artair as he and his wolf followed the path destiny had laid down before them.

Einar stepped back, signaling to the rest of the soldiers to do likewise, creating a wall of men in a circle around them.

Dag handed his sword to another *kotrondmenskr* soldier with an arrogant smile. Clearly, he believed that because of his size, he had the advantage in the more close-proximity fighting required with knives.

Artair handed his sword to Einar without demur. Einar frowned, but took the weapon in silence.

Finally, he was showing some confidence in Artair, or at least enough self-control not to express his doubt.

Einar put his fist in the air. "This is a challenge for position. Winner will be the first to draw blood three times or force their opponent to yield. This is not a death match."

The idea of fighting to the death for position considering how hard the *kotrondmenskr* found it to procreate, was abhorrent to Artair. And the expression of distaste on Dag's face said he felt the same, despite his foolish arrogance.

Good. Artair did not want to have to kill one who was not his mortal enemy.

Artair dropped into a fighting ready stance, remembering all that his laird and laird's second had taught him about fighting. As Olaf said, Artair had been taught to fight with subterfuge and the unexpected as much as with the skill of a sword, or knives.

Dag tossed his knife back and forth between his hands, in a show of confidence.

Artair effected a spinning kick that sent the knife sailing off toward the circle of onlookers on the next toss. He then tossed his own knife to stick in the dirt in front of Einar, a standing symbol of how little Artair himself feared the big Lynx warrior.

Dag laughed as if Artair had done something very stupid and rushed him. Artair's wolf howled in glee inside him and he leapt and rolled right over the back of the attacking Norseman.

Einar realized a few minutes into the fight that his mate was playing with Dag. Artair moved with blurring speed and such skill, Einar was not sure even *he* could best his mate without shifting. But Artair made no move to end the fight quickly, as if he wanted all who witnessed to see that his skill in battle was no fluke, that the place of second-in-command, he would take, was earned.

He did not need a knife to draw blood. A kick to Dag's jaw, left his mouth bleeding. Dag managed to draw blood by scratching down Artair's chest and Einar's tiger roared inside him, but Artair just laughed, swiping his fingers through his own blood and licking it. His eyes flashed amber, showing just how close to the surface his wolf was, but he did not shift.

He could have. The humans in their clan knew of the Pride that lived among them, but Artair was following the intent of the law. Einar knew he would not shift unless Dag did first.

And as fast and fierce as he knew his fellow warrior to be in his Lynx form, Einar was now convinced Artair's wolf was even more so.

Dag was a superior fighter and he showed himself well, but Artair was better. Faster. More ruthless.

It was clear that Einar's mate was not going for the easier way to win the fight by drawing blood three times. Artair would accept nothing less than Dag's submission.

Dag tried his own blow to Artair's face with a hand adorned with the large silver rings they were wont to wear, but Artair ducked, laughed and moved so fast Einar nearly missed his mate delivering a blow to the other soldier's gonads.

Dag shouted in pain, not doubling over, but not moving as quickly as he had been either.

Artair laughed again, the sound filled with joy and a wolf's bloodlust.

Atavistic chills ran up Einar's spine. In this moment, his mate was pure predator.

"You fight like a cur!" Dag threw the insult out venomously.

"And you fight like a man who does not know what it means to face a mortal enemy in battle. You think the Fearghall will stay in Scotland once they learn of your existence? You think they are the only enemies you must fear?"

Artair glared all around the circle and even at Einar. "You take your safety for granted because of your isolation. When was the last time any in your pride or the humans you live among had to kill to protect what you hold dear?"

It was true, there hadn't been a raiding party for several years. Haakon had dealt with the offenders before they could even reach Einar's father's settlement.

"All Chrechte and those they live among are at risk in these days, or do you think your Seer's words are only for other packs and prides, not your own?" Artair asked with derision.

Dag growled and leapt toward Artair, his desire to shut the Scotsman up obvious to all.

But Artair was ready for him, using the bigger man's momentum to flip him and then land on his back, putting him in a hold that would choke the life out of Dag.

Dag struggled, but Artair was much stronger than his smaller stature might imply, and he could not be shifted. Dag's face turned red.

He looked like he was going to pass out, but Dag tapped the dirt three times, indicating he yielded.

Artair released his hold, but suddenly his hand sprouted claws and he pressed them to Dag's jugular. "If I wanted your death, I could have had it many times over."

Dag coughed, dragging in gasps of air, but nodded.

Artair gave his own nod and then stood. "You are good soldiers, good fighters, and even better hunters, but you must start training to fight with intent."

And then he looked first at Olaf, and then each of the other of the newer trainees. "I have chosen the men I will train, but as second I will spend time weekly with each of the groups." He turned in a circle, giving each of Einar's soldiers a chance to meet his gaze. "May Providence help you if you do not train seriously and with the knowledge war may come, because only divine intervention will save you from my wrath."

Einar had never considered how lax they had become, training for battle more in sport than intent. The holding and Pride had relied on their *asmundr* and Einar. They had believed with an *asmundr* and a Siberian tiger protecting them, they were safe.

He thought Artair had been right as well, when he accused them of growing complacent because of and the safety of their location.

But the way Artair had just made sport of a superior fighter like Dag said much about the *way* they had to train in future.

"Your enemies will not fight for sport, but to spill your blood." Artair said, indicating his thoughts ran side by side with Einar's. "It is time you remembered your fathers were Vikings."

Einar was so proud of his mate, he wanted to grab him and kiss him, but wasn't sure that was the message Artair was trying to get across to his soldiers.

Artair walked up to Einar, grabbed his knife from the dirt and carefully cleaned the blade on his kilt, then tucked it back in its small scabbard before taking his sword and placing it in the one across his back.

Einar grabbed Artair's wrist and raised his arm. "My second, my mate!"

A loud cheer went up, even Dag joined in.

He and his mate were returning to the Long House later, when Einar remarked, "You said you never fought for position in your old clan."

Einar's gaze dropped to Artair's plaid and wondered just how much loyalty remained to his former clan.

Artair shrugged. "I never did. I did not care about position and frankly, I was a good trainer, but there were better, stronger, warriors more suited to the pack positions worth fighting for."

"Dag is a formidable fighter."

"He insulted me. He insulted my wolf. And he questioned our place at your side. With that provocation, there is no way he could win against me."

"That is a position you consider worthy of fighting for?" Einar asked, liking the idea that his normally even-tempered mate would react so strongly.

"Don't you?"

"*Ja.*" But Einar had no former mate and lifelong friendship to contend with.

"You would fight for your place by my side?" Artair pressed.

Einar growled with the deep rumble of his tiger at the very idea. "I would not allow it."

"Nor would I."

"You made that clear to all." Einar could not help the satisfaction that filled his voice at that knowledge.

Artair smiled, but the happy expression soon slipped from his features. "You doubted my strength. I could not allow that either. My wolf wanted to come out so badly and teach you all a lesson."

Einar had realized that, but he'd been surprised too. "Your wolf is much more vicious than I would have ever expected."

" I *am* a wolf and you are my mate. In blood lust, a wolf is a formidable foe. Make no mistake, if the Fearghall make their way here, they will show no mercy."

"We *have* grown complacent." It wouldn't thrill his father to hear Einar say so, but he would not lie to his mate.

"It's living so isolated for so many generations. Few challenge you. The settlement on the other side of the island is more at risk."

"It is better known for its tradable goods," Einar agreed.

"But your father is prosperous, as are his people."

"Destiny knew what she was doing when she brought you to me as my mate. Our Pride needs you."

"And you, do *you* need me?" Artair asked.

Einar stopped before they entered the longhouse and met his mate's beautiful golden-brown gaze. "I needed you most of all."

"I think Jorgen and Marie need me even more. You're likely to spoil them rotten without some tempering."

"I am not the *pa* at risk of spoiling them." Artair had shown an instant affinity to the two small children, insisting on their moving into the *jarl's* longhouse that very night.

"Yes, well, the *jarl* enjoys being a grandfather very much."

Which completely ignored Einar's accusation, but he let his mate's change of direction for their conversation pass. "He has always been good with the Pride's children despite how harsh he can be with the adults." Einar asked the question he'd been putting off. "Are you ready for our mating tomorrow?"

"I'm not sure…"

Einar's stomach plummeted.

"Do you see me as an equal now, or do I need to challenge you for my place *beside* you, too?" Artair's expression said that he would accept nothing but the full truth and that *that* truth was incredibly important.

But Einar had *not* questioned his mate's place at his side. He did not understand the need for this question. "I never—"

"It was your decision to put me with the most untried soldiers. You never wanted me to train at all."

"My nature is to protect you," Einar acknowledged. "But that does not mean that I do not see you as my equal."

"Are you sure?"

"Can you have any doubt after the lesson you gave us all today?" Learning that his mate, a man who had made it clear he didn't care about position for position's sake, would fight so fiercely and so *well* for his place at Einar's side had been a welcome shock.

"And?" Artair prompted. "Are you going to accept me fully as your second?"

It was a fair question and deserved for Einar to think before he answered, which he did. Finally, he shared the truth that was in his heart. "It will always be a challenge to let you go into danger beside me, but I am not weak-willed. I will stand proudly beside you as you take your place."

Artair's smile squeezed at Einar's heart while making his prick hard as stone. "Then I am ready for our mating tomorrow."

#

Artair had only been witness to a couple of matings between sacred mates, and none among the Paindeal of course.

So, he had no idea what to expect.

He asked the ancient Seer that evening, as the old man had decided to share the meal with them. Apparently, he dropped in for either the midday or evening meal several times in a sennight.

Artair liked the irascible old man and found it amusing how the Seer and the *jarl* interacted. Einar treated the Seer with great respect and never pressed for more information than the old man was willing to give.

Artair liked that too.

"We will travel to the sacred cave as a Pride."

"Where is your sacred cave?" Artair asked, not having run across any caves in his runs as a wolf.

"It is a half day's walk north from here, toward the coast."

Since theirs was a coastal community, most things were "toward" or "on" the coast.

"Does the Pride stay the night in the caves as well?" He could not imagine them trying to walk back in the dark.

"*Ja*. A mating is a great celebration. The human soldiers will be put in charge of security of the village."

"Do any humans come?"

"Mates of the *kotrondmenskr*," Einar offered.

"The mating ceremony will last for three days," the *jarl* added.

"Three days?" Artair asked with an unmanly squeak.

"Are matings not done this way among your pack?" the *jarl* asked, sounding like he could not imagine it. "They are the most important events within our Pride. The first ceremony is to bless the joining of the two mates. The second is a Pride ceremony, affirming our connection to one another and on the third morning, we have a last ceremony if the woman is with child from the first two nights, giving thanks for continued life in our Pride."

"There is no woman in this mating," Artair said, this time his voice as hard as he'd ever wanted it to be.

"*Nei*, but we will stay the second night regardless," Einar said, his own tone without give. "It is a tradition."

"Please tell me there's some level of privacy for the mating." Artair knew that certain aspects of the physical joining were witnessed in a Faol mating, if not watched, but to have his wedding night, as it were, held in a communal setting was not something he wanted.

At all.

"Our sacred caves have a series of chambers, never fear. You and my son will have all the privacy you need to cement your bond," the *jarl* said with a smile.

"Uh, thank you." Artair wasn't entirely comfortable discussing having penetrative sex for the first time with his soon to be father-in-law.

Artair slid his gaze to his mate and found Einar looking far from embarrassed. The only description for the look in the tiger's bright blue gaze was heated.

And Artair's body reacted to his mate's desire. Predictably.

"Stop it," he demanded of Einar, embarrassed because Artair knew all the Chrechte in the longhouse couldn't help but smell the arousal rolling off of him and his mate.

The *jarl's* booming laugh only added to that embarrassment.

But Einar shook his head. "You cannot expect any other reaction to discussion of our mating."

"Then we will talk about something else," Artair said forcefully.

He was a wolf, damn it. But he'd spent his whole adult life masking his desire for the wolf he thought was supposed to be his mate.

This openness was unnerving, but welcome just the same.

"I will never hide what I feel for you, or deny you in any way," Einar said, as if he could read Artair's very thoughts.

Would they share a mental bond once they had mated?

The walk to the sacred caves was festive, with the small Pride singing ancient songs, playing with their children and teasing Einar and Artair mercilessly about what was to come. It was unlike anything the wolf shifter had ever experienced.

His clan were close, but this was more like an extended family getting together to celebrate a holiday. Everyone shared their food when they stopped to eat. All the adults shared in watching over the children, some carrying the littlest ones.

Einar had his giant warhorse, but he did not ride it. Instead, he had the Seer on the horse's back, holding one child, or another as the day progressed.

Artair could feel the concentration of Chrechte magic as they neared the caves, a sense of the sacred that was familiar to him.

But the surroundings were not. Colder than his home in the Highlands of Scotland, some of the passages were as much ice as rock.

The Seer, who had left the horse outside the caves, pointed to the amazing blue ice walls. "These were not here when we first settled this place. It has grown colder over the centuries."

Artair inclined his head in question. "It has?"

"*Ja.* It was never the green paradise Eirik the Red tried to make it out to be to draw others to settle here as well, but it was warmer and easier to farm in the beginning."

"It still amazes me that you have lived so long," Artair said.

"Not all Seers do, you are aware?" the ancient man said.

"I thought they did," Einar interrupted, with a frown.

"*Nei.* Only the Seers given the gift of drawing forth or killing the soul of the Chrechte beast."

"You can do that?" Artair asked with shock, atavistic fear skittering up his spine.

The thought of losing his wolf too abhorrent for voicing.

"*Ja.* It is a great burden to bear."

"And the *celi di*, do they live as long as the *conriocht*?" Artair asked, not wanting to dwell on the Seer's terrible *gift*.

"If they are mated to them, yes, or what do you call it? Ah, yes, if they are *kelle*."

"Why do some live such long lives, I wonder."

"None know for certain, though we all have our own thoughts on the matter."

Artair nodded but said nothing as a hush fell over the Pride upon entering a giant cavern, a steaming pool in the center. So, water played a part in their ceremonies as well.

For some reason, this little fact gave Artair a sense of peace that had eluded him all morning. This might be the Paindeal ceremony, but at heart it was Chrechte, ancient and *right*.

A man Artair had only met briefly in his time in Greenland, stepped forward. He wore the priest's garb of the Roman church, but his scent was Chrechte. He must be the *celi di*, the Chrechte who oversaw the spiritual welfare of the pride.

Some clans, the Seer was *celi di*, some they were different people, some had only one and not the other.

Though he wore the garb of a priest, the *celi di* did not speak words of Latin, but offered the ancient Chrecht rite of mating.

Einar offered his vows in a voice filled with conviction, his expression leaving none of those present how seriously he took their mating.

Artair found himself just as determined to speak with the conviction to keep his promises that came from the very depth of his soul. This *kotrondmenskr* was his mate. His.

The Chrechte believed that the soul binding lasted through eternity.

Artair knew that whatever eternity might bring, he would be Einar's mate for their lifetimes.

The children were brought forward and recognized officially as belonging to Einar and Artair, their deceased birth parents given recognition and thanksgiving by the Pride for their part in providing heirs to the next *jarl*.

All four, Einar, Artair, Jorgen and Marie, touched the stone together, light swirling around them. At first there were green ribbons from Artair, red from Einar and a soft almost, pink from the children, and then the colors merged, turning a brilliant white. Gasps from those around them told Artair, the small *kotrondmenskr hjart* did not always elicit such an outward reaction to the joining of souls.

"Their mating must be ordained by destiny," Dag said in a reverent tone.

"He's our lord's mate for sure," Olaf agreed with clear satisfaction.

Jorgan looked up at him, his child's gaze filled with wonder. "We're a family now. A real family, *pa*." He looked up at Einar. "*Fadir*."

Marie threw her arms around Artair and started to cry. "My *pa*."

He lifted her in his arms, noticing that Einar had done the same for Jorgen and they embraced each other, so their new, small family were enclosed in a world of their own. The *kotrondmenskr hjart* continued to glow, filling the cavern with a supernatural light that felt entirely benevolent.

After their family moment, the Pride continued with the Chrechte chant of mating as they filed out of the main cavern to congregate elsewhere.

A pile of furs near the pool in the center made it clear that they were expected to consummate their mating here, in this sacred place.

Artair looked up at Einar, knowing the time had come. He was nervous, but not frightened. For so long he'd thought he would *never* have sex and now he would be mated for the rest of his life.

The scent of lust coming off of Einar said that the mating would be a robust one.

"I have no sexual experience except what we've done together," Artair reminded his mate.

Einar's smile was very satisfied. "*Ja.* I know and that makes my tiger very happy."

"You cannot say the same."

"*Nei.* But I will have no other."

"I never want to know who you have been with."

"No one from this island. Only those who have come to trade."

"Even so. My wolf will want to rip their throats out."

A very tiger like purr came out of Einar. "My beast likes your possessiveness."

Artair shook his head. "I think my wolf would like you naked."

"*Ja.* It is time for the sacred rite in the pool."

"What is this sacred rite?" Artair asked.

"We wash one another and make more promises, personal promises to each other."

A thrill of anticipation washed over Artair. "I'm looking forward to it."

Neither said a word, but they moved as one to undress each other.

As Einar released Artair's plaid so it fell to the stone floor, he asked, "How long are you going to wear your clan's colors?"

Artair paused in his own unlacing of Einar's breeches, at first not comprehending what his mate was asking, but realizing that he actually had no plans to stop wearing his kilt.

And that might not be the right answer.

"I did not think about it."

"You pledged your loyalty to our Pride."

"I did."

Einar said nothing, just looked at him, waiting.

Artair frowned, but continued to undress his mate, buying himself time to think. Which might have been the wrong tactic as Einar's naked body had a predictable effect on his own.

Still he tried to put his thoughts into order. "My plaid has always been part of who I am, revealing to everyone where I belong, even when we came on this journey to the land of the Norse and beyond, all who saw me knew I was Scot, if not of the clan Balmoral."

Einar brushed his hand down Artair's smooth chest, brushing his thumb over Artair's nipple and sending shards of pleasure piercing through him. "But now you are part of my family. My mate. *Kotrondmenskr* by pledge, if not by birth."

Artair stared up at his mate, his own hands reaching out instinctively to touch. Einar's big body shuddered at the contact.

Despite how much he wanted to simply lose himself in the pleasure of being naked with his mate, Artair forced himself to consider what Einar had asked. As much as Artair had not thought about what he wore, it was clearly of importance to the man who would one day be *jarl*.

"More importantly, I am yours," Artair said the only truth that mattered to *him* right then.

Einar's blue gaze flared with emotion as he pulled Artair into full body contact with a convulsive grip. "You are mine."

"I am."

"It is time for the pool."

They entered the pool together, their hands clasped, both their erections on full display. But instinctively, Artair knew now was not the time to touch Einar there. They still had a ceremony to perform.

Einar grabbed a bowl filled with dried herbs and sand, using the mixture to wash Artair as he made very personal promises in the ancient tongue of the Chrechte. "I will always honor your body, I will crave no other for succor or satisfaction," Einar vowed.

Artair scooped out a handful of the herbs and sand and used it and rubbed it over Einar's torso and back. "I will treasure my right to touch you as no one else ever will again. I will give you pleasure and only accept pleasure from your body and no other," Artair promised in the same tongue.

Only once every other part of their bodies had been cleansed and Artair shook with the need, did he touch his mate's engorged sex.

It was big, but Artair had no fear of taking Einar into his body. Nor did he question, that this night, at least, that was the way the claiming would go.

Einar groaned at Artair's touch. "*Ja, astin min.* Touch me."

Being called Einar's love did something to Artair's heart, healing the wounds caused by years of past rejection.

"*Mo chridhe.*" Artair grasped Einar's rock-hard cock and caressed it from root to tip. "*Mo toilichte.*"

Einar's purr reminded Artair his mate shared his soul with a tiger. "What does that mean?"

"My heart, my happiness."

Einar's smile was brilliant. "The joy we find in our mating will be without end."

"I believe you." Artair didn't expect it all to be happiness, but how could he not find joy with such a mate? With a man who called him beloved and meant it?

"I want you."

Einar growled, the sound feral and fearsome, before lifting Artair against him. Artair wrapped his legs around his mates hips, leaning forward to lock his lips to Einar's.

Einar returned the kiss with a passion that said he'd been starved for Artair's touch. It had been mere days, but this felt like he'd made Einar wait weeks, or even months, for this claiming.

To be wanted this much was in itself a powerful aphrodisiac.

They were moving and then Einar lowered them, still wet from the sacred springs to the pile of furs beside it.

Artair dropped his legs but spread them in an invitation his mate could not mistake.

Einar's blue eyes were dark with lust, his breaths coming out in harsh pants, his hands curled reflexively and powerfully around Artair's biceps as if Einar was afraid his mate would get up and leave.

No chance of that. "I want you," Artair told him again. "Today and always."

"More than you wanted Gart?" Einar asked, showing a vulnerability Artair would not have guessed at.

They were mates. Both knew that once this claiming was over, neither would ever be capable of physical intimacy with another. Still Einar needed reassurances.

"More. I want you with everything in me and I trust you to want me back," Artair said, his heart telling him how true the words were. "I always pushed away my desire with Gart, but with you I know I can let it burn hotter than the blacksmith's fire. I have never felt anything so consuming. If you do not claim me, I will die."

He didn't care how over the top that sounded, it was exactly how Artair felt. That Einar's touch was necessary to his very breath and beating heart.

Artair's words seemed to release something inside Einar because suddenly the *kotrondmenskr's* hands were everywhere, touching Artair intimately, bringing impossible levels of pleasure. He had not yet even brushed Artair's sex yet, but he felt like exploding, on the verge of climaxing.

Einar nibbled against Artair's small, male nipples and that climax grew ever closer along with the most profound sense of connection Artair had ever felt. Their souls were joining as close as Artair's human and his wolf.

"Please, mate..." But he didn't know what he wanted. To come? To have their bodies joined completely?

To kiss?

All of it.

Artair rocked against his mate, his hardness rubbing against Einar's, sending arrows of pleasure piercing through him.

Einar lifted his head and torso, just a little, enough so their gazes could meet. "You are so beautiful in you pleasure, Artair."

"Men are not beautiful."

"*My* man is."

Artair might have protested again, but Einar thrust down with his hips, increasing the friction of their sexes rubbing together.

Artair groaned and tilted his pelvis up, meeting his mate thrust for thrust.

Einar rolled back onto his haunches, his jaw hewn from granite. "Another time, we will find our pleasure that way, but my tiger demands I be inside you and finish the claiming."

Despite the atavistic fear Artair felt at that irrevocable step, he nodded. "Aye, my wolf demands the same."

"For you to be inside me?" Einar asked, his tone gritty with passion.

"Would you allow that?"

"*Ja*, of course, you are my mate."

"Good to know, but what I want, what I and my wolf need is for you to be inside me and give me the claiming bite."

Einar tipped his head back and roared, the sound pure, alpha tiger. He reached for something in the furs, lifting a small cask Artair had not noticed.

Using his teeth, Einar removed the cork and then spit it out toward the floor of the cave, away from them. Tilting the cask, he poured oil onto Artair's scrotum, letting it run down into his crease.

Then Einar reached down and rubbed the oil all around Artair's sphincter, bringing unexpected pleasure so intense, Artair could do nothing but moan.

Einar wet his fingers with the oil and then pressed one against Artair, pushing until it popped into his most private flesh. The feeling that their bodies were joined in a way that was so incredibly private washed over Artair in waves of bliss. This mating would be complete in every way, Einar would hold nothing back from Artair and Artair would never deny his body to the tiger shifter.

The intrusion of Einar's big finger burned a little, but the pleasure of being touched so intimately was there too.

Einar pressed up and touched something inside Artair that made the wolf shifter shout with pleasure as he arched up from the furs. "What was that?" he demanded with panting breaths.

"Your pleasure spot."

"Men have them?" He thought that was only women.

"We were created one for the other, naturally your body will find pleasure in receiving my sex."

Artair could not answer. He'd lost his ability to speak as Einar added a second finger, rubbing over that pleasure spot over and over again.

"Please, Einar, *mo chridhe*, I need you."

"You are very tight, mate. I need to stretch you more."

Artair shook his head in negation, but when Einar added a third finger, the burn nearly overcame the pleasure and his body acquiesced to his mate's ministrations.

Though his body shook with need and the scent of Einar's permeated the air around them, Artair's mate continued stretching that tiny opening so he could accommodate the very large and now leaking sex of his mate.

Finally, though, Einar removed his hand and shifted so his head pressed against Artair's opening. "It would be easier on you if you turned over," he said in a guttural voice, more tiger than man.

"I want to see you," Artair said, his wolf howling inside him with approval.

"You are sure?" Einar asked, his effort at holding back showing in how rigidly he held himself.

"I am. Join our bodies, Einar."

"I will join our souls."

Artair nodded, no question in his mind or heart that was true.

Einar pressed forward and Artair's body stretched.

"Push out, *astin min*, it will make it easier."

Artair followed his mate's earthy advice and suddenly Einar breached the opening to his body. Pain and pleasure washed over Artair in chills that shook him.

"Are you all right?" Einar asked, his neck chorded with strain.

"I don't know, but you have to move."

Einar pressed further forward and then pulled back, the drag of his flesh inside Artair bringing another level of pleasure.

Einar tilted Artair's body up and pressed forward again, this time managing to touch that amazing pleasure spot inside him. The careful thrusts continued until something inside Artair's body gave way and the burn turned to pure pleasure.

It was as if Einar knew because his movements changed, his thrusts going faster and harder, his body demanding a response from Artair he'd never given.

"You are mine, now and forever," Einar said in a harsh voice that touched Artair deep inside.

"And you are mine."

Einar nodded. "Forever."

The vows they spoke then were in the language of their ancients, the words coming from somewhere deep inside of Artair.

Einar leaned down and suddenly his mouth was on the place where Artair's shoulder and neck met. The bite that followed sent amazing sparks of pleasure arcing through him so big, he could do nothing but follow his own instincts to reach up and bit his mate in the way of claiming.

The moment his teeth drew blood from his mate, their climaxes washed over them, sending them both into a pleasure so intense Artair felt his heart could not withstand the pressure.

My mate. Astin min.

Artair heard the words inside his head.

Forever and always. He said in his own head, speaking to Einar in the way of soul-bound mates, tears burning his eyes.

He let them fall, feeling no shame in the profundity of this moment.

Einar brushed the moisture from Artair's temple. "You are so precious to me, mate."

"I know."

Einar was still hard inside him though they had climaxed and Artair knew their lovemaking was not finished.

"My one true mate," he said aloud. *Mo chridhe,* he said in his mind.

They spent the rest of the night making love and affirming the connection of their souls. Artair could not believe how he experienced his mate's feelings, not just the words they shared in their minds. Their connection was so strong, he had no doubts that Einar was the Chrechte destiny had truly intended to be his mate.

He was so grateful to Gart for the years of rejection and told Einar so.

"You truly feel this?" Einar demanded as they held one another in the early hours of the morning they were to return to the longhouse.

"I think meeting you would have broken the bond between Gart and me, even if we'd claimed each other." Artair's connection with Einar was that powerful.

"It is supposed to be impossible, but I believe that as well."

Later, Artair felt no grief at all when he packed away his plaid and donned the clothes Einar had gifted him with. The wool tunic under the leather jerkin and the leather breaches were warmer, but more importantly, they marked Artair as part of Einar's people, a Scottish clansman no longer.

"You look very handsome in those clothes," Einar said, the heat in his blue gaze giving truth to the claim.

"They feel right."

Einar's smile was breathtaking.

"Now, you look like my *pa*," their son said to Artair, as he and his younger sister came into the cavern.

Artair smiled. "That is a good thing since you are my son." He turned to Marie. "And you are my daughter."

She giggled, the sound so good to hear from the quiet child. "My *fadir* and my *pa*," she said with clear possession for Einar and Artair.

And their little family stayed close together on the return journey to their village.

***

Neilina ran in her human form with Dionach, weighted down with her weapons, she pushed her body to its limits, knowing the very safety of the Chrechte she had met since leaving her island could depend on Neilina's fighting stamina.

She had lost those who depended on her once because she had not been ready. That would never happen again.

Nay, not even an *asmundr* would be able to defeat Neilina now.

Though if she were to believe him, her mate would be on *her* side in the battles ahead.

Not that he treated her like a mate. Oh, he claimed their daughter, Freya as his and had insisted on spending time training the younger woman *as his right as her father*. But he did not seek any level of intimacy with Neilina.

While the Balmorals and Sinclairs searched the island for any hiding Fearghall, Neilina and Haakon trained with their soldiers, pushing both Chrechte and human to their best for the war to come.

Their styles of training and fighting were surprisingly complimentary, but Haakon never tried to leverage that rapport into something more.

There was no longer a sword in the ground between them, but the divide was there all the same. In her deepest heart, Neilina knew that if she needed him, Haakon would be there, to help her, to protect her, she who never needed another's protection.

Hadn't he already proven that?

But it was as if he had given up finally and forever on her mating.

And it was only now, that he had done so, Neilina realized that was not what she wanted. Her feelings for his father were still bordering on hatred, but Haakon's very presence here on Balmoral Island was proof he was not like the *asmundr* who had trained him.

Haakon had pledged his full allegiance to the *drago ri* just as Neilina had done. He had also acknowledged to Freya, when she had asked, that Haakon did not anticipate ever seeing his homeland again.

His murdering father would never have done as much.

As if her thoughts had conjured him, the scent of Haakon approaching came to her on the wind. She looked back over her shoulder and saw him running, his powerful legs straining the leather of his breeches.

Now *there* was a man who would look good in a kilt, if there ever was one.

Neilina nearly stumbled in her sure strides at such a thought. Aye, she'd softened toward him, but this sensual awareness was something so outside her experience, she did not know what to do with it.

She wanted to touch and be touched. She wanted him to want *her*.

Of their own volition, her legs first slowed and then she stopped entirely.

Waiting for Haakon to reach her.

Dionach ran on for only a few steps before growling in inquiry.

"All is well, dear friend," she told the bear, knowing the animal would understand her intent, if not the words.

A gift of the stone after she'd bonded the bear to her.

Haakon reached them and stopped a respectful distance away, but it felt more like a deliberate attempt to maintain their divide between them.

"Where is Freya?" Neilina asked him, trying very hard to ignore the arousal that burned inside her.

"She wanted to visit with the *celi di*."

"By *visit* you mean ask a hundred questions." Neilina smiled wryly.

Haakon shrugged his broad shoulders. "Ciara does not seem to mind."

"Nay." She stepped closer to him, needing nearness more than she needed air. "Is there need of me back at the keep?"

His blue gaze widened, but he did not move back. "Not that I am aware of."

"What are you doing chasing me down?" She asked, so confused by the feelings he elicited in her, she was cranky with it.

"I thought we could run together."

"Oh."

"That is all. Oh? No, I'd rather run with pigs, or similar?" he asked sardonically.

She wanted to say so many things, wanted to reach out and touch him, but forced herself to hold it all in and simply asked, "If you thought I would react in that fashion, why come after me?"

His eyes narrowed in unmistakable censure. "Can you really ask me that?"

"But I thought..." She let her voice trail off, not sure she wanted to admit she'd been thinking about their mating.

About their joining. About joining again. About *not* being alone in this world, but for a daughter who would die too soon, no matter what old age she reached.

"What did you think? That my beast does not crave you every second of every day," he demanded, moving so close the energy from their bodies mingled. "I know we will never be mates, but neither am I willing to drive my beast to madness if I can help it."

Wonder filled Neilina. "Your beast craves me."

She'd thought he no longer wanted her.

And it had hurt.

Even more because she knew she'd brought his disinterest on herself by refusing to separate him from the actions of his father.

"As yours does me," Haakon said with no doubt in his voice.

She inclined her head, in no mood to deny it. "So, you want to run with me and Dionach?"

"I do." Haakon nodded to the bear, giving her due respect.

"I would like that."

His brows rose in surprise at her admission, but he said nothing.

They ran for nearly an hour, his pace pushing her own as no other had since she shifted to *conriocht* for the first time.

They were a distance from the keep, when Neilina and Haakon both slowed to a walk in natural accord. "The search for possible enemies goes slowly," Haakon said.

"I wish we could help."

"But we do not know these people. How would we know who belongs on this island, and who does not? Besides, with the Balmoral and his second joining in the search, we are needed for training the soldiers as they come off their shifts of searching."

She nodded. "I have never trained anyone besides Freya. I enjoy it." And that surprised her.

"You are a natural teacher."

She laughed in disbelief. Because as much as she might find unexpected pleasure in the company of her fellow Chrechte and sharing her abilities with them, she had a hard time believing the soldiers she trained liked her methods. "I put them on their backs over and over again. How is that naturally teaching?"

Amusement flickered in his clear blue eyes. "Humility is part of learning to protect others."

"Is it?" She hadn't noticed Haakon being all that humble.

"You do not think I am modest?" he asked, proving once again their minds traveled the same paths more often than not.

"I hadn't noticed as such no."

"Trust me, a decade of rejection from the mate ordained to be mine by destiny is enough to humble any man. Even *asmundr*."

She laid her hand on his arm. "I am sorry."

He stopped walking, the shock coming off him a stringent scent to her nostrils.

She wrinkled her nose. "You need not be so surprised. Surely you realized that our meeting under the circumstances we have would change things between us."

Okay, maybe even *she* hadn't realized that, but he seemed to understand male-female relationships better than she did.

"You are saying that things between us have changed?" he asked, his tone filled with disbelief.

"Aye."

"In what way, Neilina, have they changed?" he demanded, his tone harsh.

"I do not hate you." *I want you. I don't want to lose my mate.*

The stone-like cast of his features softened by the tiniest degree. "I'm not sure you ever did, but of a certainty you hated the idea of being my mate."

"You are an honorable Chrechte." She met his gaze letting him see in her own just how much she believed that.

There were other messages there if he wanted to read them too.

"You mean that?"

She nodded, unable to the do the one thing she wanted more than anything in that moment.

Kiss him.

She craved such intimacy with him like she'd never craved anything else in this hundreds years long life.

"That is a gift I never expected to receive from you."

She stared at him in incomprehension.

"Your respect."

She swallowed. "I do respect you."

"I respect you as well, *conriocht*."

"How can you? You know my failure."

"Do you not realize yet that even the best trained *conriocht* could not defeat an *asmundr*? Even in blood lust."

"I could. Now." She was sure of it.

"Perhaps you could at that, *kelle*."

"Don't!"

"Don't what?"

"Be kind to me."

"You are my mate. It is not in me to hurt you."

"But I have rejected you." Over and over again.

"*Ja*. And as much as that has hurt, I understand your reasons for doing so. Had your father destroyed my family and all those I had sworn to protect, I do not know I would have done any differently."

"You do not mean that." How could he be so understanding? So forgiving, when she had been anything but?

"I do not lie and your senses tell you that even if you do not believe my words alone."

"No, you do not lie."

Haakon turned and started toward the keep again, feeling that it would be greedy to want more than she had already given him. Two boons she had denied him for ten years.

Her respect and her trust, at least in his honesty. It was a crack in the wall around her heart he'd believed impenetrable.

CHAPTER TEN

Later, both Haakon and Neilina joined Lachlan and Talorc in interrogating Drustin's cousin, Cleland, the young wolf who had given his allegiance to the Fearghall before returning to live with his family on Balmoral Island.

But it soon became apparent that the wolf would rather die than betray his cohorts.

Neilina stepped forward. "If you will permit me?" she asked the Balmoral laird.

He jerked his head in an angry nod and stepped back.

The young soldier laughed and spat at Neilina, his spittle landing on the floor by her feet. "As if a woman could intimidate me."

Her laughter was chilling. "You think not?"

Suddenly claws sprouted from her fingers and she wrapped them around his throat, drawing blood with the sharp points. "Listen to me carefully, you foolish child." She moved her hold on him until her claws dug into his shoulder, breaking skin and more blood flowing. "I could cut that which holds your arms to your shoulders without killing you, but the pain? Will be unimaginable."

He went pale as limestone.

But she was not done.

Neilina reached under his kilt and the pain on his face said her touch to his nether regions was anything but pleasurable. "I could castrate you with a single twist of my wrist."

She tilted her head back, sniffing the air. "Do you smell that blood? It is yours, but so little of it. I could make much more."

The smell of piss mixed with blood and Neilina's expression twisted with disgust as she withdrew her hand, wiping the moisture on the man's tunic.

"Let me loose of these shackles and we'll see what you can do to me, unnatural bitch! Demoness!"

Neilina's smile was all fierce, warrior's glee. "Remove his shackles. It is time this stupid boy learned to fear."

Though he was well past the age of being considered a man, he was nothing but a boy to one who had lived as long as she had.

The Balmoral and the Sinclair were looking at Neilina with a mix of awe and concern, but all Haakon felt was a healthy dose of lust and pride.

She turned to him, rolling her eyes. "Truly? You are aroused right now."

"My mate is stronger than other Chrechte, male, or female." He shrugged away any judgment of that fact. "My beast finds that unbearably exciting."

Haakon grabbed the keys and let loose the young Chrechte male from his shackles. "You will rue asking her for this," he promised the soldier who had betrayed not only his people, but *his family.*

Cleland tried to dive for Neilina, but she had him subdued so quickly, her movements were a blur. Then she did the unexpected, at least it was to everyone else in the room, if the scent of fear mixed with shock was anything to go by.

Neilina grabbed the boys balls and twisted, her nails once again imbedded in his flesh. He howled, but could not shift in his pain.

"You can die with your balls, like a man, or as a eunuch, but you will tell me what you know about the plans to murder so many of your brethren."

She must have let up the pressure with her hand because the disloyal soldier started to sob babbling that he did not know anything. She tightened her hand again and he screamed, the sound painful to hear. "Do not lie to me."

"Bring Eirik. He cannot lie in the dragon's presence," the Balmoral said.

"Nay," Neilina barked, anger sparking the air around her like a fire built with pitchy wood. "Our king has enough to contend with. This betrayer will tell us what he knows."

"You're supposed to try to convert me," Cleland sobbed. "If we are found out, you are supposed to try to convert us. The lairds are too weak to kill without remorse."

"Like your leaders, who have lost their souls to their hatred?" Lachlan demanded, fury filling his voice.

"I am *conriocht*," Neilina informed the ignorant soldier. "My life is forfeit to the protection of the Chrechte. *You* are a threat to that protection."

"I am too young to die."

The fool, who could betray those he'd promised his allegiance, should have considered how many more years of life he wanted before doing so. "Old enough to pledge false allegiance once. Why should we give you another chance?"

Haakon did not have the compassionate desire to *save* Chrechte who had forfeited their honor already.

"There will be no chances," Neilina decreed before Cleland could answer. "The only question is how much pain you will endure before you die."

Talorc looked like he was going to interfere and Haakon growled at him, allowing the full power of his *asmundr* nature to fill the air around them.

The two lairds and their seconds took defensive stances and Haakon wanted to bang their heads together.

Incredibly, Neilina laughed. "They do not understand yet, just how far you will go to protect them."

"But you do?"

"We are the same. Guardians."

"So are they."

"But they do not know what that means in its entirety. Not yet. They still think in terms of clans and differentiate between the Faol, the Ean and the Paindeal."

"The Ean live amongst us," Talorc said with affront.

"Please!" Cleland cried out. "Stop her."

Neilina hadn't let up on the pain inducing grip on the young man's scrotum. She flipped him with no sign of effort and backhanded him, the sound of flesh hitting flesh having a different quality than when the laird had tried to get the soldier to talk earlier.

There were too many scents in the air now that had all their beasts on edge.

Blood. Urine. Terror. Anger. Disgust.

"No one is going to stop me, you cur. You would kill babies, their mothers and the fathers who try to protect them. There is no limit to your evil."

"I don't want to kill children!"

"But you will. They are not Fearghall either."

"It cannot be helped. We would spare the children if we could." The soldier sniffled, his attitude much more the boy she called him than the man his age proclaimed, wiping at his face, but clearly cowed.

Still Neilina did not relax, her battle-ready tension obvious to any who would look. And if she was in the room? Of course Haakon was looking.

"Why can it not be helped?" She asked in a silky voice that sent shivers down Haakon's spine.

He could only imagine what it did to the weak betrayer under her power.

The boy shook his head.

Haakon considered a moment and then guessed. "Because your plan to kill cannot distinguish between the young and the old."

A spike in the scent of fear permeating the room marked how accurate Haakon's guess had been.

"Poison," Neilina said, her voice reflecting all the horror she felt. "But how? My vision had too many deaths to be from a single meal. Only some of the clan eats in the keep, but the deaths were all over the island."

"Do you have a well, or stream used by most, or all of your people?" Once, many years before, a dead and diseased animal had fallen into one of the wells of Haakon's former home.

Great distress and illness followed until they discovered the problem. Two of the aged and three human children had died before the contamination had been discovered.

The Balmoral's eyes filled with horror while Talorc cursed so creatively, Haakon couldn't help being impressed.

The young soldier was trying to deny it, screaming at them that they didn't know anything. But his very reaction revealed how right they were.

"Who? Who is going to poison my people?" Lachlan asked, this time it was his claws at the young soldier's throat.

"I don't know. I don't know. I don't know."

As annoying as the repeated declarations were, they also rang with truth. This man deluded by his bigotry didn't know who the other traitors were.

It wasn't Neilina that castrated the boy, but Lachlan and Talorc who ripped out the wolf's throat. "We will send his body to the Fearghall clan we know of as a warning. The alphas will not suffer such murderers to live."

Neilina's head whipped around. "You know of a clan that gives succor to a known Fearghall pack?"

"Aye," Lachlan said, his mouth twisted with distaste.

"And they live, why?"

"Because we are not them." Anger hardened Talorc's voice. "We do not kill without mercy."

"There is also the small matter that it is a lowland clan with ties to the English king. War with England must wait until we have dealt with more pressing matters," Lachlan offered with a frown.

Haakon almost laughed at the laird's arrogant dismissal of the country with thousands of warriors to their hundreds, but he did not. He liked it and had no desire to offend.

Neilina walked out of the tower room without another word.

"She is ruthless," Lachlan said admiringly.

"She is, but now she grieves." How Haakon knew this, he could not have told them, but he had no doubt his mate grieved the death of the Chrechte.

"He was too lost to his cause."

"*Ja*. He was, but the loss of life in one only a few years into his manhood is always cause of grief."

The two lairds and their seconds nodded in agreement, their countenances stoic but for the sadness in all their gazes.

They too grieved.

Haakon inclined his head and left to find his mate. To do what, he was not sure.

Before today he would have been certain she would not take comfort from him, but now? He simply did not know.

It took him time to track her scent because he did not want to shift to improve his ability to do so. Was not sure she would ever be ready to meet his *asmundr* form. Unlike the conriocht, he had no lesser cat to shift into.

It was the prehistoric behemoth, or nothing.

But an *asmundr* still in human form and in blood lust was as fierce as the *conriocht* form. Not that he planned to ever share that fact with his skittish mate.

Neilina was in a cave with her bear, silent tears tracking down her cheeks.

188 • Lucy Monroe

She stared up at Haakon as he walked into the cavern, her scent and the bears mixed with decaying leaves from near the entryway and the smell of earth. "He was too young to die."

"And the children he would have helped kill are even younger. His leaders have no mercy. They knew the risk to him being discovered as Fearghall and sent him in to spy anyway."

"Perhaps he could have been saved."

"You smelled his scent. He never wavered in his hatred and certainty."

"But he could have." She looked up at him with tear drenched green eyes, filled with grief. "I have wavered in mine."

And he was grateful for it. "But you do not have a heart that *wants* to hate. He did. He enjoyed thinking himself superior and even though he said he didn't want to kill children, he felt no remorse at the thought of the many who would die from the poison."

"We don't know what the poison is, or who is supposed to poison the well."

"We don't know if it is a well, either." Haakon pointed out. "The Balmoral did not say."

"But…"

"Whatever the water source, you can be certain Lachlan will have it guarded from this time forward."

She nodded.

"We might not be able to tell what Chrechte belong on this island and which do not, but we can search for the poison. You with your long life and me with the knowledge of my forebearers given to me by the stone, we have a better chance of recognizing it than most."

"You were gifted with more knowledge than navigation?" she asked, wiping at the moisture on her cheeks.

"I was."

"Oh."

He said nothing. Not sure what she wanted to hear right now. She seemed like she needed something from him, but she did not ask for it and he did not know what it might be.

Neilina sighed, the sound so forlorn he wanted to snatch her up and hold her in his lap to comfort like a child. "I need to give you back your sun stone."

"So it traveled with you, from the other place?" he asked, awed.

But maybe he should not have been so surprised. After all, the stone had disappeared from his pouch when he woke.

"It did." She bit her lip in a wholly uncharacteristic gesture. "Something else traveled with me."

"What?" he asked, perplexed. He'd given her nothing else.

"Your seed."

He could not have stifled his shocked gasp under any circumstances. "My seed?"

She nodded. "I woke with it and my maiden's head blood mixed on my thighs."

"But then...are you pregnant?"

"I do not know. It is too early for a heartbeat to be discerned from my own and I cannot tell if my own scent has changed. It is too much a part of me. If Freya were Chrechte, she would know."

He realized he did not know either. Any difference in her scent to him could be attributed to the difference between the place of *other* and actually being in her real physical proximity.

"I do not understand how what happened in that place of other can be real."

"I do not know, but one thing I am certain about my scent. It is now mixed with yours."

"I thought that was just us being sacred mates."

She shook her head. "No. We did not claim each other but we are bound as surely as if we had."

"We were bound before that night." He had tried to tell her, but she had never wanted to hear.

"Yes, we were. If we had not been, I could never have trusted you enough to let you into my body."

Because his father, *asmundr* like Haakon, had killed her entire pack.

He sat down beside her, and she did not move away. Not sure he was doing the right thing, but unable to stop himself, Haakon put his arm around her shoulders and pulled Neilina to him.

She collapsed into him like she'd been waiting for this very thing and he wrapped his other arm around her.

"If I'm pregnant, I don't want my child to die."

"We will not let that happen."

"But these Fearghall, they are worse than your father ever was. They want to destroy all Faol who do not follow their beliefs and all Éan just for existing."

Her belief that there were Chrechte worse than his father was nearly as shocking as the way his mate accepted the comfort of his touch.

"There have always been evil men."

"Aye, I remember McAlpin's betrayal."

"I have heard the story from my father." His dislike of the wolves had been intense, even though Haakon had not realized it, and the way McAlpin had betrayed his own race was a story Haakon's father had been only too happy to tell.

"Your race, and even the royal descendants, survived his attempt to kill any who might threaten his right to the human throne."

She sat back, her emerald gaze filled with worry. "You are saying we will survive again."

"*Ja.*"

"But not without casualties. The Faol survived your father's marauding ways, but they went more than two centuries without a *conriocht* among them." She frowned, looking away. "But perhaps that is as much my fault as his."

"You were grieving."

"For two centuries?"

"Your fear of letting your people down again was too big to overcome." He tilted her head up and drew her gaze to his again. "Until the time came for you to step into the gap."

"How many perished because I abdicated my place among my people?"

"If Bjorn had faced you again in battle, he would have killed you." He'd killed the other *conriocht*.

And that knowledge was a burden Haakon would have to carry for the rest of his many years of life.

"You feel as badly about that as I do about hiding in my forest home for so long."

"Worse, as you did nothing to hurt your fellow Chrechte."

"Neither did you."

"He was *my* father." And as ashamed of those horrific actions Haakon was, he still loved his father.

Bjorn the Destroyer had become Bjorn the Protector and he had loved his son, training Haakon to be the best *asmundr* he could.

"And you have redeemed the honor of the *asmundr*."

That claim hit Haakon like a blacksmith's anvil.

"You believe this?" he asked in shock.

She nodded.

"Neilina." That was all he could say. Her name.

After ten years of her vilifying him, her sudden approval had both him and his beast in shock. And filled with lust like never before.

"I do not want to spend the next two hundred years alone." The longing in her tone was too much for Haakon to ignore.

He pulled his beautiful mate, weapons and all, into his lap and kissed her with all the tenderness he had ever wanted to give her.

Her lips parted against his, a soft sound coming from her.

The kiss went on and on, their souls merging as they had only done once before. As he had never expected to experience again.

She moaned against his lips, her body pressing into his, like she was trying to crawl inside him. And he understood.

Her wolf needed the full connection of their joining as much as his own tiger gone from history.

She began undressing him, no hesitation, no maidenly timidity.

Not his warrior princess.

She broke the kiss, pulling back and tugging on his leather jerkin. "Get this off," she demanded in a growl that would have done her wolf proud.

He nodded, yanking at his clothes and weapons with little care for seams or scuffing scabbards. Though, he was *asmundr,* so he placed the weapons within easy reaching distance.

Fully naked, he pulled her to him for another scorching kiss, that melted through the ice that had formed in his soul over the past ten years.

Then he was helping her take off her weapons and clothes, her hands as eager as his in removing every barrier between them.

Cupping her luscious breasts, he deepened the kiss, the scent of her arousal mixing with his own, a heady fragrance that only added to the needy lust driving him.

"I want you," he growled. "Need to be inside you."

"Yes." She grabbed his hand and tugged him deeper into the cave. They entered the chamber she had been using to sleep since arriving on Balmoral island. Two pallets of furs were on either side of the small cave.

The mixed scents would have told him that Freya slept here if he didn't already know. *He* had spent his nights on the ground outside the cave, protecting that which he considered his own.

Dropping down to the furs, her beautiful body on full display. Her nipples jutted from the feminine mounds of her breasts, enticing him to touch and taste. Dark curls covered her most intimate place, taunting him. Her long legs moved restlessly, making him crave those very same legs wrapped around his hips as he joined their bodies.

She reached up and pulled him, a silent invitation.

Neilina led him to her pallet to join her, but he resisted.

"What is it?" she asked. "Don't you want me?" Her gaze filled with wounded uncertainty.

The vulnerability in the usually invulnerable woman was not something he could let stand.

"Of course I want you, mate, but I will retrieve our weapons first."

Her eyes widened in shock. "I didn't even think of them." She looked around herself, her gaze focusing in a way it had not before, her expression not a good one. "I can't... This is..."

But he would not let her retreat. This was meant to be, and she knew it. "What we have both needed for more than ten years, princess."

"But I *never* forget my weapons."

"It is all right to trust me with your safety, Neilina. Your wolf knows this, so you did not think of it." How could she still be so ignorant of that basic truth?

"My wolf trusts you." Neilina shook her head as if trying to understand it. "She *does*. Even with Dionach on watch, I don't forget my weapons."

"Dionach has been a good companion to you, but she is not your mate." He made no effort to soften his tone. It was time Neilina accepted that she was his to protect. Always. "I *am* the only one you will ever trust this deeply."

"Do you trust me?" She laid there proudly naked, her beautiful green eyes challenging him.

"*Ja*. But mate, I am *asmundr* and that means my deepest, most primal instinct is to protect. And because you *are* my mate, that instinct is even stronger when I am with you."

"But I am *conriocht*. I *never* forget my weapon."

"But even a *conricocht* can know with certainty that will give your beast peace that this *asumundr* will always protect you. *And* that I *can* protect you."

"Your father really let down his own nature, didn't he?" she asked in a sort of wonder.

The pain of that truth pierced, even in this moment of knowing that finally his mate would bond with him completely. "He did."

"But you never have."

"Never."

She nodded. "Get our weapons."

He made quick work of retrieving not only their weapons, but all their clothes as well.

He left Dionach guarding the entrance to the cave. Though the bear looked to be napping in the sunshine, her position in front of the opening that would prevent any from entry told its own story.

When Haakon returned to the sleeping chamber, he stopped to take in the sight of his perfect, proud and too alluring mate in all her naked glory.

No blush indicated embarrassment at his appraisal and he smiled. "You were made for me."

"As you were for me." She was doing her own looking and if the heated expression in her emerald gaze was anything to go by, she very much liked what she saw.

His tiger roared inside him, insisting they join with their mate.

Scars that announced her as warrior, marked her body. Her muscles were honed so that he could not doubt that she trained as hard as he did to protect their people.

"You are so beautiful," he told her. "Ideal for me."

"I am marred by scars." From battle with his father, she did not add.

But still, it was a silent knowledge between them.

"Your scars mark you as protector of your people. Nothing could be more beautiful to me."

"You really mean that." She said with some wonder. "You are not bothered I dress like a warrior."

He knew that some of the clan Chrechte found Neilina an uncomfortable presence among them. She was too confident. Too powerful for those not yet certain of their own place in the world.

But to him? She was everything a woman should be.

"I find everything about you perfect. You are *conriocht*. How else would you dress?"

"Right now, I am not dressed at all," she said in a low voice, filled with seduction.

He had no words as his body reacted with such intensity, he could barely stand.

"Come to me," she invited, her hand out.

He needed no second invitation and joined her on the furs, his hard as granite shaft sliding against her hip as he lay down beside her.

A groan tore out of him, the pleasure of touching her so intimately too good to deny.

She reached down and grasped his hard flesh, her fingers exploring with a lack of hesitation he found even more arousing.

"I cannot believe I have already had this inside me."

"It was not without pain," he said. He had not forgotten a single moment of their time together and even now wished he could have spared her the pain of first penetration.

"It was also not without pleasure." Her smile was all feminine allure.

He could do nothing but kiss her in that moment, his tongue taking possession of her mouth as she gasped against his lips. She kissed him back with intent, her lips sliding against his own, her tongue tangling with his.

He cupped her nape with one hand, the other journeying down her body to map curves he had craved for too long. Her nipple beaded against his hand as he cupped her breast. He brushed his thumb back and forth over it, loving how it grew harder and more erect in her passion.

She pulled her head back, panting. "That feels so good."

"This will feel even better," he promised before dropping his mouth over the tender bud and suckling.

She moved her body against his, sounds of pleasure spilling from her mouth.

He kept up his ministrations even as he rubbed himself against her hip.

"I want you inside me before you climax, mate," she warned in a tone that said she would not be denied.

Pure pleasure at the demand arced through him and he shifted so he was over her. Her thighs spread, making it clear this was exactly what she wanted.

He moved so his leaking erection rubbed against her clitoris, bringing them both pleasure. She cried out and he groaned around her nipple.

He could come this way, *would* climax if he didn't have a care. She was so perfect for him, like living fire.

"Yes, Haakon! That is so good."

He agreed, but like her, he wanted more. He moved down her body, intent on having more and more and more.

Her protest cut off mid rant when his mouth closed over the most private flesh between her legs. Her scent was like almonds, but so damn sexual, his beast roared with need inside Haakon.

He tasted her, taking in her essence and giving his beast some of what the tiger needed. Haakon tongued her clitoris until she was bucking against him, soft cries of desire sounding around them.

He pressed a finger inside her and she arced up with a shout. "What are you doing to me, Viking?"

Moments later, he slipped two fingers inside, helping soft tissues to adjust for his possession, but also seeking that sweet spot inside her.

She screamed and he knew he had found it.

He brought her to climax, needing this time between them to be nothing but pleasure. No pain for her body.

When she came, moisture gushed from her and he lapped at it, thoroughly enjoying this proof of her body's reaction to him.

Neilina tried to be upset that he had not listened to her about coming inside her, but the pleasure still pouring through her body would not let her.

And she trusted him.

Trusted that the mind-altering pleasure she had just experienced was not all there was.

196 • Lucy Monroe

Her trust was justified only moments later when he began anew, touching her in ways that led to increased arousal, building the pleasure inside her until she was once again on the verge of explosion.

Only then did he surge up and press his big member against the opening of her body.

But he did not push inside. He stopped, his neck corded with tension. "Are you ready?"

"Yes, Viking, I'm ready."

"I will claim you with my bite this time," he warned her.

She met his gaze and realized this was more than the sex she had expected. He had taken her admission that she did not want to spend the next centuries alone to heart.

"I will not love you," she warned him, her own words causing her pain in the region of her heart, but ignoring *that* pain.

He winced, but that was all. No anger emanated off of him. "I cannot make the same promise, but you will be my mate."

"I am already your mate," she admitted.

His blue gaze flared with heat and something else. Absolute satisfaction.

"*Ja.* You are."

"I will bite you too," she warned.

His smile was all predatory male. "I would have it no other way."

"Then join our bodies, mate." She tilted her hips provocatively.

He growled and pressed forward, sliding inside so much easier than the last time, but still he went slowly. So very slowly.

And there could be no doubt that to do so cost him. His big Viking's body was rigid with his effort, his gorgeous face set in fierce concentration.

If the first time had been entirely at her pace, this time he was in control of the timing. And every move of his hips showed just how measured that was going to be.

This would be no quick mating, with pleasure the only goal.

He was taking possession of her soul as surely as he was giving her ownership of his. And the latter terrified her.

To be responsible for another on such a deep level after how she had let her own family and pack down was not something she had ever wanted.

"I can't do this," she voiced her fear.

He stopped immediately, the grimace of pain that caused him right there for her to see. "We will stop. Just give me a moment."

But she wrapped her legs around his hips, stopping him from pulling back. "No."

"Damn it, princess, please..."

His vulnerability with her was almost as frightening as the responsibility for his soul. Or perhaps it was all part of the same thing.

"I don't want to stop."

"Then what did you mean?" he asked through gritted teeth as he held his body immobile over her.

"Be responsible for you."

His smile reached inside her and warmed the ice around her heart, melting walls that had taken two centuries to build. "We will be responsible for each other."

"What if I cannot protect you?"

"I will never allow you to lose me as you did your pack, *elskan min*."

"You cannot make such a vow."

"I can. I do."

"You are so arrogant."

His laughter warmed the very air around her. "This is something I think we have in common."

"What if I fail you?"

"Have you ever failed Dìonach?"

"She's a bear."

"Have you failed her?" he pressed, no give in his voice or hard body poised so rigidly above her.

"Nay."

"Have you ever failed Freya?"

"I almost did. If not for you, we would have died."

"It is because *you* are my mate that you did not."

"I am not afraid." The acrid scent of the lie revealed the truth to the both of them.

"I am."

She stared up at him. "You are afraid of nothing."

"I am terrified I will not be enough for you. You are so damn independent, powerful enough to protect these packs without my help. But I will never allow it," he warned, like he thought she'd get ideas.

"I need you," she admitted.

"And when you don't? Will you reject me again, send me away from you?"

"Nay. I could never do that."

"Then you cannot fail me."

Moisture burned her eyes, but she blinked it away. "I want to believe you."

"Then believe." And he started moving again, pressing deep into her body on the next thrust. "Believe, my princess."

As she opened her body to her mate, Neilina chose to believe in her own strength and for the first time in too long, opened her heart to hope.

Their joining was even more incredible than before. There was no pain. Only pleasure. No sense of doom hanging over Neilina despite her visions.

Nothing but a profound sense their two souls merging as one would change everything.

Everything for her.

And everything for those she was meant to protect.

Together, she and Haakon could and would protect those in their care.

Her thoughts splintered as the pleasure in her body wound tighter and tighter, his soul caressing her own even as their bodies joined.

Haakon stopped moving and she cried out in protest, but he waited until she met his gaze.

"Are you ready for my bite?"

"Aye." No hesitation could live in this profound moment so filled with power.

He started moving again and she thrust up, building the passion between them, drawing his body's unfettered reaction with her own.

He made a primal sound that had to come straight from his beast's soul and dropped his head, his mouth pressing against the join of her shoulder in an open-mouthed kiss.

Her entire body suffused with pleasure, even as something moved inside her that she had never felt before. It was her wolf, but her beast as Neilina had never experienced it. Ferocious and satisfied, powerful and filled with knowledge that was beyond Neilina's many years.

And then he bit her, his teeth too sharp for a human, but he had not shifted. She felt her skin break under sharp canines with no pain, only a dark, primitive pleasure her beast approved of completely.

And as Neilina came apart with pleasure, she reached up and bit into the flesh where Haakon's shoulder met his neck, his blood filling her mouth as sweet as any nectar.

Green and red lights glowed around them, mixing together until white light filled the cavern. They had not spoken Chrechte vows and yet, as she screamed with her climax, her soul joined with his in infinite connection.

The stone walls around them melted away and suddenly they were surrounded by Chrechte whose backs were to Neilina and Haakon, joined in the deepest of intimacies.

These Chrechte were strangely familiar and suddenly she realized they were her pack. Her parents. Her grandparents. The *celi di* and alpha. All of them were there, chanting the ancient words of the Chrechte mating.

Her pleasure mixed with joy so intense tears burned a path down her temples as they had not done in two centuries. "Haakon," she said in an awed whisper.

He lifted his head from where he'd bitten her and turned it one way and the other to take in those surrounding them. "They have come to bless our mating."

He stiffened and she turned her head to see what, or who, he was looking at.

Even though his back was to them, there could be no mistaking the *asmundr* standing beside the wolves he had killed.

Haakon's father.

Neilina reached up and gripped Haakon's face gently, turning his head so their eyes met again. "They have *all* come to bless our mating. It is a gift."

His own beautiful blue eyes were awash with moisture, but he nodded.

Then Haakon spoke, promising her all that her soul could ever long for in the tongue of the ancients.

She said her vows with a joyful knowledge that this moment had been ordained by destiny. God had given her a second chance to be as he'd created her to be. *Conriocht.* Divine protector. *Kelle.*

Haakon found completion with a roar that would have shattered stone.

When he finished, they drew apart with gentle touches and he made sure she was covered by her cloak from neck to ankle, but only took the time to put on his own breeches before he touched the shoulder of the *celi di.*

It was if the entire assembly received the sign, because they all turned to face them, their faces suffused with joy.

"We thank you for coming to bless our mating," Haakon said to the *celi di.*

The spiritual leader smiled in her gentle way. "We could not have come if the power between you two was not so great."

"There has not been a mating such as yours since many centuries before my own birth," Bjorn, the Slayer, pronounced.

"You are both blessed by the sight, though it is more powerful in Neilina," her *celi di* added.

Her mother's eyes were filled with such approval. "You are *kelle.*"

"I failed you all," she admitted the truth that had haunted her for two centuries.

"*Nei.*" Bjorn denied fervently. "You fought with courage and a willingness to die for your people. It was I who failed those I was born to protect, turning my strength against the very beings I was meant to keep safe."

She could not deny those words, but still... "If I had been stronger—"

"You failed no one," the *celi di* said with certainty.

Her alpha stepped forward and laid a hand on her shoulder, which caused Haakon to growl. "It was our time, *kelle.* One life is meant to be lived until old age and another ends in the cradle. The pain is for those left behind, but you did not fail. I was proud of you every day you were under my care as pack and I am even more proud now."

"How can you say that? I've hidden from my responsibilities for so long."

"You have taken up the mantle of *kelle* once again. You and your mate have already made the difference."

"What do you mean?"

"The Fearghall will not succeed in their murderous intent. You will not only stop them poisoning the Balmoral, but sharing your wisdom has already insured they will finally ferret out the remaining of the Fearghall among them."

"You are certain."

"I am certain." He indicated his grandmother, the Seer that had been in their pack for longer than Bjorn had been *asmundr*. "She has spoken."

The old woman came forward, her steps slow, but her eyes glowing with timeless knowledge. She reached out and took Neilina's hand, then reached for Haakon's clasping them together. "By this mating shall all Chrechte be saved. You have spoken your allegiance to the *Dragon Ri* and by so doing, brought the ways of the ancients back to your people. This will save the lives of not hundreds, not thousands, but tens of thousands of Chrechte into the future."

She tapped their hands. "You will have children and those children will serve their people as you do. Bring your oldest daughter to the stone and she will have her first shift at the next new moon."

Could she be saying what Neilina thought. "Freya?"

The old woman nodded. "Your eldest." But her look was for both Neilina and Haakon, making it clear to all that Freya was both their daughter.

"I told you she was mine," he said with some smugness.

Neilina could do nothing but smile. Her daughter would shift and once she shared her nature with the wolf would then be even safer. There was nothing Neilina could find to fault in that.

"We must go now, but just as the ancient *kelle* visits Princess Ciara, mate to the *Dragon Ri*, we will come to you, child as we are needed. Our wisdom will always be yours to seek out in the place of *other*," the *celi di* promised.

Neilina surged toward her parents, her little brother, her older sister and hugged them all, even as she knew she had to let them go. But from this time, she knew they would always be with her.

Had always been with her.

Amber light flashed and then her pack was gone along with Haakon's father and mother.

"You didn't even get to speak to your parents," Neilina said with apology in her voice.

He smiled down at his mate, while the cavern she had been using as her sleeping chamber came back in focus around them. There was a lightness to her soul he could feel through their connection and he could not grieve the lost opportunity.

And so he told her.

"But..."

He placed his finger against her lips. "There is naught to concern yourself with, my princess. We will see them again. To see this joy inside you is worth anything."

"We are mated," she said with bemusement. "I mean really mated, blessed by the *celi di* and ordained by the alpha. I never thought to have such a thing."

"And we're going to have more children, your Seer said so."

His words affirming Freya as their firstborn touched her deeply.

The smile that came over Neilina's features was like the sunrise. "And we will keep those children safe."

"We will."

"I will still doubt some days."

"And I will remind you that you are never alone."

Her smile turned to something else entirely, something that made his beast growl with want. "I think we need to do our utmost to create life between us, don't you?"

"Are you suggesting we make love again?" he asked, not even wincing when he used the word she refused to apply to him.

She didn't seem to notice, only nodding and indicating the furs. "Lie down, I have a desire to control things this time."

"As my *kelle* wants."

They both fell into a doze after orgasms even more shattering than those that had called her former pack to the place of *other* to bless them.

Haakon jerked awake when Neilina sat straight up and screamed, clawing at her throat.

"Neilina!" he shouted and then shook her.

Her eyes opened, their emerald depths so dark they were almost black. "We have to find the poison. They mean to poison the underground river that feeds the wells throughout the island."

Any poison strong enough to kill Chrechte would destroy all the wildlife as well. Balmoral Island would become a wasteland.

"Did you see where it is?" he asked.

"Dìonach knows."

"Your bear?" he asked, thinking he had to have misunderstood.

But Neilina nodded. "She likes to explore. Especially caves."

"She is a bear. How can she know?" As a good companion was, Dìonach still had the intellect and instincts of an animal.

"I did not say she understands what she knows," Neilina said with more patience than she usually gave him. And he smiled. "However, my vision was certain. She has seen something that does not make sense to her bear's instincts."

Dìonach was still guarding the opening, when Haakon and Neilina emerged, once again fully dressed, their weapons in each scabbard as necessary.

Dìonach surged to her feet and head butted first Neilina and then Haakon.

Neilina smiled. "Yes, old friend. I have taken a mate."

The bear's growl was so clearly approval, it warmed Haakon. The animal understood that he and Neilina belonged together. Even if his mate was still fighting the inevitable emotional connection of their mating. Their souls were joined.

Of course, she would love him. When she finally let down that final barrier stopping her from doing so.

Neilina rubbed her head against Dìonach, then pulled back. "You saw something in the caves. Something you did not understand. Can you show me?"

Dìonach jerked her head up and down and Haakon could not doubt that she was nodding.

Neilina stared into Dìonach's eyes, her brows drawn together in concentration.

"It's a pile of blacksmith slag in an underground cavern." Neilina shook her head. "But why would that be so strange, for the blacksmith to have a place to dump his slag?"

"Deep underground? In a cavern that other Chrechte and human do not go?" The blacksmith in his old home buried his slag after all precious metals had been melted off. He didn't cart it a distance away and pile it up in a cave.

"How can you be sure that is the case?"

Haakon explained his reasoning and added, "I do not think Dìonach would have noticed it otherwise."

Neilina's beautiful, strong features were creased with confusion. "But slag is not poisonous."

"The slag of certain metals can be very poisonous if water, or another liquid is used to draw out that poison. Ingested, it can cause a wasting disease that cannot be treated and will ultimately lead to a long drawn out and painful death."

Horror dawned in Neilina's emerald gaze. "As would happen if it was dumped into the underground river."

"It would take time. Weeks, even months, but no one would be the wiser while the poison leached into the water supply. Not even the superior senses of the wolf would smell the change in the water."

"And because the water is used for growing too, the food would be contaminated. The evil of such a plan is beyond my comprehension. None would be spared from babe to grandfather, to the animals that drink from the streams."

"*Ja,*" he agreed grimly.

"We have to find that cave." Fear and urgency infused Neilina's tone.

Haakon pulled her body to his with one arm and cupped her cheek with his other hand so their gazes met. "We will find it. We will stop this evil. Together, none, not even the treachery of the Fearghall can stand against us."

She nodded.

Nothing more, but she believed and that was all Haakon needed from her.

Dìonach led them to an entrance into the earth a distance from the sacred caves used for Chrechte rituals. The bear shook her head toward the opening, clearly not wanting to return inside this particular cave.

"Stand guard while we are inside," Neilina instructed her large companion.

Dìonach settled to one side of the cave and Neilina led the way inside.

The passage was narrow at first and dark. "I'm surprised your bear came inside the first time," Haakon opined.

"We are bonded. The spirit that sends me visions probably compelled her, but she certainly wasn't coming back inside this time," Neilina added wryly.

Torches, that indicated others had visited the cave before them, lay on the ground, the smell of tallow strong to Haakon's sensitive nose. He dug in his pack and came up with his flint rock, making quick work of lighting two of the torches and handing one to Neilina.

"Have you always gotten visions?" Haakon asked her as they started out again.

"I used to have really intense dreams, before I lost my clan, but they stopped for many years. Then I saw Dìonach in the forest, wounded. I found her upon waking. She was just a cub, her mother killed by hunters. I bonded her to me once she was grown. Until I started having visions of the catastrophe we are trying to avoid, the only other one I had was about Freya."

"Always you are given the insights you need to save."

"But not when it came to saving my clan. I did not have any visions before the Slayer came."

"And our Seer did not know my father's first mate would desert him and take his child away to mate and marry a wolf, thus beginning an avalanche of events that led to death and much grief among our people. We are not responsible for what we do not know."

She stopped, as if stunned by the idea. "You don't think I was too weak to see, too young?"

"The *kelle, celi di*, and Seer have no control over the wisdom they are gifted with."

"Only what we do with that wisdom."

"*Ja.* And how can you ever be responsible for being too young? You do not ordain the day of your birth."

"Or death."

"Not for yourself, or those you protect."

"I wish I'd let you in before."

He kissed her. How could he help it? He wanted to. She needed the connection, even if she didn't know it. And despite their need to hunt, she let herself melt into him for timeless moments. But then they both pulled back and began their search in earnest.

It would have gone faster in his beast form, but Haakon scented the air for that which did not belong. The scent of man or wolf.

Neilina caught it first and he followed her through winding tunnels that split off into different directions until they came into a low cavern. And against one wall was a big pile of slag.

The scent of water said that the source of the island's wells and streams was near. Haakon made his way to an opening in the other side of the chamber and struggled through the tight space to come into a giant cavern with stalactites dripping form the ceiling and a fresh, crystalline lake even bigger than the one above ground near the keep.

"It's beautiful," Neilina said from beside him, her voice tinged with awe.

Light came from cracks in the ceiling above, one spot sending a shaft of sunlight glinting off the water.

"*Ja*. Too beautiful to be used for such nefarious purposes."

"Why haven't they dumped the slag in already?" Neilina asked out loud, not really expecting her mate to have an answer. "Or have they?"

"Nei. The ground around the lake is undisturbed." Haakon waved his torch in both directions, making his point. "There are marks where we have stepped, but that is all." He frowned, looking more forbidding than she'd ever seen him. "As to why not yet, I think the would-be murderers are still on the island and do not want to risk their own deaths."

The righteous anger of her *conriocht* protector nature filled Neilina. "Good."

"*Ja*. We will track them and bring them to justice."

Or kill them. Whichever felt right at the time, but Neilina did not say that. Haakon's expression said he'd thought the same thing.

They returned to the small cave and her mate leaned down and sniffed the large pile of slag, his frown turning to a feral smile. "They left their scent on the slag. Three distinct scents, all strong enough to track."

"They are here in the cave as well." It was those three scents she had tracked to lead them to the pile of slag. They had been faint, and she hadn't been sure of the number of scents mixed, but now she could distinguish between them.

"Your ability to track scent is stronger in your human body than mine is," he admitted freely.

And she kind of adored that about her super confident warrior mate, even when she'd been a distrustful harridan, he had not ever held back from acknowledging her strengths.

She nodded her agreement but leant down to inhale deeply of the scents around the slag. She wanted no chance of losing their tracks by missing something. "Now, we hunt."

His expression was deadly. "*Ja.* Now we hunt."

She started stripping, but he did not follow suit.

"What are you waiting for?" She wasn't relying on her human senses for this hunt. It was too important.

"Nothing."

"But you can't shift with your weapons on. They will hinder your beast, not help it." He knew this, so why she had to point it out, Neilina did not know.

"I will not shift."

"But your sense of smell will be stronger in your *asmundr* form." Again, he *knew* this.

"I will not shift into my giant cat in front of you."

"You would withhold your beast from me?" she demanded, affronted. "We are mates." His beast belonged to her as surely as Haakon did.

"For your own sake."

Understanding dawned and with it came a powerful surge of emotion. Haakon always put her first, if she had but realized that a long time ago. "Your father never shifted in front of me. He destroyed my *conriocht* without ever taking his beast form."

Haakon did not look surprised.

"You knew," she marveled. "That in your human form, the *asmundr* has the strength of a fully shifted *conriocht*."

"In blood lust, yes, we do. It is the Berserker form. Our eyes shift, our muscles become bigger, but we do not take on our beast."

"I do not fear your beast," she assured him, was positive she would not even fear his Berserker form. "He is my mate."

She did not expect the kiss that came with that admission, but she fell into it with all the enthusiasm of a woman who had discovered how much she enjoyed physical intimacy. And his kisses made the world seem a better place.

When he stepped back, Haakon made quick work of his weapons and clothing.

Naked and proud, he stood before her. "Are you sure?"

"Aye. More than." She was no weakling and finally she accepted that for the absolute truth it was. "Show me your beast."

His shift was as fast as any she had ever performed. Much, much faster than other Chrechte.

She stood in awe at the sight before her. He was like the tigers her mentors had told her about, but so much bigger. She was tall for a woman, but still on all fours his giant head, with its fangs as long as her forearm, was at the same level as her own.

Haakon made no sound. He did not move. But she could feel his beast reaching out to her.

She stepped forward and touched his head with both of her hands. "I am filled with awe, mate, but no fear. Scent the air. You know I tell the truth."

Then instinct told her to rub her head against his and she did. The purr that sounded from him went through her like a wash of the tenderest emotion.

Her shift came over her without thought. First to the wolf and she wended her way through his legs, under his belly, marking him with her scent, taking his scent into her own fur. They tussled until she lay on top of his giant back and shifted to her *conriocht* form.

"You are amazing, and my beast adores yours."

Haakon just purred in reply, but then she heard, *My beast will always protect you.* In her head.

We share a soul bond.

We knew that.

But I was fighting that truth.

You fight it no longer?

Nay. You are mine in every form and at every level.

The purring of the big cat grew louder, but she forced herself to climb off and to stand there in all her *conriocht* glory. "It is time to hunt the betrayers of our kind, *asmundr.*"

He surged up and roared in agreement, then they left the cave in one accord, moving so fast no other Chrechte would have been able to keep up with them.

They caught the scents they searched for in a group of village huts an hour's walk from the keep. Slowing down, they both stalked the scents, she followed one trail while he followed another.

Screams sounded from near one of the huts, but Neilina ignored the fear of those who were innocent. She only sought the guilty. Children ran from her beast form, seeking sanctuary with mothers and fathers who had run in from the fields at the first cries.

The scent trail Neilina followed led to the farthest hut and inside an old Chrechte man, sitting in a chair, whittling like he had not a care in the world. When his own actions would cause the death of the entire family that shared this home with him. And he was clearly unconcerned by the cries of others who lived near him.

Neilina threw her head back and howled in fury and condemnation.

His head jerked up, fear filling his expression along with knowledge. He knew he'd been found out.

He jumped to his feet. "You'll not take me, demon!"

Neilina moved too fast for the other wolf to track and smacked the knife he wielded away from him. The sound of a bone snapped came just before he screamed and cradled his wrist to his chest.

"Da?" A young Chrechte woman stood in the doorway, her expression filled with horror. "*Conriocht*? Why are you here? What have you done to my father?"

Neilina lifted the old man by the neck so his feet dangled above the floor. "Betrayer. Murderer."

"Nay," the woman wailed, dropping to her knees in grief, her fist going to her mouth to stifle instant sobs.

"You would have killed your own family." Neilina shook the old man and dropped him.

"She mated a human. She betrayed her race. My grandchildren are nothing but half breeds, weak with his human blood."

The woman's sobs grew louder.

Neilina dragged the old man out of the hut by the scruff of his neck, the sound of a prehistoric tiger's roars coming from another hut.

She threw the old man on the ground. "Run and I will catch you and gut you where you stand. You will not die quickly and your agony will be great." Her words were guttural and hard to understand because of her elongated muzzle, but his fear said he knew just what she'd promised.

Other Chrechte and people had come out of the huts, the scents of fear, curiosity and grief permeating the air around them.

She motioned to one of the women. "Go to his daughter. She needs comfort."

The woman nodded with a jerky movement and skirted widely around Neilina before rushing inside the structure Neilina had just left.

Neilina followed the scent of her mate and found him menacing, not one, but two Chrechte, with his giant beast, his fangs dripping saliva, his roars bone chilling.

She tilted her head to take in the scent and confirmed that the man and woman were the other scents from the cave.

"Betrayers. Murderers," she condemned for a second time, as was her right as *conriocht* to the very people they would have destroyed.

The woman leapt for the *asmundr*, her hand coming up with a sword in it. She drew his blood before he tossed her with his powerful head.

The scent of her mate's blood sent fury unlike anything she'd ever known, even when her clan was under attack, through Neilina.

She leaped across the floor, landing in front of the offender and grabbed the woman from the floor. "You will die."

"Nay," the man yelled.

But it was her mate's head butting into her back that brought Neilina back from the brink. *She is no threat to us, my princess. We will take them both before their council to face judgment.*

The woman's mate shifted and ran, but it took very little effort to run him down and Haakon carried him to the keep like a naughty cub in his giant maw. Neilina shepherded the older man and the woman with a clawed hand tight on each of their napes.

By the time they reached the keep, there were dozens of clansmen both human and Chrechte alike following them at a distance. Word must have reached Talorc, Lachlan and Eirik, because all three stood waiting for them with stony expressions that said nothing good about the three guilty Chrechte's futures.

Neilina and Haakon dropped their prisoners in front of the two lairds and the *dragon ri*.

The clan kept their distance, casting wary glances at Haakon's beast and Neilina's *conriocht* form.

Allowing the shift to come over her, Neilina waited to speak until she could do so without hindrance. "Here are your betrayers."

Freya walked up with a cloak. "Cover yourself, mother. I think the men in the clan are as in awe of your beautiful body as they are of your *conriocht*."

The sound of Haakon's laughter from behind her said he had shifted as well. "I think our daughter is right."

Neilina turned her head. "The women don't need to be looking at what belongs to me either," she informed him.

And in a very timely fashion, Ciara arrived just then with one of the Ean's leather kilts. Haakon winked at Neilina before putting it on.

"How do you know these three are the betrayers?" Lachlan asked, grief making his gaze dark. "Their family has been in our pack for many generations."

Haakon remained silent, allowing Neilina to explain about her vision and finding the slag in the cave.

The lairds looked surprised when she shared Dìonach's part in finding the cave, but Eirik's did not. She'd noted before that the Éan seemed to have more memory of the ancient ways than the Faol.

"I think you have much to teach us about the ways of the Chrechte we have lost," Talorc said, confirming Neilina's thoughts.

"It will be both my and my mate's honor to do so," she assured him.

"So, you've accepted your mating then?" Freya asked with clear delight, grinning between Neilina and Haakon.

Despite the very serious tone of the situation, Neilina allowed herself to smile at her adopted daughter. "I have."

"Our ancestors have blessed the mating," Haakon announced. "But there will be no place among them for the likes of these." He spat on the ground by where the three betrayers huddled.

The woman yelled invective at them, but neither Neilina nor Haakon paid the femwolf any heed. Her hatred blackened her own heart but could not touch them.

Lachlan gave instructions for the slag to be removed from the cave and for a new regime of guard duty to take over protecting the island's water supply.

"Take them to the prison tower. They will face the council and sentencing tomorrow."

"He must be interrogated by the *drogon ri*," Neilina indicated the old man Chrechte. "He knows far more about the Fearghall than he will pretend."

She did not know how she was so certain of that truth, but Neilina knew she was right.

"I submit to no demon!" the old man yelled.

"I will not ask for your submission, old man, but I will demand your truths," Eirik said in a tone of otherworldly power that sent shivers cascading over Neilina.

"Come, we will return to our cave. Our *dreki kongr* does not need us to get the betrayer to speak." Haakon put his hand out to Neilina.

And for the first time, Neilina did not hesitate to take it.

"I think I'll stay here in the keep and give you two some privacy," Freya said.

But Haakon shook his head. "It is time your mother and I discussed what the future holds for us and you are part of that future, daughter."

Freya's smile was brilliant, her beauty undimmed by the scar on her face.

They returned to the cave, joined by Dìonach, and told Freya about their mating's blessing by Neilina's clan.

"I wish I'd been here to meet them all, but maybe I wouldn't have seen them." She wrinkled her nose. "And I'm pretty sure I wouldn't have been comfortable being here while you two were *bonding*, even if my back was turned."

Neilina felt a wholly unaccustomed blush steal up her cheeks

But Haakon just laughed. "I'm sure you are right, daughter, but I believe once you have had your time with the stones, you will be gifted to see the place of *other*."

"But I've already had my ceremony and I'm just human."

"There is no just about human," Neilina reminded her daughter.

"However, this time we will take you before the Faol Chridhe and I will touch my sword's *kotrondmsnkr hjarta* to it, drawing your energy to join with both your mother and mine."

And that is what they did.

They had traveled back to the mainland with the *dragon ri* after he extracted necessary information from the betrayers. All three had been sentenced to death with the sentence carried out within a day of their trial before the council.

It took several months, but all the Fearghall spies and underminers within the allied clans were routed out. This time, every single Chrechte had been required to speak a very specific pledge of loyalty to the *dragon ri* and their own clan and to publicly denounce the Fearghall and all they stood for.

The old man had revealed, in fury and with accusation, that the Fearghall numbers were dwindling. He blamed the weakening of the Chrechte packs with their intermatings, but in fact, the opposite was true. By denying true mates, fewer children were born among the Fearghall sympathizers and the clan that harbored them had one of the smallest Chrechte packs known.

The MacLeod pack had been an exception only because it was not all Fearghall, only led by a small minority of them. The intermarriage they denounced was what was actually saving the Faol and Éan from extinction.

They had Freya's ceremony in the ancient sacred caves on the Sinclair land that used to belong to the Donegal clan.

Ciara, *celi di* and mate to the *dragon ri*, presided over the ceremony.

Haakon squeezed his daughter's hand when he felt her shake beside him. "You have nothing to fear from our sacred stones."

"The power in this place presses down on me. I feel like I should be kneeling," Freya whispered back to him.

"Then kneel," Neilina instructed her daughter.

And the three of them approached the stone so that Freya could kneel as she placed her hands onto the stone. Neilina put her hand over Freya's and Haakon put his hand on top of both of theirs using his other to press the stone in the hilt of his sword against the bottom of the Faol Chridhe.

Light shown around them in flashes of brilliant colors and then Freya's head fell back and she cried out, her body rigid.

The shift came over her and moments later, a beautiful *conriocht* appeared, the same light covering of white fur as her mother sprouting from Freya's skin.

There were gasps of surprise from those within the chamber.

For, if any proof that the nonshifting Chrechte were called by the stone as their shifting brethren was needed, here it was.

Freya, who smelled wholly human had just taken a guardian form.

Neilina shifted to her own *conriocht* form and embraced their daughter, emotion swirling in the air around them.

Love and relief.

Haakon sheathed his sword and put his hands on the shoulders of his wife and his daughter. "My family. Protectors of all Chrechte and holders of my heart."

A resounding cheer went up and the joy in the cavern could not be questioned.

Another protector of their people now stood between them and any who might try to destroy *any* honorable Chrechte.

Neilina joined her husband in their private chamber deep in the warren of the ancient ritual caves. "Our daughter is *conriocht*."

"We are truly blessed."

Neilina chewed on her lower lip. "But it is a heavy burden for her to carry."

"A burden she will not have to carry alone."

Neilina nodded. Her mate had a tendency to see the best side of things. She was trying to learn that trait from him.

She pulled him down to their furs and placed his big hand over her stomach. "Can you sense our baby?"

"You're pregnant?" he asked in clear awe.

"You did not know?"

"I thought I was imagining the subtle shift in your scent. I cannot hear the second heartbeat yet."

"I had a vision. In the cavern, as the lights swirled around us."

Her *asmundr's* eyes filled with moisture. "A baby?"

"Our baby." She smiled. "Freya will be the best and most protective older sister ever."

"She will."

"But you?" Neilina said, her heart in her throat. "Will be the best father."

"You believe that, despite what my own father was?" Haakon asked, clearly moved.

"There is no man alive more honorable than my mate," Neilina offered him that truth without reservation.

"And no woman more integrous and strong than my mate." He kissed her with tender passion. "Nor as beautiful. I love you, Neilina, with everything in my soul."

Moisture burned her own eyes as she returned his kiss and then whispered against his lips. "I lied when I said I would not love you. I cannot imagine life without this powerful feeling inside me. You are the center of my world."

He pulled her to him in a frenzy of need, as if her words had sparked unbearable passion and they made love with an urgency they had not met to this point.

They continued to join their bodies deep into the night, whispering words of love and devotion over and over again.

Neilina had thought she lost her chance at happiness when she failed her clan, but the joy and love that filled her belied that belief entirely.

She would never face another daybreak alone, and though she needed no protector, she had one. For all the centuries left of her long life.

"I love you," she said one last time as sleep came to claim her.

His reply, "And I love you, more than life," followed her into dreams no longer filled with the dying but showing a future as glowing as the sun.

EPILOGUE

Ten years later, Haakon and Neilina returned to Iceland for the first time, bringing their family of not only Freya, but a nine-year-old son named Colin for Neilina's father and a four-year-old daughter named Astrid for Haakon's mother. His son had Neilina's fierce nature, but their daughter had all the gentleness Haakon remembered of his mother.

They had spent the last decade traveling from pack to pack, teaching Chrechte the old ways and how to draw on gifts long forgotten.

But the time had come to introduce his family to his uncle and cousin and all those Haakon had spent his first decades of life living among and protecting.

They were accompanied on this trip by the *dreke kongr* and his wife. She had seen that she was to preside over the coming of age ceremony for Einar and Artair's two children. That ceremony had been filled with power and shocking to most who attended, Einar and Artair not excluded.

Their daughter was gifted with the power of the Seer who could call forth *and* banish the beast nature of her Chrechte brethren. Their son took on his second father's wolf form and then shifted almost immediately to a Tiger of the Rus like Einar. Having two forms was unheard of in a child born of parents of the same Chrechte race and/or human.

But gifted he had been, and the entire holding rejoiced when the *jarl* officially named his grandson successor after Einar.

Marie spoke as Seer for the fist time with her hand on the *kotrondmenskr hjart*. "My brother, both Faol and *kotrondmenskr* will share my longevity of life. Many generations from now, he will lead the *kotrondmenskr* from Iceland to rejoin our Paindeal brethren."

Chills washed over Haakon at his young cousin's words. Whatever led to that migration would be permanent, he knew, just as he knew that his place was no longer among the *kotrondmenskr*, but at his mate's side as they served *dreke kongr* together, protectors of all Chrechte, not just a single race.

The future held challenges and joy, but through all of it, he would have his beloved *kelle* by his side and their children that would lead and protect the Chrechte in generations to come.

~ The End ~

MORE BOOKS BY LUCY MONROE

Other Paranormal Novels by Lucy Monroe

ENTHRALLED

Other Novels in this Series:

MOON AWAKENING

MOON CRAVING

MOON BURNING

DRAGON'S MOON

WARRIOR'S MOON

For more information on Lucy's books, including her Harlequin
Presents and contemporary single titles, visit

http://www.lucymonroe.com.

ABOUT THE AUTHOR

With more than 7 million copies of her books in print worldwide, award winning and USA Today bestseller Lucy Monroe has published over 70 books and had her stories translated for sale all over the world. While she writes multiple subgenres of romance, all of her books are sexy, deeply emotional and adhere to the concept that love will conquer all. A passionate devotee of romance, she adores sharing her love for the genre with her readers.

Follow Lucy On:

Facebook
Twitter
Pinterest
Goodreads
Instagram

Email her: http://www.lucymonroe.com/contactmail.htm

Printed in the USA
CPSIA information can be obtained
at www.ICGtesting.com
LVHW092312081224
798650LV00036B/675